Murder at Drake's Anchorage

Murder at Drake's Anchorage

E. Lee Waddell

COACHWHIP PUBLICATIONS
Greenville, Ohio

Murder at Drake's Anchorage, by E. Lee Waddell
© 2021 Coachwhip Publications edition

First published 1949
Eleanor Lee Waddell, 1905-1975
CoachwhipBooks.com

ISBN 1-61646-504-2
ISBN-13 978-1-61646-504-9

1

Clarence Pidgeon: Truant

A fat boy caromed through the revolving doors of the hotel and halted so abruptly that a taxi driver, following with his bags, narrowly avoided colliding with him. Mrs. Gordon Maxwell II, who was waiting for Gordon Maxwell III to return from the gentlemen's lounge, watched the fat boy settle for his fare and tip the driver. His mannerisms, the way he stuck his fists into his pockets and jerked his chin back in a gesture of dismissal, were those of a boorish adult. Mrs. Maxwell thought that she would probably dislike his father. As the boy's head pivoted above his unyielding torso, his glasses threw off reflections of the lights which circled the lobby. Mrs. Maxwell watched him approach the hotel desk, wondering whether he would carry through his transactions there with an equal assurance. Mrs. Maxwell still felt the loss of Gordon Maxwell II when she had to deal with hotel clerks.

"O. K., Mom. Let's go!" Her own thirteen-year-old son stood before her. She smiled up at him. Gordie had been at work upon his black hair. He had triumphed temporarily over its tendency to curl forward. One drop of water lingered on his forehead and another hung from his ear.

"Isn't that one of the boys from the school over at the desk?" she asked him.

A frown shadowed her son's face as he looked across the lobby. "Oh sure. That's old Clarence Pidgeon. Come on, let's go! Shall we?" He gave her arm an urgent tug.

"But don't you want to say hello to him? Maybe we could drive him out to the school. He seems to be alone."

"Oh shucks, Mom. They'll be sending the station wagon in. I don't want—"

Mrs. Maxwell suppressed a sigh. She did so want Gordie to be a manly man, at home with his fellows. "All right, darling. Ask them to send the car around."

Clarence Pidgeon caught sight of Gordie as he was returning from the entrance and came across to join him as he arrived beside Mrs. Maxwell. Clarence's attitude was condescending but she heard uneasiness in his voice.

"Hello, Gordie."

"Hello, Pudge. Mother, this is Clarence Pidgeon, one of the fellows—"

Mrs. Maxwell and Clarence shook hands. The contact was unpleasant. His fat hand was cold and damp. Inwardly she agreed with Gordie, "He does seem to be a little stinker." Aloud she said brightly, "May we drive you out to Drake's Anchorage, Clarence? Were just about to start."

Clarence giggled. "Oh thanks, Mrs. Maxwell, but I'm not going out to Drake's Anchorage," he asserted. "I'm not going back at all!"

"Not going back! What are you here for then?" exclaimed Gordie practically.

"I'm going to have lunch, now," said Clarence, "and I'm going to have two desserts."

"But if you aren't going back to school, why'd you come back from Texas?" persisted Gordie.

Clarence pouted. "Well gee, I started back, but on the plane I got to thinking of everything. So when I got into the airport, I called up my father and I told him I didn't want to go back. I just said— Well, you know what's been going around," he summarized belligerently. "Jeepers, he was mad!" he added, awed by the ease of his victory. "I didn't know he'd be that mad." The eyes of Clarence and Gordie locked and carried forward a wordless communion.

"But why is it you don't want to go back to school?" Mrs. Maxwell intruded herself into it.

A wave of red started at the base of Gordie's neck and traveled up till it suffused his forehead. Clarence didn't hear her.

"Jeepers," Clarence repeated in hushed tones. "He hit the ceiling. He said to wait right here till he came. He's bringing Mother too. I guess they're on the way now. He's going to tell the Head what he thinks of him."

"Mrs. Maxwell, your car is here," said the doorman.

Mrs. Maxwell stood up, retaining around her shoulders with one negligent hand her short coat of silver fox. With her other hand, and an inconspicuous twist of her hips, she brought her black tailored broadcloth into lilting conformity with her erect figure. At her throat, full but clean-lined like Gordie's, there was a minute fluting of sheer white lawn. It was as provocatively innocent and as expensively flawless as the feathery whorls of her mouse-black hair that encircled the black velvet monk's cap that crowned her head.

"Well, I suppose if your parents have asked you to wait for them here—" She drifted into hesitant silence, baffled by the curtain that the two boys seemed to have drawn between their world and hers.

Gordie pulled her arm through his and led her toward the door. Neither of them offered further words of farewell to the boy they left behind them in the hotel, nor did they speak to each other for some moments after they were alone in the car. Mrs. Maxwell devoted herself to negotiating the traffic on the steep San Francisco hills. Her son sat silent beside her.

She found Van Ness Avenue, made her way past its series of marble-columned automobile agencies, blatantly bannered used-car lots, and traffic lights, and finally turned left on Lombard with a sigh of relief. She was now on the road that would take her across the Golden Gate Bridge, into the hills that stretched down from the red-wood country to form the northern peninsula—as the land of San Francisco and the towns below it formed the southern peninsula—that flanked the seventy-mile-long Bay of San Francisco. In the sixteenth century, having come through the Straits of Magellan to explore the Pacific shores of the New World for navigable harbors and Spanish loot, Sir Francis Drake had failed to see the waterway between these two peninsulas, had sailed on north some thirty miles to drop anchor. On one of the high points of land on which Drake may have set up his brass plaque claiming the land for Queen Elizabeth—the plaque which was picked up three hundred and fifty years later near San Quentin by an Oakland clerk—now stood the school, Drake's Anchorage, to which Mrs. Maxwell was returning her son.

"I hope they haven't drowned Toots' kittens," said Gordie. "The Head said they wouldn't. They wouldn't if he said they wouldn't, would they, Mother?"

"I hope not, dear." Mrs. Maxwell fumbled in her bag for her coin purse, while cars lined up behind her at the toll gate. She always wondered why she hadn't put fifty cents where she could get at it easily.

"Thank you," said the toll collector, as he lifted the coin from her gloved hand. He had to express gratitude. It was one of the regulations.

"Mrs. Bjornstrom promised to take the all-black one for the Doghole, and Miss Parelli said she might take one home. I don't think they'd drown any of them, do you Mother?"

There was a fog bank moving in under the bridge. An invisible boat bleated. The sound seemed to come from immediately under the car. Mrs. Maxwell started, and swerved instinctively. She didn't like to drive. Her thoughts turned not to Gordon Maxwell II but to Alrik Lind, headmaster of Drake's Anchorage. He handled the wheel of a car with ease. He had, indeed, handled with unreflecting assurance any challenge she had ever seen him face. How would he meet Clarence Pidgeon's father who was flying up from Texas to tell him what he thought of him?

"No dear, I don't think they'll drown any of them. What was it that Clarence told his father that made him so angry?" Gordie turned on his knees in order to reach down behind the seat to bring up the new bridle that had been his one Christmas request. He settled down again with it on his lap and appeared to become lost in a contemplation of its splendid silver mountings. There was a long pause before he spoke. "Golly, Mom, Horace is going to look swell in this!"

"You haven't answered my question, Gordie."

They had left behind them the lofty northern terminal of the suspension bridge. As it wound its way down to the level of the bay, the highway cut titanic swaths through the Marin County hills. The wind brought the fog down the seaward hollows and drove it cater-cornered through the cuts in disturbing intermittent blasts. Mrs. Maxwell tentatively switched on the windshield wiper and stole a moment to glance at her son. He had raised his head and was staring into the fog. His face had a closed look which frightened her. She turned off the windshield wiper. It made matters worse.

"Gordie," she urged again.

"It isn't the sort of thing you talk about to your mother," he said coldly.

"But darling—"

How would Gordon Maxwell II have met this? It was difficult to imagine. For his ship had gone down in the Marshalls when Gordie was ten, and before that time he had never thrown more than a passing glance at parenthood. Neither of them, in truth, had done more than look into the nursery occasionally, before a dinner or after a polo match, until the war had come along. In the war years she had become more interested in Gordie. She had believed she saw sprouting in her son all the graces she had found it increasingly more plausible to remember in her husband the longer he had remained away.

Perhaps she had best leave the problem to Alrik.

Alrik and Gordon had been at college together, and just before Gordon's death they had run into each other again in some port in the South Pacific. While on his terminal leave, Alrik had stopped off to see her at Coronado Beach. During his stay there, which had lengthened into several weeks, Alrik had been rudely critical of her preoccupation with her son. "A hothouse plant," he had called the child. Then the sudden death of his grandfather in San Francisco had taken him north, and Alrik had dropped out of her life as abruptly as he had dropped into it, leaving her feeling hurt and angry and unappreciated. But they had many mutual acquaintances, and back in New York she had found herself listening with unwilling interest to all news of him. That winter she had heard that he had inherited from his lumber-baron grandfather a fifth interest in a boys' school out on the Pacific Coast. Alrik, they said, was actually running it himself. You could always expect Alrik to do the unexpected.

That spring Gordie had been twelve, and hysterically unhappy in his New England preparatory school. On the advice of its suave headmaster, she had taken him out of the school before the end of the semester. He was flunking everything anyway, and the headmaster had suggested that perhaps they were pushing him too fast. Perhaps a long vacation and then a tutor. She had taken him to a guest ranch in Montana. There he had been afraid of the horses, awkward and unhappy in the riding lessons she had forced on him, and she had been able to do nothing about his depressions and his fits of temper. At last, she had written to Alrik, and that fall had entered him at Drake's Anchorage. For the first few weeks she had stayed close at hand, telephoning almost nightly, coming out weekends to see how he was getting on. Then Alrik had put his foot down. "Go away," he had said, "and stay away till Christmas. How can you expect the boy to get anywhere when you're always hanging on his neck?"

This time she had not felt hurt by his bluntness. Like the others who circled around him in his domain at Drake's Anchorage, she had fallen under the spell of his magnetism. He was a Viking superman returned from the sagas. Humbly she had accepted his criticism, and meekly she had done his bidding. At the midyear holidays she had not even called for her son at the school, but had awaited his arrival with the other boys in San Francisco. And the improved Gordie she had gotten back had reinforced her faith in the school. Whatever cloud was looming up on the horizon in the person of Clarence Pidgeon, she reflected, Alrik Lind would dispel.

While she mused, they had gone around the east side of Mt. Tamalpais, through the sunny towns it sheltered. Now at San Rafael, the county seat, they turned to head back over its northern shoulder toward the coast, through the wilder country of the Sir Francis Drake Highway. Gordie began to see landmarks that reminded him of momentous occasions of the preceding semester.

"There's where we ate, Mother. Look! Down there. Oh, you're too slow! I wanted you to see the bridge I put Horace over."

"Bridge? I didn't see a bridge. When was that?"

"You're not listening," Gordie accused her. "I was just telling you. It was on the November All Day Ride. We trotted all the time. It rained all day. We trotted right through the mud and the puddles and splashed each other. I was wet all over, Mother, and the water ran down the saddle horn and squashed where I sat!" Gordie's eyes were shining with the glorious memories he beseeched her to share.

"That must have been wonderful. And you didn't catch cold?"

"Shucks! No! You never catch cold outside, the Head says."

"But that place you stopped. It was beside the road. Did you come by the road? I thought you followed bridle paths."

"Bridle paths!" Gordie expostulated. "Mother! Trails!"

"Trails, then," Mrs. Maxwell accepted the correction equably. "I thought you followed trails."

"We do, most of the time. But back this way there aren't many, and over Bolinas Ridge they haven't been opened up since the Fire. I told you about the Burned Area, Mother. You can see a little of it soon. Look quick when I tell you."

As the road left the redwood groves and took to the uplands, Gordie sat forward on the edge of the seat, peering out of each of the car windows in turn at the ridges above them.

"We've been awfully busy with trail work," he continued. "Everybody has to do it. But only we responsible fellows can work in the Burned Area. It's dangerous, you know. The Head says he can only use fellows he can trust. You have to look where you're going and test out everything. Some of those old trees— You don't know when they're going to take a notion to keel over, the Head says. There mightn't even be any wind. He's had men in there, felling the big ones and hauling them out in trucks. We use them for firewood. The fellows who get demerits have to chop."

"Have you had to chop?" probed his mother.

"Well, yes, some," Gordie acknowledged reflectively. "Twice I forgot my laundry—"

As Gordie meditated on other unrevealed sins, they topped the highest ridge and caught their first full view of the Pacific. The sun, concealed from them by fog banks, glinted on the long horizon line. For a time, they drove across downs, matted with low-growing chaparral and bush lupin. They were almost as high as the summit of Mt. Tamalpais. In every direction, the land swept away from them in yellow-green valleys and blue-green ridges. Here and there a rusty black spine showed where the last forest fire had climbed to a summit. Then they descended to meet and turn south on the old coast road at a group of frame houses named, by the road sign, Olema.

"Never in my life," said Mrs. Maxwell, "have I seen a human being walking around this place. Does anyone live here?"

Gordie considered. "I don't remember any but I guess they do. Ranchers," he said judicially. From here on this was his country, and he was unwilling to admit ignorance concerning any of its aspects.

They followed a narrow valley south, the ocean hidden from them once more by the highlands on their right. After several miles, their way on either side was lined with evidences of the fire, partially overgrown with new greens. Of the trees, only the redwoods still lived.

"They tried to stop the Fire along the creek bottom here," explained Gordie, "but it jumped the road." The fire had been before his time but he knew the epic by heart.

"There's the road the trucks go in," he pointed out when they were passing through thickets of willows again.

"They made it with just a tractor to take the logs out. It goes clear up to the top of the ridge, and we've almost met it from the other side. We've got the trail marked out that far. You know how we lay out a trail, Mother? We call it blazing, but we don't hack the trees till we are sure where it's going. We tie little white rags on bushes. By next spring, we'll be across this road, and working up the Bolinas Ridge—

"Here's our road, Mother, here's our road! You'd better go into low!"

Mrs. Maxwell caught her lower lip between her teeth, swung sharply to the right up a steep dirt road, and shifted gears just before the engine stalled. When the car picked up power in the lower gear, she leaned back thankfully. Three miles of this, but the crucial moment had been passed. They wound upward in long switchbacks under the trees. Redwoods gave way to madrones, to live oaks, to bays, finally to highlands dotted with bunch grass and an unbroken view of the sea. The sun was out again. Now its light picked out the faraway towers of San Francisco and the long crescent of surf on its beach until, as their road dropped south, they were obscured once more by nearer headlands.

"Seems to me," breathed Mrs. Maxwell grimly, "it would be easier to get here by boat."

"There are the corrals!" sang out her son happily. "There's the polo field! Look at our woodpile! You can see from here that it's longer than ever! It goes clear past the tool shed. Let's stop at the barn, Mother, and see Horace and Toots and Walter and everybody. I want to show him the bridle."

"Show whom? Walter or Horace?"

"Horace, of course. Please, Mom!"

"No. I'm going to deposit you at the Office. After that, as far as I'm concerned, you're on your own."

"But I'll have to unpack! Mr. MacDowell will make me unpack and stand inspection!"

"Then I'm afraid you'll have to unpack—unless you want to get busy on the woodpile your first night back," decreed Mrs. Maxwell. She wished Alrik could hear her.

"Aw, Mom," mourned her son reproachfully.

They left the barn and corrals behind. They followed the road in its final sweep to the south and west, out on a promontory from which grasslands dipped steeply to cliffs five hundred feet below, then finally north and east up the gentler slopes before Drake's Anchorage. The school backed up against the last ridge they had come over and faced the sea.

Alrik Lind, grandfather of the man who stood now before the open doors of the Great Hall, had built solidly—for the years and the storms. The white plastered walls of Drake's Anchorage were set on gray rocks and reinforced by vertical timbers, reminiscent of stockades. Above these logs, where the small windows were cut in, the adobe revealed itself to be at least a foot thick. The low roofs rested on heavy beams which protruded several feet beyond the walls. Behind the Great Hall, the series of open courtyards and small cell-like rooms furthered the impression that the whole construction had been conceived as a fort. A nostalgia for a more primitive era must have overtaken Lind the elder and his four friends in their declining years. Having stripped their profits from the forests of the West Coast and retired to opulence in Chicago at the turn of the century, they must in time have become dissatisfied with the lives of their sons and of their sons' sons. For in the twenties they had established this school.

The Head was talking to a tall blond youth and a small blonder woman. The boy's name was Peter Van Tassel. Mrs. Gordon Maxwell II did not remember what the mother's name was that year.

"Darling! How perfectly *wonderful* to see you!" called Van's mother as she hastened across to where Mrs. Maxwell and Gordie were getting out of the car. Her heels pattered on the cross sections of redwood trunks that paved the terrace in front of the school. Mrs. Maxwell felt she was about to be kissed and hastily held out her hand.

The Head remained where he was with a hand on Van's shoulder. A sweat shirt and a pair of nondescript jeans covered his huge frame. Grease-spotted sneakers suggested that he had been down working on the boat.

"Welcome back, Maxwell," he said. "How are you, Frances? Van, see if you can run down Mr. MacDowell." He shook hands solemnly with Gordie and smiled at Mrs. Maxwell.

"Yes, sir," said Van. "Come along, Gordie. Here, I'll give you a hand with that duffel."

"Oh, Alrik!" exclaimed Van's mother before they were out of hearing. "You big beautiful brute of a man! How *do* you make him like that?"

Mrs. Maxwell turned back toward the car. "I'm not stopping now," she said as she got in. "But I'm going to be in the city for a while. If Gordie needs anything— I mean, just tell him I said good-bye."

The Head followed to close the car door. She told herself resentfully that the look he gave her was not hers, but the one he used to speed all departing mothers on their way. Damn that woman. She had wanted to tell him about Clarence Pidgeon.

"We'll take care of him," said the Head. "He'll write to you Sunday."

The sun had abandoned the January afternoon. Vapor collected on the windshield as she circled the school and started up the ridge behind it. When she drew up to take a last look back before descending into the trees, the world beneath her had vanished in white opacity. No city to the south, no ocean, no black rocks, no school. She hurried on, fleeing the insupportable solitude of empty space. A small unacknowledged corner of fear in her own heart accompanied her.

2

Miss Breckenridge: School Secretary

Behind the stockaded main structure of Drake's Anchorage, on the steepish trail that led up to the corrals, there was a small stone cottage. According to a tale told at least once to each generation of new boys, the cottage had originally been erected for Mr. and Mrs. Gudmund Bjornstrom. It was said that when Mr. Bjornstrom had been a lumberjack working for Lars Aakrog, one of the school's founders, he had saved Aakrog's life, and at the same time suffered the injury which had shortened his left leg. The Bjornstroms were said to have been settled in Stone Cottage and running cattle on the ridge long before Drake's Anchorage had been thought of. Then there was a story about another of the founders which held that Stone Cottage had been built for Miss Eliza Breckenridge, now the school secretary. Whatever secrets of bygone days were locked in the stones of the cottage, when Alrik Lind came to the school, Miss Breckenridge was in residence there, and the Bjornstroms were occupying rooms in the barn. One of his first acts was to build another and larger stone cottage south of the main building and install there the Bjornstroms and the six smallest boys in the school. Mrs. Bjornstrom became known as the housemother of the small boys and Mr. Bjornstrom as the superintendent of buildings. The new cottage, through somewhat obscure processes of association, was called the Doghole.

None of the boys or younger teachers ever considered asking the three old people about their origins. Their bearing did not invite questioning. Like the lichen-covered rocks and the manzanita bushes, they were accepted as part of the school. But on rainy evenings around roaring fires, in the Games Room, in the Faculty Common Room, in the studies of the masters and the suite of the top-form boys, stories about them were handed down. What claim Miss Breckenridge was said to have had on the founders powerful enough to oust the Bjornstroms and place her in possession of Stone Cottage differed with the age level and the disposition of each raconteur. It was generally agreed, however, that Mrs. Bjornstrom and Miss Breckenridge had not exchanged a word with each other within the memory of anyone at the school.

At six-thirty Tuesday morning—the morning on which the second-semester classes were to begin—the headmaster knocked at the door of Stone Cottage.

"Miss Breckenridge," he said. "I want to talk to you."

It was still dark. Miss Breckenridge had lit her oil stove but she had gone back to bed. Her hair was in curl papers and her nightgown was flannel.

"You will have to wait," she said rising, "until I make myself presentable."

"I can't wait. What do I care how you look? Open the door. I want to come in."

Miss Breckenridge flung a Paisley shawl over her couch and a Cashmere shawl over her curlers and a mackintosh over her nightdress and opened the door.

The Head stepped inside and closed the door. His own mackintosh, bulky and stiff with the cold, glistened where the fretted window of the oil stove threw yellow lights on it. He seemed to fill the room.

"Now listen carefully to me and don't talk," he said. "I don't want to stop long."

She sat down in her platform rocker, pulling the trailing ends of her costume around her. "Well, speak then."

"I'm on my way to Chicago. Walter is driving me over to the coast road to catch the bus. Last night something came up." He stopped speaking, clenching and unclenching his fists as if he were censoring what he would allow himself to say. "I don't know when I'll be back. The school is to go on as usual. You will be asked where I am. Say I have gone to consult with the founders in Chicago on the policy of the school. That's all you know. Stop there. Don't speculate about anything else that you will hear with anyone. What you know keep to yourself. You are to carry on in every way as usual. Have you got that? Now, where have I gone?"

"You have gone to Chicago to consult with the founders on school policy."

His voice had told her some things but she wanted to see his face. Miss Breckenridge stretched her bony hand toward the bead-fringed lamp beside her chair.

"Don't turn on the light," he said harshly.

Miss Breckenridge returned her hand to the arm of her plush-covered rocker. When she spoke, her tones were uncolored by their official relationship, and the timbre of old age was muted. "What's the matter, Alrik?"

Loons wheeled above the lifting fog, laughing to each other. The boom of the waves in subterranean caves reverberated up a fissure in the rock behind Stone Cottage.

"And don't ask questions."

He hesitated again with his hand on the door latch. Whatever it was that he considered saying or doing, he decided against it. His bulk loomed briefly against the gray outdoors, and then the door had closed on him.

Miss Breckenridge remained quietly in her chair. Of the five founders, two were dead. Cnut Sorenson had

preceded Alrik's grandfather by a year, and now his grandson's second wife held Cnut's share of the school. She was
living only thirty-five miles away, over the shoulder of Mt.
Tamalpais in a town called Ross. She had coined a crazy
hybrid name. Mrs. Cnut-Sorenson, she called herself.
Miss Breckenridge was glad she was being ignored. Alrik
was going to Chicago. He was going to Lars Aakrog, Rog
Torvaldson, and Oscar Liljeborg. They were all three in
or nearing their nineties. For twenty years they had been
crotchety old men. What had they to offer now to Alrik
but their money? And not so much of that any more. Miss
Breckenridge knew that Drake's Anchorage, founded as an
eccentric gesture, had become their chief source of support. In one of his fingers, Alrik had more of the strength
that had once been theirs—the strength that they had not
known how to pass on to their sons—than remained in all
three of them. Then why was he going to Chicago?

Sounds of a bar being rattled rapidly around the inner
sides of an iron triangle clanged through the morning air.
Breakfast in half an hour. Miss Breckenridge pulled red
velvet curtains across her windows and lit her lamp.

She removed the shawl, the mackintosh, and the flannel nightgown. She pulled on a long-legged, long-sleeved
wool and rayon union suit. She dropped a black silk pet-
ticoat over her head and drew it together around her waist
with gathering strings which she tied in a bowknot behind.
Then she put on a white muslin corset cover and puckered
up its ruffles with the drawstrings at the neck and waist.
In all her seventy-two years, Miss Breckenridge had never
donned a corset or a brassiere. Her wool stockings she
held up with ribbon-covered garters. Next she slid into
a green crocheted mercerized-silk jumper. When she had
laced up her black leather shoes, she stood before a mirror
in a gilded oval frame to remove her curl papers. Her iron-
gray hair was short and fine, and before she had combed

it out, the skin of her scalp showed in the wide parts between the curls. She fastened a black ribbon around her throat with an amethyst brooch. Miss Breckenridge's outer covering was a generously roomy tweed suit. Perhaps blues and grays had once predominated in it. In the memory of the school, which was not long, it had seemed to derive a protective coloring from the landscape around Drake's Anchorage. When she had placed five rings on her veined hands and hung an amber pendant around her neck, Miss Breckenridge tidied up her room, put on her mackintosh once more, and went down to breakfast.

To reach the southwest corner of the school, where the dining room was, from the northeast corner where she had entered the stockade, Miss Breckenridge had to follow a series of cloister-like passages. For the school was built around three open courtyards, extending from the east and rear quarters, which consisted of classrooms and the older boys' suite and the Games Room, to the west and front, where the general living rooms were. Facing the ocean, the library and Faculty Common Room flanked the Great Hall to the north, and the dining room to the south. Opening on the six covered passageways which ran east to west along the three courtyards, were the rooms of the boys under fifteen and over ten years of age. Centered in each of these rows was a master's room and study. Between the most northerly corridor of boys' rooms and the outer stockade, lay the infirmary and the headmaster's rooms. In a similar position along the south wall, lay the kitchen, its related rooms, and Miss Blossom's suite and schoolroom. Miss Blossom oversaw the scholastic life, as Mrs. Bjornstrom oversaw the domestic life, of the smallest boys.

Miss Breckenridge preferred to reach the Great Hall just before the five-minute warning gong was sounded. Experience had taught her that at that time the conscientious had already returned from the washrooms, and those who had overslept had not yet started for them. But this morning she had been delayed. The five-minute tocsin caught her as she was approaching Mr. MacDowell's door. He charged out of it to cross the courtyard clad in shorts and undervest, towel in one hand and toothbrush in the other.

"Dod blast it, Miss Breckenridge, you're off your beat!" he shouted cheerfully as he passed her. "Happy New Year, anyway!"

Other doors banged. Bathrobed figures scurried along all sides of the court. Shrill trebles, sliding croaks, and a few uncertain basses rent the air. "Who's got some soap?" "Hi, Neil! Did you get that ax?" "Good morning, sir! Yes, sir! I'll be there on time, sir!" "Beaumont! You old horse! Is that a razor? Look, Van, Beauty's got a razor!"

In the Great Hall, several of the faculty and about a dozen boys had already arrived. Mr. and Mrs. Bjornstrom were standing before the fire between the dining-room doors with their small boys lined up, polished and shining, to start the new term. Their shoestrings were tied, their flannel shirts were pushed into their jeans all the way around, their parts were straight, and their neck scarves were correctly knotted and tucked between the first and second buttons of their shirts. Not a demerit in sight. Miss Breckenridge reflected with unwilling admiration that Mrs. Bjornstrom must have got them out of bed a half hour before the rising bell to see personally to their grooming. She wondered whether the Head had told the Bjornstroms he was leaving. She rather thought not. They looked complacent, waiting to be admired.

But Mr. Weber had not shaved! Miss Breckenridge was startled. It was the first time in almost two years that she had seen that salt-and-pepper stubble spreading out around the sideburns on his pudgy cheeks. In former years, that

had been a storm signal of bad days to come. This morning
he had retreated to the northern end of the Great Hall,
and stood with his back to the fireplace there, hands in the
baggy pockets of his rumpled gray suit, gazing through the
open half of the Dutch door at the gray Pacific. Mr. Weber
was a brilliant mathematician. Years before, he had lectured, and written treatises, and commented adversely on
the treatises of his colleagues in the University of Vienna.
He had also had political views and lectured about them.
In what order of cause and effect he had been shunted
from European universities, through American Midwest-
ern colleges and Southwestern boarding schools, to heave
to at Drake's Anchorage in the late thirties, Mr. Weber had
never revealed. Whether his political views had brought
about his expulsions and in turn his alternating bouts of
hard drinking and soft cynicism, or whether his drinking
had come first and his expulsions followed, Miss Breckenridge did not know. He had muddled through eight years
at the school. He had a way with children. In defense of
the concept of curved space, he might once have been savagely rude, but when inviting a beleaguered and desperate boy to enjoy with him the logic which underlies the
process of long division, he was very gentle. However, in
the war years he had fallen so far in the graces of Drake's
Anchorage, which was itself at that time just hanging on
to academic standards by a shoestring, that only the short-
age of male teachers had kept him on. With the coming of
the new headmaster, he had spruced up. The rest of the old
guard, Monsieur Trougnac, Mr. Dingle, the Bjornstroms
and Miss Breckenridge, had awaited his first lapse with
interest. It had never occurred. Alrik Lind's expectations
of people were simply incontrovertible.

But this morning, Mr. Weber had not shaved. He knew
the Head had gone. Did he know more than Miss Breckenridge? She went to stand beside him.

"Good morning, Mr. Weber. Be sure to come in after breakfast for those textbooks you ordered. They came last Thursday. The Head said to let you give them out, and to charge the accounts of the seventh-grade boys. There are eight of them, and a desk copy. That's right, isn't it?"

Mr. Weber rubbed the bald spot behind his halo of gray curls and looked up at Miss Breckenridge. Miss Breckenridge was five feet six and he was five feet four, but the contrast between their bony structures and the amount of flesh upon their bones made them both feel that the difference between their heights was much greater than it actually was.

"Now why did I do that? Well, since you say I ordered them, I'll try to remember to pick them up." He began to quote without enthusiasm, "If three men are pouring cement into a form four feet deep— Miss Breckenridge, what hourly labor rates do you suppose this new edition quotes? A nice problem in prognostication."

He hadn't begun drinking yet.

The doors into the dining room were propped open by one of the waiters. Those who had collected in the Great Hall began to move toward them, continuing their talk of vacation experiences. Latecomers, among them Mr. Mac-Dowell, slid to precipitous halts in the adjoining court-yard, righted themselves, and sauntered in to make up the tail of the crowd at the dining-room doors. Locomotion in the main group ceased, but the chattering went on. The minute hand of the grandfather's clock jumped to two minutes past seven-thirty. The door which led across the passageway to the school office opened and Monsieur Trougnac and Mr. Dingle entered. Monsieur Trougnac's long thin face was set in the severe lines it assumed when-ever he was about to step aboard the *Golden Hind* on which he invariably became seasick. Mr. Dingle was for once without his affectations. No light quips tossed deftly right and left. Without mannerisms he seemed positively undressed. His face looked as if he were on his way to the funeral of someone he didn't know well.

Miss Breckenridge and Mr. Weber, who alone had remained at the far end of the Great Hall, exchanged a speculative look and moved down to join the others. The crowd parted for Monsieur Trougnac and Mr. Dingle and then followed them into the dining room. It took the boys several minutes to find the seats they had drawn by lot for the new month. When the confusion subsided, some half-dozen of the seats remained unclaimed, and Monsieur was standing behind the chair at the head of the head table.

"For all that we are about to receive may the Lord make us truly grateful," he intoned.

Chair legs scraped stone floors, the babble of voices arose once more, and the school settled itself to what might be considered the official opening of the new term. There were eight tables in the dining room. They were presided over normally by the headmaster, Mr. Bjornstrom, and the six masters. These latter were Monsieur Trougnac, who taught French, Mr. Dingle, English, Mr. Weber, mathematics, Mr. MacDowell, science, Mr. Pyke, history, and Mr. Arbuthnot, Latin. Each table had a second in command who sat at the opposite end. Mrs. Bjornstrom supported Mr. Bjornstrom; Miss Blossom, Mr. Weber; and the school nurse, Miss Burtt, was at Monsieur Trougnac's table. This morning, she had gone around to its head. Miss Parelli, who came in by the day to do bookkeeping and assist Miss Breckenridge in the Office, ate lunch at Mr. Arbuthnot's table. Miss Breckenridge lent balance to the vagaries of Mr. MacDowell. The seats at the foot of the remaining three tables, those of the Head, Mr. Dingle, and Mr. Pyke, were positions of honor, assigned directly by the Head to the boys who were to occupy them, once a term.

Miss Breckenridge saw that Peter Van Tassel had made
the seat at the end of the Head's table. He had just turned
sixteen. He had been at the school five years, passed
along automatically from grade to grade, without having
learned to read, to the sixth grade where he had stuck. He
was fourteen and still there when Alrik Lind came to the
school. By that time he had shot up to almost the height
he had now. He had been skinny, with long hands and long
feet that fell over things. His mother, who flitted in and
out at term ends but seemed never to read his reports, always commented playfully on his awkwardness. The Head
had moved him into the seventh-grade science and history
classes that fall, arranged Mr. Weber's schedule so that he
had an hour a day alone with him, and spent two peri-
ods every morning with him himself. During that time,
the headmaster and the boy had been more often outside
than in, taking the initiative about the physical upkeep
of the school with Mr. Bjornstrom in limping pursuit.
There had been parts to order for the boat's auxiliary engine, charts to study of the school's wiring and plumbing
arrangements, and other such listing and ordering. Somehow, during the course of these projects, Van had discovered himself reading. The following fall, at fifteen, he had
entered the ninth grade, still two years behind his age
level, but well adjusted. His frame had filled out, and he
had been discovered to be good at long-distance running,
bringing glory and honor to the school by his showing in
the annual cross-country Dipsea Race. In a field of sixty
experienced runners, he had placed fourth. His tan was as
dark as his eyes, darker than his hair. "Golden Boy," his
mother had called him fatuously last night. Miss Breckenridge resented his mother. Miss Breckenridge resented
most of the mothers.

Fitzsimmons Eubank sat at the end of Mr. Dingle's table.
That would be a rude shock to Mr. Dingle. He would have

preferred to have somebody like Nathaniel Vaughan, and
this the Head very well knew. Fitz was the husky, trucu-
lent grandson of a man who had gone from cowpuncher
to owner of Chicago stockyards. His father was the political boss of a middle-Atlantic state. His mother had re-
married railroads—that is, railroad dividends. Fitz was a
bully who had been ousted from two Eastern schools when
he arrived, simultaneously with the new headmaster, at
Drake's Anchorage. That fall he had mistreated the horses
he was forced to ride until Walter had forbidden him entrance to the corrals. This, Fitz had explained to other
boys with similar disinclinations but less enterprise, was
the way to get what you wanted. In the science lab he had
produced a number of successful explosions and a variety
of evil smells. He had established an all-time record for
tardiness, and fomented sit-down strikes on the woodpile.
But unlike his cronies, Wyman Gould, Jr., and Clarence
Pidgeon, he had placed first or second in every class on
every examination he had been present to take. He had
punctured even Mr. Dingle's aplomb and they had had
several head-on clashes. The one last spring had resulted
in so many demerits that Fitz had had all work and no
privileges throughout the balance of the term. The Head
had supported Mr. Dingle, but with the opening of the
fall term he had gone to work on Fitz. And Fitz had been
worthy of his mettle.

Sparks flashed as steel met steel. What took place on
the cruises of the *Golden Hind,* for every one of which that
fall Fitz was a member of the crew, was whispered from boy
to boy and did not reach Miss Breckenridge's ears. From
them, Fitz came back weary and subdued and once with a
black eye. He remained mute about his troubles. He had
no surplus energy with which to bedevil the other boys
and looked as if he might have welcomed their sympathy.
They had none for him. But finally, in late November, his

luck changed. A storm which had been skirting the area made a sudden shift in its course while the *Golden Hind* was out beyond the rock-infested waters of the North Farallons. The little schooner, unable to make the cove in time, had to ride out the squall on the high seas. The Head and four boys were gone all night. Monsieur Trougnac decided hourly to call the Coast Guard, and hourly reconsidered. Mr. Pyke, and Mr. Bjornstrom, and Walter were all against it. The following midmorning the wanderers returned, bedraggled but alive, and Fitz emerged as a hero. The three other boys admitted honestly that when they had collapsed with nausea and fatigue, Fitz had continued to work the pumps, to handle the tiller, and in all ways to respond to the commands of the ship's captain.

In the four weeks that remained of the term, Fitz enjoyed with becoming modesty the worship of the small boys, and was somewhat shy of the masters. He had conceived a hero worship of his own during the storm, and the sensation was so new to him that he was uncertain how to act. Now he had been promoted to a position in which he was to be regarded as responsible for the conduct of the other boys. It seemed rather rashly soon to Miss Breckenridge, and it would certainly seem so to Mr. Dingle. Fitz would follow the Head through hell and high water, but the Head was gone. What would he be like while Monsieur Trougnac uneasily held the reins of government?

The third seat of honor, at the foot of Mr. Pyke's table, was held by Neil Truesdale II. That was a conventional appointment. Neil was an upright and serious lad for whom good sportsmanship was not a hectic new enthusiasm but a natural law. He was almost unique in the enrollment in that his sojourn at Drake's Anchorage was occasioned neither by a record of recalcitrance, nor by scholastic ineptitude, nor by the marital projects of his parents, but by allergies. Inexplicably, in the fogs of the Marlin County coast, he did not have asthma. Neil was Foreman of the Trailbreakers. For at least two hours several days a week, he labored with unfailing enthusiasm on trail maintenance. He throve upon it, and set such an example of arduous activity for his gangs that they could not resent him as he drove them on toward ever-receding goals.

Miss Breckenridge addressed herself to her baked grapefruit. Some of that new nurse's folderols again. She was dietician as well as nurse, and planned the menus. When would she learn that when the Head had decreed that a boy could not be excused from the table until he had eaten everything placed before him, the old ways were best? Gordon Maxwell III, seated on Miss Breckenridge's left, was already bogging down.

"Put a little more sugar on it, Gordie," suggested Miss Breckenridge. She followed her own advice and then offered the bowl to Gordie.

"I don't think it would help any, Miss Breckenridge," replied Gordie. He accepted the sugar bowl politely, but set it down, and tentatively pushed his grapefruit plate to one side. "It's bitter. I think there's something really wrong with it."

Robert Wintringham, one of the small boys, joined in from Miss Breckenridge's other side. "There *is* something wrong with it. Mine must be the other half." He laid down his spoon. "May I start my cereal, now, Miss Breckenridge?"

"No," replied Miss Breckenridge. "Finish it up, both of you, and no nonsense. There's nothing wrong with it. That's the way it tastes when it's cooked. It's good for you."

"I don't like it cooked," said Rab.

"Look. It's all red down at the bottom. Maybe it's rusted, or something," said Gordie, still hopeful.

Miss Breckenridge did not deign to reply. It was indicative of the security of her authority that Gordie and Rab ate the rest of their grapefruit without demurring further. Not the juice, not the third of the fruit which a hasty knife had left attached to the sides, but at least the loose pieces disappeared. Miss Breckenridge thought that was enough. She noticed that Mr. MacDowell was having even less success at his end of the table.

Monsieur Trougnac left his place early in the meal, and Mr. Dingle followed him soon after. No one rose to make any announcements. Mr. Pyke, a stalwart ex-Navy officer, ex-shipmate of the headmaster, nominally teacher of history, but principally concerned with polo, got morosely to his feet and lumbered off. The tables emptied rapidly. Soon, up and down the dining room, there remained only a half-dozen of the more painstaking adults, spotted around with mournful, slow-chewing boys.

"May I be excused, Miss Breckenridge?"

"Miss Breckenridge, may I be excused?"

"Sir, may I go now? This piece is burnt."

Miss Breckenridge followed Monsieur Trougnac and Mr. Dingle into the office where she had seen them disappear. What were the two of them cooking up? She didn't trust them.

3

Monsieur Trougnac: French, and Mr. Dingle: English

Miss Parelli dropped three little Parellis by the mailboxes, where the county school bus would pick them up, and drove on up the coast road to take the steep turn for Drake's Anchorage. There were nine Parelli children living. From babyhood up, they had pulled weeds, scrambled over the rocks and sands to dig for clams, milked cows, had Saturday-night baths, got somehow over the wet dark hills to school in the hand-me-down clothes of older Parellis. They had fought with each other, and played with each other, and passed one after the other through the stages of learning to read and to write and to figure without ever having realized there were emotional hazards involved. However, Miss Parelli felt that the family would have fared better all along the line with more cash. In common with the other maturing Parellis, she had felt this so strongly that she had viewed her education exclusively in terms of how to equip herself to get a job. When she had been offered a position as bookkeeper, immediately after she graduated from high school, at a place near enough to the ranch to enable her to live at home and commute to work in the family 1934 Ford, she had accepted her good luck gratefully.

After a year and a half at Drake's Anchorage, many things she saw and heard there were still surprising her. But her abiding surprise was that there were people who would pay a cool $3000 a year to have produced synthetically for their offspring a childhood which, with minor modifications, so closely approximated her own.

Miss Parelli's form and features retained traces of the Rubens cherub that all Parellis resembled in childhood. She was competent, limited in range but not in intensity of experience, and nineteen.

On this Tuesday morning she entered the Office at Drake's Anchorage at five minutes before eight. Miss Breckenridge was concluding a telephone conversation. Monsieur Trougnac and Mr. Dingle were at the other end of the room, talking to each other. They stopped when she came in.

"You, Mademoiselle!" ejaculated Monsieur Trougnac.

He was in his usual costume, olive-drab over-long shorts, black turtle-neck sweater, black beret. Since they had exchanged New Year's greetings yesterday, when he had come into the Office upon his return from the holidays, why should he seem so unpleasantly surprised to see her turn up at her regular time today? He continued to stare at her apprehensively as she threw out her automatic good mornings to each in turn and settled herself at her desk. He paced the width of the room twice before he halted tensely beside her.

"Mademoiselle," he said, "there are things serious you must understand."

"*Faites attention à la petite!*" interjected Mr. Dingle. "*Elle pourrait nous faire du scandale.*"

Miss Parelli gave Mr. Dingle a cloudy look.

Mr. Dingle was dressed as usual too. It could not be said that he wore his usual costume, for he had many. This morning his coat was— Well, to mention colors in describing Mr. Dingle was necessary but misleading. She had tried it at home, and her brothers hadn't believed her. The blendings he achieved were too subtle to be spoken of as colors. To say that he had on a green coat, purple trousers, and a lemon suede vest was immediately to defeat yourself. And still you would not have mentioned his tie, his shirt, his socks, his handkerchief, his shoes, all intrinsic units in his design.

"What's new?" inquired Miss Parelli.

Mr. Dingle lifted his elbows, placed the palms of his hands together, leaned forward and opened his mouth to speak. As he did so, the phone rang, and he remained in that position, tilting his head to listen and to look at Miss Breckenridge who was answering it.

"Good morning. This is Drake's Anchorage. . . . He's not here today, Mrs. Cnut-Sorenson. . . . He's gone to Chicago to consult the founders on school policy. . . . That I couldn't say, Mrs. Cnut-Sorenson. . . . I have no information I am withholding. . . . Perhaps he didn't feel it concerned you—"

Mr. Dingle wrested the phone from Miss Breckenridge's hands.

"Luella, good morning! We were waiting to call until we could feel we weren't disturbing you. . . . Frightful! But did they go to see you? They agreed last night to do nothing further if we complied with their conditions. . . . My God! She *did?* . . . She *has?* She'll have to be muzzled— tactfully, of course—or she'll create a situation that's irretrievable. . . . *Ab*solutely necessary. . . . You may be sure we are. . . . That would seem to be the only possible course. A tragic thing. . . . Monsieur Trougnac and I will look forward to that eagerly. Make it as soon as you can. . . . Good-bye, Luella. . . . Thank you. That is very heartening. . . . Good-bye."

Mr. Dingle replaced the telephone on the desk and returned Miss Breckenridge's glare coldly.

"Miss Breckenridge, I fear you have failed to understand the seriousness of our position. We must not antagonize *anybody*. The continued existence of the school is in jeopardy."

"I'm not worried. If people would follow the Head's instructions and keep out of what isn't any of their business, the Head would settle things all right."

"The Head, my good woman, as you seem not yet to have grasped, is unfortunately out of the picture."

"He is not! And I'll thank you to get out of this Office and keep your mouth shut!"

Mr. Dingle threw up his hands and turned to Monsieur Trougnac. "The woman is impossible! We can't carry on like this!"

"Say, what is this?" said Miss Parelli.

The telephone rang. Mr. Dingle and Miss Breckenridge both reached for it. Miss Breckenridge won.

"Good morning, Drake's Anchorage. . . . Yes, this is Olema R-5. . . . Yes, this is Drake's Anchorage. . . . The headmaster is not available just now. This is his secretary speaking. . . . That is extremely unfortunate, Señora de Herrera. They will miss the opening days of classes. . . . Possibly so. . . . We'll hope for tomorrow, then."

Miss Breckenridge hung up and turned to her desk without a glance for the waiting Mr. Dingle. Monsieur ventured into the silence that followed.

"The de Herrera boys are delayed, Miss Breckenridge?"

"Yes. Bad flying weather." Miss Breckenridge addressed herself energetically to her typewriter. "I'm sending a note to Mrs. Bjornstrom."

"Mademoiselle," Monsieur turned once more to Miss Parelli. "You observe that we are distraught. It is most unfortunate. The headmaster—er—Mademoiselle your extreme youth! Most unfortunate. But it is necessary the utmost discretion. One ill hint. How shall I say? The school, she is like a woman. In short, Mademoiselle— *Mon Dieu, M. Dingle! Comment dire à l'enfant que l'on accuse le chef de saloperies envers les gosses?"*

Monsieur Trougnac had plunged into syllables which communicated only his desperation and Mr. Dingle took over.

"—In short, Miss Parelli, hear no evil, see no evil, and most important, *speak* no evil. In very short, speak not at all— Ah, Mrs. Maxwell! You brave our early morning fogs!"

Mr. Dingle cut short his homily to assume a demeanor of exquisite courtesy toward Mrs. Gordon Maxwell II who had knocked and thrown open the door without waiting. Miss Parelli observed her clothes with approval. Like these others, Mrs. Maxwell appeared to be "distraught" but she was if anything lovelier than ever to look upon.

"Oh Monsieur! Oh Mr. Dingle! What are you doing about this—this unspeakable outrage?"

"Madam," said Monsieur, "we are taking all the steps necessary to protect the children from its effects. I may say with confidence that that is the concern most profound in the heart of every member of the staff."

"But Alrik! What about him? Where has he gone? What is he going to do?"

Miss Breckenridge spoke like a Victrola record from the other side of the room. "He has gone to Chicago to consult with the founders on school policy."

Mrs. Maxwell was not calmed. "What can *they* do? He ought to have a good lawyer. At once! Can you reach him? Tell him I want to get him the best lawyer in the country."

Monsieur Trougnac was solemnly condolatory. "Madam, regretfully, he can not fight this. You must see that his hands are tied. You must know of the committee who delivered their ultimatum last night."

"I know. I was there when they started out." Mrs. Maxwell all but ground her pearly teeth. "Because one little pip-squeak tells his father dirty stories, eleven supposedly adult people forget everything else they ever knew about Alrik and go hog-wild! What about the other parents? There must be some sensible ones!"

"However wild the accusation against Mr. Lind is, my dear Mrs. Maxwell," said Mr. Dingle in tones of profound mourning tempered by fortitude, "it has been made. And only his quick action has kept the news of it from going further. If he had not left the school within twelve hours, they would have withdrawn their boys this morning and given the story to the papers. However deep our sympathy was for the ruined man, the only course the faculty who were present at the interview could follow was to advise him to capitulate immediately." Mr. Dingle shook his head warningly at Mr. Weber who had come to stand in the doorway. He continued with gentle persuasiveness to Mrs. Maxwell. "You must steel yourself to recognize that, Mrs. Maxwell, for the situation is still grave, and we need your help—to protect the fair name of the school—to shield the innocence of your son—to make sure that this scandal travels no further. That is what Mr. Lind asks of us."

"Those damned sanctimonious legal whores!" exclaimed Mrs. Maxwell and burst into tears.

Miss Parelli looked at her with new appreciation. Mr. Dingle put a soothing arm around her shoulders. Mr. Weber advanced solemnly to lean over Miss Breckenridge's desk. He put his hands on it and seemed to be addressing Miss Breckenridge alone in phrases which took the confounded Miss Parelli back to senior English.

> 'Foul whisperings are abroad. Unnatural deeds
> Do breed unnatural troubles; infected minds
> To their deaf pillows will discharge their secrets;
> More needs she the divine than the physician,
> God, God forgive us all!'

"Your textbooks, Mr. Weber," said the indefatigable Miss Breckenridge, picking up a package and handing it to him. "You'd better go to the kitchen and get some coffee. The first-period bell will ring in five minutes."

Mr. Weber accepted the package, inspected it curiously, and started for the door. When he came up with Mr. Dingle, he paused to counsel him,

> 'Look after her;
> Remove from her the means of all annoyance,
> And still keep eyes upon her. So, goodnight:
> My mind she has mated, and amaz'd my sight.
> I think, but dare not speak.'

He tottered through the doorway and disappeared down the passageway.

Monsieur said, "Pardon," jerked himself to attention before Mrs. Maxwell, and hurried away after Mr. Weber.

"Whatever in the world?" inquired Mrs. Maxwell, dabbing her eyes with the handkerchief Mr. Dingle had sacrificed to her needs.

"Disregard it," said Mr. Dingle. "Mr. Weber has a romantic Viennese soul. Monsieur Trougnac will see to him. And now, my dear, let us take a turn on the terrace. You can regain your composure in the ocean air, and I have interesting things to tell you about young Gordon."

Miss Parelli and Miss Breckenridge were left alone. Miss Breckenridge's back did not invite conversation. Miss Parelli opened her journal and began making entries from the petty-cash book. Her posting was meticulous but her mind was not on it.

There was something screwy about this place. She was not really surprised that catastrophe had overtaken it. It wasn't natural. Nothing about it was natural, although there was nothing you could put your finger on. Indeed,

she had always fiercely defended it and the way of life of
its clients when her brothers had criticized their extrav-
agance. If they had the money, why shouldn't they do as
they wanted with it, she had always demanded. And the
boys were nice enough little kids. They had beautiful manners. And although she was overcome with stage-fright in
his presence, she admired the Head tremendously. What
had he done, anyway, that was so terrible he had had to
run away in the night, and that was so shameful Monsieur
blushed when he tried to talk about it? That Dingle! He
was a cool one. And Miss Breckenridge sure had it in for
him. And Mr. Weber—drunk and quoting Macbeth right
after breakfast. She tried to remember the lines. "Foul
whisperings. . . . Unnatural deeds—" Had he meant anything by them or was he just spouting? She suppressed the
giggle that rose in her throat as she thought of Mr. Dingle
as a "deaf pillow," for she stood in awe of Miss Breckenridge. Miss Breckenridge told everybody, including the
Head, where to get off. Mr. Arbuthnot was scared to death
of her. Miss Parelli was more familiar with Mr. Arbuthnot
than she was with any of the other masters because she ate
lunch at his table. Mr. Arbuthnot was a rabbit. He was so
colorless he was almost an albino, and his nose quivered
when he got excited. He also got pink. Miss Parelli had
tried a bit of persiflage with Mr. Arbuthnot and he had got
very pink. He had even seemed afraid of Miss Parelli. She
had decided that his masculinity was as dead as the lan-
guage he taught and had lost interest in him. If she could
only have had the same chance with Mr. Pyke! Now, there
was a man worth getting! But Mr. Pyke had never noticed
her. Mr. Pyke seemed not to be interested in anything
feminine nearer than San Francisco. Mr. Pyke, she felt in-
tuitively, kept business and pleasure expediently separate.

There was one thing that she knew about all the masters that she didn't condone. They were always in debt.

Their salaries were large—that is, they were three times as large as hers—but they were always asking for their pay checks a couple of months before they were due. They seemed to think they should live on the same scale as the boys' parents did. Last fall, that good-looking Mr. Mac-Dowell had got back to school head over heels in debt to the Super Oil Company. He boasted that he had got all the way across the continent on a credit card, even borrowing on it for food and lodging. He'd been tutoring the son of one of the owners and he'd had a note saying he was to have all courtesies shown him. Miss Parelli didn't approve of living beyond one's means. It wasn't sensible.

The course of Miss Parelli's reflections brought her back to Mr. Dingle's words, "The continued existence of the school is in jeopardy." Did that mean her job too? Miss Parelli had no debts, but she had obligations, and she also had intentions. The events of the morning had practical aspects. What would happen if the Head never came back? How could anything go on here without the Head? Surely, surely he would come back and save them all from whatever was threatening. Miss Breckenridge believed he would. Surely she was right and the rest of these nincompoops were wrong. Miss Parelli felt a new affection for tough old-lady Breckenridge. She determined to help her hold the fort.

Miss Parelli looked at the electric clock. The school was still called to its meals by the hand of the cook upon the iron triangle that hung from a beam outside the kitchen door, but its academic progress was ordained by a network of bells animated at set intervals by this clock. Mr. Bjornstrom had been skeptical when the Head had installed the system, but so far it had only once been thrown off schedule by a storm-uprooted tree. Miss Parelli saw now that the first period was nearly over. She gathered together a pile of letters and rose to her feet.

"Well, I guess I'll go distribute the mail, Miss Brecken-ridge. It's about time for the bell."

Miss Breckenridge did not look around and her voice was a little muffled.

"Very good," said Miss Breckenridge.

4

Nathaniel Vaughan: De Profundis

Nathaniel Vaughan's heart was throbbing in that old suffocating way that it had. His cuff caught on the end of his ruler and flipped it off the desk. When he reached down to pick it up, his fingers scuffled over it and pushed it still farther under his seat, and his blood seemed to rush to his head and pound there. When he came up with it finally, the other hoys were sitting ready and he still had no pencil. He began searching through his pockets, but he couldn't locate it. His breath caught in his throat and he started to cough, a dry surface cough that brought no relief. He stopped looking for the pencil to place his thin-boned fingers over his mouth, fingers that no amount of sun and wind had been able to roughen.

Mr. Weber did not notice that Nathaniel was not ready. He was seated at his own desk, looking down at a booklet like those that had been distributed to each member of the seventh-grade arithmetic class. He read from it in a monotone:

"Do nothing until I tell you to begin. Then work quickly but carefully until I tell you to stop. Do not ask questions. Find the answers to the problems and write them on the dotted lines. Use the margins to figure on. When I say 'Stop,' lay down your pencils. Now, turn to page one. Begin."

Seven pages rustled, and each of seven boys began competing against his own precarious ability to think and act under pressure for the little figure that would go down on his permanent record card opposite "Achievement Test, Advanced Arithmetic." The eighth boy, Nathaniel Vaughan, stopped coughing to dog-ear the corners of his booklet. When he had finally got it open to page one, he leaned over it, ruffling the remaining pages, tearing bits off the corners and rolling them into little balls. He was unaware that he was still without a pencil, for he had forgotten that he was supposed to be using it. Nathaniel was living again the hours that had led up to what had just happened to him at the classroom door. Mr. Weber did not look up from his desk.

Wyman Gould had got back to school after dark last night, only a short time before lights out. Nathaniel had been present in the washroom when Wyman had come in and slapped everyone he could reach on the back.

"Hello, and I hope, good-bye!" said Wyman.

"Cut it!" sputtered Ward Frazier. "You almost made me breathe up my tooth powder. What do you mean, good-bye? I thought you and the Head had a heart-to-heart talk and you were going to lay drains across the Cliff Trail all through January."

"Oh that?" said Wyman. "I just lost my grip there for a while. He took advantage of my pre-Christmas mellowness. And then, old Pudge hadn't yet struck his blow for freedom." Wyman threw water on his face and began rubbing it vigorously with a large bath towel. "Fact is," he said from under its folds, "I haven't even made up my mind to unpack."

"What's Pudge done now?" piped a voice from one of the showers.

Wyman came out from under his towel. "Who's that? Young Ballantyne? The very walls have ears. Sorry, fellows.

I'm under contract not to spill it. Give me some of that stuff, Ward." Wyman began on his teeth at a bowl next to the one where Nat was standing. "But if you know what's been going around—you can put two and two together. Now, Nat, here, would be sure to know. Ask Nat to tell you about the facts of life. Well, would you look at him blush?"

Wyman had gone out grinning around the toothbrush he held between his teeth, and Nat had fled after him to avoid the questions of the older boys. Wyman's jibe had started up the demons of fear and guilt that were always lurking in the pit of Nat's stomach ready to clutch at his heart. He had taken one of his pills and turned out his light before the bell. Then he had crawled in between the cold sheets and tried to remember the things the Head had said to him some months before. Nat hadn't told him about it. He had never told anybody about it, but the Head had seemed to know. Maybe everybody knew! His skin crawled at the thought. But the Head had said it would be all right, he had reminded himself. The Head had said that everything would be all right.

This morning he had gone back to sleep after the rising bell, and then hurried feverishly in order not to start the new term with a tardy mark. The Head occasionally missed meals when he was busy somewhere else, so although Nat had been disappointed not to see him at breakfast after he had managed to get there on time, he had thought nothing of it. He had returned to his room, readied it for inspection, been agreeably surprised that Mr. Weber, his rooms master, had failed to arrive to check on him, and gone to his first-period class. At the end of that period, Van had approached him in the courtyard with a question which had shattered his thin shell of security. Nat had gone cold with fright and tried to get away from him without speaking, but Van had caught him by the arm and persisted.

"I've *got* to know," Van had said. "The Head's gone. Do you realize what that means? He can't come back till I've found out who started this. Come on, Nat. Give me the truth."

"I've never told anybody. The Head took me to the nurse for something once, but I've never told anybody. Let me go. Let go of me! The others are looking!"

"They won't if you stand still. Told anybody *what?* That's what I've got to find out. I'm asking everybody. Not just you."

Nat's heart had thumped harder and harder till his whole body pulsed with it, and little dots vibrated before his eyes. "Now it's happening," he had told himself, as Van's face and the voices of the other boys in the courtyard seemed to be going farther and farther away. "I'm going insane. Soon I won't know anything and I'll start hitting him."

The bell for second period had reprieved him. "Think it over," Van had said. "You've got to come clean. I'll see you again at milk lunch." Nat had stumbled into Mr. Weber's classroom.

Now he gazed unseeing at the achievement test. Tears gathered under his eyelashes and threatened to splatter on the page below. He hadn't hurt anybody. Nobody but himself. Van had no reason to ask him anything. What had been going around that Wyman was sure he would know about? Was it about him? What had Clarence Pidgeon to do with it? He remembered coming into the showers one day after polo practice. Clarence Pidgeon and Culpepper Gaines had stopped talking to look at him and then grin at each other. He had thought it had been because he was never any good at polo and had fallen off his horse when he missed a shot that day. Now he wondered whether they *had* been talking about that. Could his secret bane have become a public joke? He ached with loneliness, but loneliness had been his refuge. His instinct to flee the school was blocked by memories of life at home. Everybody was against him. He put his head down on his arm. He wasn't going to say a word to Van. They couldn't make him. Nobody could make him. His hair fell over his white forearm in silken ripples and the nape of his neck looked very young to Mr. Weber who had been regarding him in mild perturbation for the last five minutes.

Attitudes stemming from divers traditions contested with each other for control over Mr. Weber's drink-muddled impulses. In the environs of the classroom, that of the pedagogue had so far maintained supremacy. A test was going on. If he spoke or moved he would invalidate its conclusions. That he not only didn't care a damn about the conclusions but also would have doubted their significance if he had cared was under these circumstances irrelevant. But prostrated before him was a soul-sick child who was in the process of learning that he could not run with the pack. The spectacle threatened to overcome his pedagogic inhibitions. Mr. Weber had learned that lesson well himself. If he had spoken, it would have been to utter a string of oaths garnered from decades of experience in defending his own ego against the norm. But such conduct, he foggily realized, would not have been considered by the headmaster to be suitable therapeutics. What *would* the Head have done with the child? Could this soft golden head be the rock on which the Head's arrogant ship had foundered? Why was the boy crying?

Mr. Weber examined his watch. Fifteen minutes more until the end of the period. Five minutes more of the test. Mr. Weber looked out the high window at the level crests of wind-groomed bay trees and saw the fifth of bourbon that was still unopened in the small cabinet in his study.

"Stop," said Mr. Weber at exactly nine fifty-five. "Bart, bring the papers up here. Tomorrow's assignment is on the

board. Get done what you can of it in the next ten minutes. Bart, stay up here at my desk and see that there's no
talking."

With the achievement tests under his arm, Mr. Weber
closed the door of his classroom on academic life and
walked purposefully along the rear passageway toward his
study. It was too late to duck when he realized that the
clicking noises on the damp stones at the northern end of
the passage were coming from the white canvas-covered
wooden heels of the nurse. Her starched silhouette materialized briskly out of the shadows. Mr. Weber had no
appetite for an encounter with anyone so certain of the
nature of rectitude as Miss Burtt. They met in front of the
science laboratory which opened on the center courtyard.
Mr. Weber attempted to pass by with a bow, but Miss
Burtt stopped.

"Mr. Weber," Miss Burtt accosted him, and hesitated.

As she thumbed a cascade through her loose-leaf book
of recipes as if it were a deck of cards, she seemed slightly
less than usual like the supervisor of a metropolitan hos-
pital. The spreading circles of uncertainty had evidently lapped against her. Momentarily, Mr. Weber wondered
whether she were about to appeal to him as one human
being to another, but his stirrings of fellowship were dispelled by her words.

"What has upset the boys? Where is the headmaster?
Why aren't you in your classroom?"

Mr. Weber regarded her with distaste. He shifted his
papers and attempted to stand without swaying. He wasn't
sure that he was succeeding, but he spoke with dignity,
"None of your questions, Miss Burtt, concerns anything I
wish to discuss. You will excuse me—" He bowed himself
around her and around the corner which separated him
from his rooms in one sweeping hazardous arc.

Miss Burtt compressed her lips. Two vertical lines deepened at the corners of her mouth. She looked speculatively down the center courtyard toward the north windows of the Office before she went on past the rest of the classrooms toward the kitchen and her daily wrangle with the cook. The woman who had preceded her at Drake's Anchorage had not accustomed the cook to supervision, and the kitchen was the one section of Miss Burtt's domain that she considered she had not satisfactorily regularized. Now she was beginning to suspect that in another graver field she had been remiss. She would take that up in good time.

Miss Burtt's predecessor had been a self-effacing elderly woman who had been with the school almost as long as Miss Breckenridge and the Bjornstroms. When she had departed the previous spring to care for an ailing relative, her going had removed so little from the life of the school that the headmaster had been tempted not to replace her. Mrs. Bjornstrom was there, and he was in the process of hiring Miss Blossom. He was disinclined to make further provision for pampering. But the school's doctor had said that he would not be answerable for the health of the boys unless there were a registered nurse on the grounds. So the headmaster had capitulated and left the responsibility of securing a person who would satisfy him with Dr. Sterne. Shortly before the opening of the fall term, the doctor had turned up with Miss Burtt. Some consideration of health was supposed to have influenced her retirement from a more active life, but it was difficult to associate any form of weakness with Miss Burtt. She had established a routine of dispensary hours and health checkups and pressed her dietary schedule ruthlessly on the easygoing, full-bellied cook. She had neither offered nor invited intimacy with any of the other school personnel, and had even snubbed poor Miss Blossom who that same fall had been introduced into the school to teach the small boys. That Miss Burtt had cared to go to Drake's Anchorage to become the caretaker of sniffles and menus should have puzzled anyone who paused to adjudge her apparent professional qualifications, but in the four months since her arrival, her associates had rarely wandered into such considerations. For there is an immediacy in the ordinary life of a school, carried on from bell to bell, an urgency welling eternally from the springs of childhood, that tends to push into the background of its personalities all that is not relevant to the activity of the school.

Indeed, on this first day of its truncated existence, Drake's Anchorage was carried forward mainly by the bells and the imperatives of childhood. Then at teatime came a lull, and most of the uneasy staff came to reconnoiter in the Faculty Common Room.

It was four o'clock. The sun, hanging low over the Pacific, flooded horizontally into the room, leaving the rafters and the floor in shadow, dimming the flames that were curling up over the recently lighted logs in the fireplace. The Common Room lay at the northeast corner of the school, immediately above a cove that cut into the shore line. The headmaster had had the windows of this room enlarged, and it was possible to stand beside them and gaze down the cliff to where the breakers dropped their thunderous weight on the rocks that had fallen from its face and then raced up a narrow finger of sand to hurl themselves in discordant involutions through the caves at the head of the cove. Also visible were stretches of the trail which led down and around to the opposite side of the cove where a point of land jutted out to shield the small inlet that provided anchorage for the *Golden Hind*. If the weather were good and the tide right, at this time of day it would be natural to look out over the flat expanse of ocean to search for a scrap of white sail. This would be the

Golden Hind coming in to run the gantlet of the breakers. Two or three boys might already be gathered importantly around the small skiff drawn up on the beach of the inlet, standing by to take off the crew of the *Golden Hind* after it had dropped anchor. And along the mile of trail there might be a half-dozen others, conferring sagaciously with each other on the state of wind and tide and the seamanship of that day's crew. But today, although the sky was clear and the breeze fresh, the *Golden Hind* dipped quietly at anchor and not a boy was visible on the trail.

Miss Blossom turned her back on the window and tried to puzzle out the undertones in the desultory conversation that was going on around the fireplace. Miss Breckenridge was pouring. Mrs. Bjornstrom was present. This, in itself, was unusual. Ordinarily, where one was the other wasn't.

"No sugar, Mr. Arbuthnot?"

"Thank you, that's right, Miss Breckenridge."

Mr. Arbuthnot blinked as he rose from his corner behind the chimney to face the sun and accept his cup. Mr. MacDowell, who was reclining on the chimney seat, allowed his knees to collapse and his feet almost to fill the corner Mr. Arbuthnot had been crouching in. Unable to see the feet in the shadow when he returned, Mr. Arbuthnot sat down upon them, rose so hastily that he spilled some of his tea, sat again with timid perseverance on the extreme edge of the seat, and pushed back as far as he could go.

"A tennis tournament at this time of year, Monsieur, would be a farce," said Mr. MacDowell. "Nothing but a series of postponements. And besides, who's in the mood for it? I'm not. The boys aren't. Nobody would sign up for it. No, sir," Mr. MacDowell concluded, setting his cup on the floor and folding his arms, "you're not going to railroad me into that."

"Granted, my dear fellow, that the idea at first glance is bizarre," Mr. Dingle answered for Monsieur Trougnac, "but the times are bizarre. You must contrive to present it in such a way that it does appeal to at least a dozen or so of the boys."

"Humph," said Mr. MacDowell. "You get up some charades!"

Mrs. Bjornstrom looked up from her knitting. "Now why don't you do that, Mr. Dingle, over at the Doghole? I'd like real well to take the little boys right back there after dinner these evenings." When Mr. MacDowell laughed she buttoned up her lips and smoothed her plump short lap. "Such goings on!"

Mr. Dingle retrieved her ball of yarn from where it had skittered under the tea-table and returned it to her with faintly insulting dexterity. "A delightful invitation. I shall consider it."

"Perhaps you can get Mrs. Cnut-Sorenson to help you," drawled Mr. MacDowell.

"Miss Blossom would be equally charming, and so much more accessible, don't you think, Mr. MacDowell?" said Mr. Dingle. "Miss Blossom, you haven't had your tea yet. Do come and join our happy circle."

"Are there boys on the Cliff Trail, Miss Blossom?" asked Monsieur Trougnac. "Have you seen any go down? No? Have your tea. I shall exchange places with you."

Miss Blossom accepted her tea, took the chair that Monsieur had vacated, and looked back across the room at his outlines, gilt-edged by the last rays of the sun. There was a hawk-like watchfulness in the set of his narrow shoulders and his nose was lengthened by the line of light upon it.

"We must have a plan," he said. "We must have order. How do we know that they are all outdoors now? Mr. Arbuthnot, do you know what your boys are doing at this moment?"

"They're up at the polo field with Mr. Pyke," replied Mr. Arbuthnot.

"All six of them?"

"I—only five have come— That is," Mr. Arbuthnot revised his approach nervously, "Humphrey Enders and Spencer Kydd went up to the polo field."

"And Fitz Eubank?" asked Mr. Dingle.

"I'm not quite certain. I know he wasn't in his room."

"That is not satisfactory, Mr. Arbuthnot," said Monsieur sternly. "Where are your boys, Mr. MacDowell?"

"Good lord," muttered Mr. MacDowell into his chest. "Do you want to run the place like a reform school? I saw Maxwell and Culbertson and, I think, Capon start off toward the corrals. I suppose they went on to the polo field. They usually do. If not, they're around up there somewhere with Walter, I don't know what happened to the others. Maybe some of them have sneaked back into their rooms to play blackjack. It's not going to ruin them for life."

"*Hélas,*" said Mr. Dingle, glancing at Monsieur, "*Si ce n'était que du blackjack!*"

"Maybe Mr. Weber has a game on," suggested Mr. Mac-Dowell, biting his thumb at Monsieur. "Hadn't you better go check up on him?"

"Mr. Weber!" exclaimed Monsieur, rising to the bait too easily to afford Mr. MacDowell a sportsman's thrill. "Where *is* Mr. Weber?"

Mr. Arbuthnot cracked his fingers in the stillness that followed Monsieur's question, and then in haste to generalize his inadvertent sounds, he rose and made for the door. There he had the ill-fortune to come face to face with Miss Burtt.

"Mr. Arbuthnot, I was looking for you. You haven't reported to me that Clarence Pidgeon isn't back yet. Is he ill?"

"Er—" Mr. Arbuthnot cleared his throat. His attitude suggested to Miss Blossom, who was not overly imaginative, that of a cornered animal that was about to make a

dash for it. What was there about the name of Clarence
Pidgeon that froze all the men in the room into a cautious silence? None of them seemed to be going to come to
Mr. Arbuthnot's assistance. It was Miss Breckenridge who
spoke harshly, and in attack.

"Well, tell her, Mr. Arbuthnot. You know what's the
matter with Clarence Pidgeon better than anyone else,
don't you?"

"Ah, lay off him, Miss Breckenridge," said Mr. Mac-
Dowell unexpectedly. "How in hell would you expect him
to know anything?"

"And you, young man," went on Miss Breckenridge,
crashing her teacup down as if she had come to the end of
her patience, "are more to be blamed than he is! You make
me sick. The lot of you. Charades! Tennis tournaments!
Lists!"

"Miss Breckenridge," Mr. Dingle went toward her.
"Have mercy on our humble proposals. We have, however
ineptly, to carry on—"

She shook his hand off her shoulder and rose. "Don't
you come worming yourself around me with your pretty
ways! I know how you've been using them this many a year,
and how you think you're going to get what you want at
last. But you're wrong. You couldn't hold the school together a month without him!"

"Miss Breckenridge, if you do not put yourself in control I discharge you!" Monsieur Trougnac's voice broke
shrilly across hers. "Order! Order! Now! At once! On this
instant!"

Miss Breckenridge laughed scathingly. "*You* discharge
me! I am responsible only to the headmaster, and I shall
remain so."

"Tschk, tschk! Such manners," said Mrs. Bjornstrom.

"Hypocrite," replied Miss Breckenridge. She marched
to the door to face the nurse.

"Miss Burtt, Clarence Pidgeon will not be back because he has lied, and his father has lied with him. The headmaster is absent, attending to the damage they have caused. While he is away, he expects his staff to continue in the duties he has assigned them. You should have been told. It should not have been left to me to tell you.

"But these miserable fools are all too busy taking advantage of his absence and pretending innocence. They think he isn't coming back. They *hope* he isn't coming back, because he made them be men." She turned to face the room balefully. "I know what has happened in the past and I see what you are up to now, and I won't forget. You had all best drop your poses and get down to brass tacks. What are you going to do to stamp out this lie? Miss Burtt, you help them thrash it out. I despise them too much. Miss Blossom, come with me."

Miss Blossom gazed around the room, dark now save for the firelight since the sun had gone. Monsieur Trougnac was gripping the back of the chair that Miss Breckenridge had left, hunched over it, breathing fast. Mrs. Bjornstrom still held her knitting but her fingers were not moving. Her gray hair, parted in the middle, fell over her forehead uniformly, like a wig. She was looking, without expression, at Miss Blossom. Mr. Dingle had retreated to the gloom by the window and she could not see his face, but his head was turned toward her. In fact, everyone in the room seemed to be staring at her, Miss Burtt and Mr. Arbuthnot from the doorway and Mr. MacDowell from where he stood in front of the fire. His legs threw weaving shadows across the tea-table. Miss Breckenridge had flung a command over her shoulder and disappeared. Naturally they would look to see whether she would obey it, Miss Blossom told herself, but still she was frightened. These people had become strangers—people she didn't know.

They were hostile. They were dangerous because they were hiding secrets.

Little Miss Blossom ran after Miss Breckenridge, out of the room and out of the northeast gate of the stockade. To her left, a dozen yards away, was the beginning of the Cliff Trail. To her right, the road she was standing on led along the wall to the lean-to under which the faculty parked their cars. There was space enough to turn a car easily on the ledge, graded and surfaced with gravel, but when getting hers out Miss Blossom invariably felt that she was backing right off the cliff. She could see the light from Miss Breckenridge's flash bobbing on the bumpers of the cars as she passed them. Miss Blossom hurried to catch up with her.

"You wanted me to come with you?" she panted.

Miss Breckenridge turned her light on Miss Blossom's face. It was an ordinary face, distinguished chiefly by youth and a coronet of heavy brown braids—a gingham, small-town face. Miss Blossom put up her hand, palm out, to shield her round questioning blue eyes.

"Please! What is it? What's happened to everybody?"

"You shouldn't be here," said Miss Breckenridge, starting to walk on, "but since you are, you can at least stay out of the row I've stirred up in there now. Get along to your room and stay there when you're not on duty."

"But Miss Breckenridge, why? What—"

"Good heavens, child! Just do as I tell you. I've got enough on my mind without playing nursemaid to you. There now, there's the bell. Run along and dress."

Miss Breckenridge gave her a little shove toward the gate before which they had paused and started to ascend the trail which led to Stone Cottage and the corrals. Several boys were leaping down its familiar turns, scattering pebbles before their careless boots.

"You, there," said Miss Breckenridge, catching them in the beams of her flashlight. "Stand still, and let me by, like little gentlemen."

The one in the lead slid obediently to a halt. "Hold everything, fellows! Good evening, Miss Breckenridge."

"I doubt it," said Miss Breckenridge, and picked her way past them up the trail.

Miss Blossom went through the gate the boys held open for her and on toward her rooms. The courtyards were cheeringly enlivened with the hum normal to forty or so boys in the half hour before supper. When she came to the door on her right, at the south end of the passageway, which divided her suite from the rest of the school, she didn't want to leave the noise behind. As she walked up her narrow windowless corridor, past the doors of the schoolroom, the bathroom, and her study, their voices became fainter. In her bedroom, backed up against an empty laundry, the only sound that came to her was the deep heaving of the ocean which was always waiting at Drake's Anchorage to seep into man-made silences.

5

Neil Truesdale: Trailbreaker

Miss Parelli arrived unusually early at the Office on Wednesday morning, for her curiosity was whetted. Even so, Miss Breckenridge, Monsieur Trougnac, and Mr. Dingle were already gathered there. This morning they scarcely noticed her. Miss Parelli settled herself pleasantly and prepared to listen until the hands of the clock should point to eight o'clock. Miss Breckenridge's back was turned toward the two men, but you felt that it was taking part in their conversation. The faces of both Monsieur Trougnac and Mr. Dingle were showing signs of wear.

"There is too much time," said Monsieur, "between the end of the study hall and the lights out. You saw, last night. It is impossible that we be everywhere. The small groups of two and three they are most serious. And especially the washrooms. The masters must look more often into the washrooms." He scribbled nervously with a silver pencil in a notebook that he took from the pocket of his shorts.

"The devil of it is," said Mr. Dingle, mopping his forehead with a spare handkerchief from an inside pocket, "that there's no way of ascertaining how much they know, or which ones know it. For example, I don't like the attitude of Fitz Eubank. Although he's clever enough not to be obvious, I could have read double meanings into almost everything he said at breakfast this morning."

"But of course. He was intimate with the Pidgeon child. You must be on guard. And also, his rooms master." His pencil hovered over his notebook. "And that is—" He frowned.

Mr. Dingle sighed. "That is Mr. Arbuthnot."

"A pity. He should have a stronger hand."

"The whole north courtyard needs a stronger hand. One doesn't expect much of either Mr. Arbuthnot or Mr. Weber."

"Ah yes, and that suite of older boys!" Monsieur Trougnac lowered his voice as if speaking of the condemned cells. "If we could appoint one of them in there to watch the rest of them? Perhaps Van?"

"Most unwise, Monsieur. Most unwise. I would not advise that we discuss this with a single boy. I wouldn't be surprised if this whole situation had not been precipitated by just such indiscretion."

"That is true, that is true. We must find another way to strengthen the supervision in the north courtyard." Monsieur Trougnac paced back and forth. "It is a place of serious difficulty. Nathaniel Vaughan was there. Miss Burtt tells me he has had one of his old attacks. She has isolated him in the infirmary. I wonder—" He stopped his pacing to look fearfully at Mr. Dingle.

"Indeed," said Mr. Dingle. "And he is in Mr. Weber's row—"

Monsieur Trougnac was reminded of another harassment. "Ah, Mr. Weber! Mr. Weber I have not seen since the noon hour of yesterday. All evening he did not come in! It was Neil who called Miss Burtt." Monsieur took his notebook out again and scribbled, "Such conduct can not be suffered."

"Under these circumstances, Monsieur, I would suggest that either you or I move into the headmaster's rooms." Mr. Dingle's tones intended casualness but did not quite succeed.

Miss Breckenridge ripped paper and carbon sheet out of her typewriter, crumpled them up, and threw them in the wastebasket. She got out a stenographic pad and began to make notes of her own. Mr. Dingle looked across to see what she was doing, but Monsieur Trougnac was too engrossed with his own reaction to Mr. Dingle's words to notice her.

"Move into the Head's suite? At this time? It had not occurred to me, but perhaps, as you say, under the circumstances—" He filled his narrow lungs and straightened his narrow shoulders. Then his eyes met the ingenuous interest of Miss Parelli's regard and he deflated. "But—then my own corridor, and the center courtyard—"

Mr. Dingle stood up. "Your hesitation is understandable. Mr. MacDowell, opposite you, is not always reliable." He paused, and seemed to wait gently for Monsieur Trougnac to be the one to continue the development of their deliberations.

"Whereas," Monsieur followed through eventually, "you would leave Mr. Pyke in charge of your courtyard if you were to move."

"Exactly, and although Mr. Pyke's scholastic contributions to the school are negligible, he does have a strong hand."

Miss Breckenridge's grunt was almost inaudible, but its effect on Mr. Dingle was electric. He whirled like a dervish, and the question seemed to be wrung from him against his will. "Miss Breckenridge, *what* are you writing?"

"When the headmaster returns," said Miss Breckenridge imperturbably, "he will want a record of what has taken place in his absence."

Mr. Dingle's face was pale as he fought to regain an appearance of suavity. When the phone rang, he abandoned the attempt and fairly leapt across the room. But the instrument was on Miss Breckenridge's desk and she had it in her hand before Mr. Dingle could reach her side. He stood over her as she spoke into it. From her words it became apparent that the person on the other end of the line was inquiring whether it was true that the headmaster had resigned. Miss Breckenridge cut the conversation short with a bald negative and hung up. Mr. Dingle was shivering. Miss Parelli noticed that his otherwise immaculate jacket was darkened with perspiration for a good three inches around the armpits.

"Mr. Dingle," said Miss Parelli in tactless surprise, "I believe you're ill!"

"My God, not yet," said Mr. Dingle from between his teeth, "but I will be, if this woman continues to inhabit this Office!" He attempted to light a cigarette, but his hands were trembling too much to bring the tip of it and the flame of the match into alignment. He threw both the match and the cigarette violently at the wastebasket, folded his fingers so that only his elbows were flapping, and addressed Miss Breckenridge in a voice which with a supreme effort he managed to keep level. "In your demoniacal soul, Miss Breckenridge, what possible motive can you have for alienating every parent that rings up? I forbid you to answer that phone again. Miss Parelli will take the messages, and call Monsieur Trougnac or me when necessary."

Miss Breckenridge said nothing but began to write again in her notebook. Mr. Dingle gazed down at her pothooks, his pale lips pressed shut, breathing audibly through his nose. Before he had found the phrases he was mustering, Walter lounged into the Office. A weather-beaten Stetson was pushed back from his weather-beaten face, and the high heels of his muddy boots were run down. He was six

foot three, broad of shoulder, but lanky. He jostled Mr.
Dingle away from the telephone without appearing to notice that he was there, and gave a San Rafael number to the
operator in a Texas drawl.

"Yeh, Pasquinucci? Huggins. . . . About those horses.
Tell Newt I'll take all four of them. All but that little bay.
. . . No. No, he knows I can't use her. . . . Yeh, sure I will,
right away. . . . Oh, I'll pick them up the next couple of
trips to town. . . . Well, I reckon I can get in Thursday and
Friday. . . . Say, that load of hay ain't turned up. . . . Well,
get on to him. Be seeing you."

Walter hung up and went on in the same easy tones,
"Miss Breckenridge, you can send a check for a hundred
and ninety dollars to the Pasquinuccis. They ain't fixed to
wait till the end of the month."

Mr. Dingle, who had reassembled himself at the far
side of the room while this was going on, arrested Walter's
saunter toward the door.

"By whose authority?" asked Mr. Dingle.

"Mine," grinned Walter, and began to drift again.

"Then it is evidently necessary to make our situation
more clear," said Mr. Dingle crisply. "Mrs. Cnut-Sorenson
has placed Monsieur in charge of the school. Miss Breckenridge's signature may still be recognized by the bank
through Lind's arrangement, but it may also have already
been canceled. Miss Breckenridge's signature will not be
authorized by Monsieur Trougnac. You will have to consult
Monsieur Trougnac about the purchase of those horses."

Walter sucked a hunk of something and looked as
though he wanted to spit. He got the hunk into one cheek.
"I take my orders from the Head. I haven't heard any different. He wants those horses. I'll take my chances on the
check's being good. Mail it, Miss Breckenridge."

"Now let us not talk too quick," said Monsieur Trougnac uneasily, "Walter, we shall wait about the horses until

our affairs are in order. Yes? Call back the man and tell
him there is delay."

Walter returned to spit trenchantly into the wastebasket. He was accurate, and its metal base clanked the frac-
tion of an inch across the stone floor.

"I'll tend to my business and you tend to yours," said
Walter. "My business is the corrals. You keep out of the
corrals." He appeared to reflect. "The horses might step
on you," he concluded, and turned a dead pan on Miss
Parelli before he walked out.

"*C'est le comble!*" sighed Monsieur. "Mr. Dingle, it is
time for the bell."

"About the north courtyard?" Mr. Dingle reminded him.

Monsieur glanced at Miss Breckenridge's stiff shoulders. "Let us not move too quick there also," Monsieur
hedged. "*Allons!* The bell!" Monsieur Trougnac escaped.

Mr. Dingle shifted his coat collar, smoothed his hair,
dusted his shoulders, and followed. Miss Parelli watched
Miss Breckenridge lock her notebook in a drawer and stand
up. When Miss Breckenridge looked at her, Miss Parelli
could read nothing in her expression except an awareness
that Miss Parelli had not yet attacked her morning's work.
Miss Parelli turned to her books, and Miss Breckenridge to
the south windows of the Office.

Centered at the other end of the south courtyard was
the mathematics classroom. To the south of it, lay the
history and Latin rooms, to the north of it, the French
and English. Miss Breckenridge arrived at the windows
in time to see Mr. Pyke turn the far corner to the right,
and Mr. Dingle the one to the left. Boys streaked along
after them. The headmaster had established ironclad rules
about tardiness. Mr. Weber's door stood open, and the last
boys threw themselves over its threshold just as the final
bell sounded. Immediately, what had been bedlam became
cloistered quiet.

Miss Breckenridge was about to turn away from the window when Wyman Gould, Jr., and Buddington Wright reappeared in the doorway of the mathematics room. They reconnoitered the passageway. Then after gesturing to others still inside, they walked out into the courtyard. After a short interval, Houghton Kennard, Porter Philpott, and the Chevalier twins followed. They appeared to confer. Wyman thrust his head once more inside the door, but jumped out again backwards in mock alarm. He rejoined the others and said something which made them laugh. Upon that, Neil Truesdale II plunged through the door to land in the middle of the group, scattering it. He spoke rapidly with gestures, but not loudly enough for Miss Breckenridge to hear him. Wyman responded, and Neil's arm shot out. Then there was a flurry of flailing arms and legs, partially hidden from Miss Breckenridge by the cheering circle around it. Monsieur approached from the north and was lost in it. Mr. Pyke dived in from the south, and came up with the collar of a boy in each hand. The commotion subsided as he set them down, retaining a firm grip on each of them, and looked to Monsieur. Other boys were leaking from each corner into the courtyard. Monsieur's staccato tones penetrated the Office windows as he ordered them back to their classrooms. When only the two culprits remained, Monsieur went his way with Neil Truesdale, and Mr. Pyke disappeared with Wyman. Almost immediately thereafter, Peter Van Tassel came loping down the courtyard. When he arrived in the Office, Miss Breckenridge was seated again at her desk.

"Miss Breckenridge," said Van, "I have a message for you from Monsieur. He says Mr. Weber must be ill. He wants you to go see what's the matter with him, and he wants Miss Parelli to go teach his class."

"Me? Teach? Me?" exclaimed Miss Parelli who, not having witnessed the fight, was somewhat behind on events. "I never heard of such a thing!"

"Well, you have now. Thank you, Van. Tell Monsieur I'll attend to it. You'd best go back to your class." Miss Breckenridge shooed him from the room and turned to Miss Parelli. "And you'll probably hear of a lot worse before this is over. Get along. Review the multiplication table. You'll manage all right."

Miss Breckenridge went off toward Mr. Weber's rooms in the north courtyard.

As there was no response to her knock on the door of his study, she opened it and walked in. The door of the inner room stood ajar, and she could see a lump which was evidently Mr. Weber in a disordered bed. She could also smell him, and hear his snores. An empty bottle lay on the floor beside him. Miss Breckenridge shook him roughly by the shoulder.

"Damnation," said Mr. Weber. "Go 'way."

"Get up," said Miss Breckenridge. "You're late for class."

"What of it? Can't you see the writing on the wall?"

"We'll keep going till the Head gets back. Get up, I say. Here're your trousers. Get something on and I'll bring you some coffee and you'll be in time for the second period."

Mr. Weber sat groggily on the edge of the bed and pulled on his trousers and some shoes.

"He's not coming back." He paused in tying a shoe to look up at Miss Breckenridge with tears in his eyes. "He won't show his face here again, the poor damned fool!" He sobbed, and pounded on a snarled shoestring. "The lying bastard!"

"Shut up," said Miss Breckenridge. "Here's your shirt."

"Didn't even have enough sense to cover his tracks!"

"You're drunk," said Miss Breckenridge, "but that's no excuse. I have a mind to slap you."

Mr. Water struggled to his feet and began to get into his coat. "You dried-up old virago! What do you know about it?" He held his head and felt his way along the wall toward the door, telling himself as he went, "Nothing at all. She doesn't know 'thing 't all—"

"Comb your hair and wash your face. You can't go to class that way."

"Not going class. Going town."

He fumbled in his pockets, peered at his bureau where his keys were lying, and started to grope across the room in that direction. Miss Breckenridge met him halfway, pushed him off balance and back down on his bed. He began to whimper. She picked up the keys and went out, closing both doors behind her, and paused in the passageway to consider.

Somebody was going to have to keep track of Mr. Weber. Mr. Bjornstrom was probably somewhere about, but Miss Breckenridge did not relish having to appeal to him. She set off toward the infirmary. In spite of the fact that the new nurse shot herself with insulin before every meal, she seemed to be a levelheaded person, Maybe she had something up her sleeve she could do with Mr. Weber. Miss Breckenridge crossed the courtyard, rounded a turn by the Faculty Common Room and entered the infirmary. The entryway and the dispensary were empty. Miss Burtt must be out on her rounds. Miss Breckenridge remembered what Monsieur had said about Nathaniel Vaughan and looked into the isolation room. Nat was there, lying face down without a pillow, but he turned over when he heard her step.

"Oh, Miss Breckenridge," he said at once. "I've got to see Van. Please, Miss Breckenridge, ask Van to come here. She took my clothes."

She felt his cheek. It was hot, and a pulse was visible in his throat. "Now, what have you been doing? Running up hill again?"

"I'm all right. I mean I'd be all right if I could see Van. Please tell him!"

"Well, well, maybe I will, but what's so important about Van? Miss Burtt wants you to keep still and not see people."

He looked up at her pleadingly. "It's something I've got to—do. Don't make me wait any longer! She doesn't understand."

"All right, sonny, I'll tell him." She patted his cheek again. "And you tell Miss Burtt, when she comes back, that I want to see her."

As Miss Breckenridge went past the north courtyard, she noted that Mr. Weber's door was still closed. She intended to go on to the kitchen on the chance that Miss Burtt might be there, but as she came by the empty Office, she heard the telephone ring. She went in to answer it, dropping Mr. Weber's keys on her desk as she did so. It was Mrs. Cnut-Sorenson, asking for Mr. Dingle.

"He's in class," said Miss Breckenridge.

"Will you have him call me, please, at his earliest convenience? The matter is urgent."

"School business?" asked Miss Breckenridge tartly. "I can handle it for you."

"Really, Miss Breckenridge!" Mrs. Cnut-Sorenson's voice came over the wire with a musical hint of annoyance. "If I say that I wish to speak to Mr. Dingle, obviously it is Mr. Dingle to whom I wish to speak."

"In the headmaster's absence," replied Miss Breckenridge, "I am referring all school matters to Monsieur Trougnac. I shall let him know you called."

"Miss Breckenridge," said Mrs. Cnut-Sorenson, an unpleasant edge cutting up through her throaty tones, "I have had complaints from the parents about your insolence. Mr. Dingle has spoken to me about it. Your long association with the school has made you careless, but I must remind you that it is not a life tenure. These are difficult days, and I am loath to make changes, but do not doubt that I shall remove you if it becomes necessary. I shall consider it necessary if I hear of your making one more obstructionist move. Let Mr. Dingle phone me during the morning recess. Good day."

As Miss Breckenridge slammed down the receiver, the bell signaling the end of the first period sounded. "Presumptuous hussy," she muttered.

During the five-minute interval between classes she watched the boys circulate. She kept an eye on the door of the mathematics room, but Miss Parelli did not appear in it. "So far, so good," she went on to herself after the second bell. "Now, where has that nurse got to?"

She found her with the cook. The cook had his hat on.

"Just take off that hat, Olie, and quit bluffing. You know you're not going to walk off when the headmaster needs you so badly," said Miss Breckenridge, "Miss Burtt, what are you up to?"

"Juice, she wants now," said Olie. "Squash juice, bean juice, carrot juice! Labeled, in bottles! And what do I make soup with, I asks her!"

"I have explained that to you, Olsen," said Miss Burtt. "We won't discuss it any further now. Miss Breckenridge, you wished to speak with one of us?"

"Yes, you. But first I will say that I agree with Olie. You mean well, Miss Burtt, but you're finicky. No male, young or old, likes innovations in his food. Forget about that stuff in that book of yours and give them meat and potatoes. Throw in one vegetable, if you want to, and we'll stuff that down 'em."

"Miss Breckenridge, as you yourself suggested, I am continuing in the duties I have been assigned. I'll thank you to do the same."

Miss Breckenridge was a realist and she needed allies.

"Well, all right. Then go see to Mr. Weber. If he's not one of your duties yet, he soon will be. Get him washed up and back in the classroom before little Miss Parelli gets into algebra. I doubt whether she's at home in it, and I need her in the Office. You'll find Mr. Weber in bed—I hope.

"Do you have any coffee made, Olie? You'll probably need a pot of it, Miss Burtt." Miss Breckenridge nodded to them both amicably and left the kitchen.

Olie filled a small coffee pot from a larger one which had been sitting on the back of the stove, and got out a cup. "Do you want I should take it to him, ma'am? I'm used to his ways."

Miss Burtt thrust her notebook in the pocket of her white sweater and took the tray from his hands. "No. I'll see to it. He's done this before, then?"

"In the old days, ma'am. Not since the headmaster came."

"Deplorable. Well, you have your menu for today, Olsen."

Olie rested his fists on his hips and watched Miss Burtt march off, shaking his head mournfully. He sighed audibly as he removed his hat.

"Bad days, bad days," said Mr. Bjornstrom from the laundry whither he had retired at the time of Miss Burtt's arrival.

"Too many interfering women," agreed the cook.

Mr. Weber, had he been able to hear the words, would have concurred. Miss Burtt put him under his shower. The water was cold. When the bell for the third period rang after milk lunch, Mr. Weber was in his classroom, and Miss Burtt was in her bedroom changing into dry clothes.

While she was there, the telephone rang in the dispensary. Her line was an extension of the one in the Office. After a minute, she heard the buzzer that signaled that the call was for her. That would no doubt be the school doctor. She buttoned the flap of her skirt and moved without hurrying to where she could pick up the instrument.

"Yes? This is Miss Burtt speaking."

"Dr. Sterne, here. Er— Thank you, Miss Breckenridge."

There was a click as Miss Breckenridge hung up.

"I expected you to get in touch with me yesterday," said Dr. Sterne.

"I'm sorry. I thought you would be coming out."

"Five parents have tried to see me! I thought it wisest to be able to say I had no information until I'd heard from you what the conditions were out there. Do you realize that my professional reputation is at stake? Your negligence has placed me in an impossible position. Worse than negligence! How on earth did you bungle so? Didn't you see what was happening?"

"I have a patient here in the infirmary that I think you should see, Doctor."

"Oh! There now? Who is it?"

"Nathaniel Vaughan."

"Damnation!"

"Yes, Doctor."

"Well, I suppose I must go out. God damn! This thing is dynamite. Did you talk to the headmaster? What is he going to do?"

"I think it would be advisable for you to come out this afternoon, Doctor. There are several matters on which I need to consult you."

"Well, arrange it so we can talk without being overheard. I'll be there at about two o'clock."

"I usually go over to look in on the small boys during the rest hour."

"That's no good. Stay there in the dispensary."

"Very well, Doctor."

6

Miss Parelli: School Bookkeeper

Mr. MacDowell walked into the Great Hall after lunch behind Miss Parelli.

"There's a story going around, Miss Parelli, that there was a duel fought over you this morning. And Brock Chevalier couldn't eat his dessert. Is it true that he sent you a dozen red roses?"

Miss Parelli was quick on the uptake. "Why, I thought they were from you, Mr. MacDowell!"

"I only wish I'd thought of it. Look, my angel, tonight's my free evening. What about having dinner with me somewhere cozy?"

Miss Parelli was not sure whether the invitation was part of his joke or to be considered seriously. "Well now," she parried, "I'll have to think that over. Do you think it would look well?"

"I think it would look very well indeed," said Mr. MacDowell, apparently on the level.

Miss Parelli dropped into one corner of a long couch and inspected him from under her lashes. Mr. MacDowell flopped down beside her. Robert Wintringham and Sterling Abernathy, who had a checker game going on the other end of the couch, caught the checkers as they slid downhill and replaced them in their proper squares in righteous silence.

"What are you doing with those things in here?" Mr. MacDowell said. "Take them into the Games Room where they belong and they won't get upset."

"We've only twelve minutes till rest hour, sir," replied Rab. "It'll be all right," he added magnanimously, "if you don't move around."

Mr. MacDowell heaved a sigh. "Would you care for a stroll on the terrace, Miss Parelli?"

"I'd rather just sit." Although she had a comfortable confidence in her power to charm, Miss Parelli suspected that something more than met the eye underlay his sudden display of interest. He wasn't really thinking about her, even now. His eyes were following Miss Breckenridge and Mr. Pyke as they came out of the dining room together and walked the length of the Great Hall to disappear into the library.

"What—" said Mr. MacDowell, and then broke off to lift himself gingerly off the couch. He turned his back on the checker players and smiled down on her intimately. "I'll drop into the Office later this afternoon if you can have that information ready for me, Miss Parelli."

"I can't promise anything," said Miss Parelli.

"It would be a great kindness." He went toward the courtyard doors.

Monsieur Trougnac relinquished a group of older boys whom he had been addressing with determined brightness. "Mr. MacDowell, I would have a few words with you. We will walk together."

When they had gone, Miss Parelli sensed a hollow cheerlessness about the Great Hall that she had never before been aware of. Ordinarily, almost everyone drifted in there after lunch. The long morning of classes was over. The boys had been fed. Very shortly they would have to retire to their rooms for an hour. In the few minutes before the bell, rival projects for the afternoon were hatched and passionately promoted. There always seemed to be so many more undertakings bidding for attention than there could possibly be time to enjoy. Young and old, the weary and the innocent, everyone in the room would unconsciously absorb vitality from the hubbub. "The world is so full of a number of things that I'm sure we should all be as happy as kings." Miss Parelli realized now that that prevailing attitude must somehow have been set in motion by the presence of the headmaster. For today he was not there, and no one seemed to want to stay in the room. There were only a few boys left, and none of the faculty. The boys to whom Monsieur Trougnac had been talking wandered dolefully out on the terrace. Miss Parelli went off to renew her lipstick and powder her nose.

Early in the afternoon, Dr. Sterne brought the de Herreras into the Office. Dr. Sterne was a large, smooth-shaven, firm-cheeked man who always had creases in his trousers and a fresh handkerchief in his pocket.

"The Señora Francisco de Herrera," he said as he opened the door, as if he were announcing royalty.

An enticing odor accompanied the Señora into the room. Her two small sons followed her. They were the issue of a previous marriage she had made with an Australian, but the Señor de Herrera had reclaimed them for Mexico and his hacienda by legal adoption. He was well on in years and had never had children of his own. Juan, the prospective heir, had large dark eyes and a narrow chest and a fixed idea that he was a failure. He was eleven years old. Alonzo, who was nine, was sturdy in body and spirit. He always thought he could do anything and would keep on trying to do it until forcibly restrained. During the exchange of words among the adults which ensued, neither of them spoke, but whereas Juan remained listlessly in the exact geographical location into which he had eddied in his mother's wake, Alonzo inspected the entire room and manipulated everything movable.

"Miss Breckenridge," said Dr. Sterne, "perhaps you will arrange it so that the Señora can have a talk with Miss Blossom and Mrs. Bjornstrom. I understand the headmaster is not here."

"You are so kind, Doctor." The Señora offered her soul to him with her eyes. "The taximan was quite lost when you rescued us." She sank gracefully into the chair that he pulled out for her and arranged a cigarette in a long holder. Dr. Sterne struck a match for her. As he leaned over, she added with a directness that contrasted inauspiciously with her earlier manner, "I shall wish to see *you,* you know, when I have left the children with the good Mrs. Bjornstrom."

He straightened up. "A thousand apologies, Señora! But I am here on a flying visit. I shall be an hour late at my office as it is. You will forgive me." He closed the door on himself rapidly.

The Señora smiled a slow smile at Miss Breckenridge. "He is not anxious to talk, that one." She made a leisurely *moue* and produced a smoke ring. "And you," she continued softly. "How very very sad it is for you. You loved him so much." Her voice was like a violin.

Miss Breckenridge was angry, but her sharp tongue failed her under the direct attack of the limpid panther eyes. It was useless to dissemble. "I'll take you to Miss Blossom," she said gruffly.

"But I have no interest in Miss Blossom," objected the Señora, using a higher, clearer string. "She does very well what she is paid to do. Let this young girl take the children to their housemother. Go now, Juan." She touched the boy's shoulder lightly and turned her cheek toward him. "Kiss me, darling." He did as he was bidden. "Come,

Alonzo, Alonzo!" The repetition of his name penetrated Alonzo's preoccupation with the adding machine. He turned undazzled eyes upon his mother. "Come here, little one." She held out her other arm. "Miss— You will have to tell me your name again—" The Señora was now smiling persuasively at Miss Parelli.

Miss Parelli looked at Miss Breckenridge. She hoped and expected that she would object to the arrangement that the Señora was making. But Miss Breckenridge failed her. She said nothing. She had turned her face away. Awed by Miss Breckenridge's unusual submissiveness, she took Alonzo by the hand and led him to his mother. "Mary Parelli," she said.

"But of course. I am stupid to forget." The Señora elicited a kiss from her second son. "Good-bye, my darlings. Go with Miss Parelli."

Miss Parelli had to leave just when things were getting interesting.

The Señora waited until the door had closed. "It is all too incredibly naive, too stupidly disastrous," she said. Miss Breckenridge maintained her silence. "Oh come, Miss Breckenridge," said the Señora with a touch of impatience. "You can be frank with me. I talked with Mrs. Maxwell at the hotel this morning. Where is the headmaster?"

"He is in Chicago," replied Miss Breckenridge doggedly, "consulting with the founders on the policy of the school."

The Señora made a gesture of distaste. "Everyone has been stupid, but he has been most stupid!" She paused to turn on Miss Breckenridge's stiff face eyes that understood and forgave the sorrows of all the world. "I am very sorry for him." Then she went on with crisp definiteness, "I am willing to buy his share of the school. These founders, I will buy them out too. For I want the school to continue. It is what I wish for my sons. Try now to see if you can reach him by telephone."

"The school is not for sale," said Miss Breckenridge flatly.

Anger flickered in the Señora's face although not a muscle moved.

"You do not help him that way," she said, after an interval in which she had become gentle again. "I am making an offer he will be glad to avail himself of, and he is not in a position to refuse."

More than anything that had gone before, this woman threatened Miss Breckenridge's tenaciously cherished belief that Alrik could not go down to defeat. Almost, her hand reached out toward the telephone. At that moment, the bell signaling the end of the rest period echoed through the courtyards. Miss Breckenridge went to the window. Instantaneously, the school came to life. Before the bell had ceased ringing, boys were shouting to each other, clattering back and forth in their heavy riding boots, swooping down upon the large wooden bowl of red apples that was waiting for them outside the Office windows. This resiliency was the talisman she needed. It was like being again in the physical presence of the headmaster. He had known these things when he had stood beside her in Stone Cottage only yesterday morning, and he had gone out to fight.

"I have my instructions, Señora," said Miss Breckenridge. "The school *is* continuing. I have nothing further to say." She turned her back on the Señora de Herrera, and appeared to consult a filing cabinet.

Señora de Herrera rose also. Her patience was exhausted. "Imbecile!" She spat out the word. "Do you suppose that I can not arrange it without your assistance?" She went to the window and opened it. "Monsieur," she called out to Monsieur Trougnac who was hovering nervously near the group around the apples, "I wish to talk with you."

When Monsieur Trougnac recognized her, he came eagerly into the Office. "Señora," he exclaimed, bending over her extended hand. "How happy I am to see you! And the little boys? Juan? Alonzo? They are with you?" he asked anxiously.

The Señora smiled. "Do not excite yourself, Monsieur. They are here. But it is not of them I wish to speak. I am here because it is my intention to buy Drake's Anchorage."

Monsieur Trougnac lifted his head slowly to gaze into the Señora's madonna face. "Señora," he breathed, "your heart is large."

Miss Breckenridge, who had been watching the tableau, did an unheard-of thing. She abandoned the field of battle. She seized her mackintosh from its hook and went out across the Great Hall to the terrace where she could look out to sea. As the wind whipped at her coat and the mist dampened her hair, she did not exactly have thoughts. Images passed across the screen of her mind. Their passing blurred the harsh determination of her face and posture. Finally she said aloud a thing that she had never said, nor even ever thought, before.

"I am grown old."

She wanted rest. Most of all she wanted solitude. She walked the length of the terrace, her eyes lowered to follow the contours of the redwood flagging—rings within rings within rings, recording the passing of the years in which these dull blocks had been living trees. At the corner of the Common Room, she hesitated. The trail up to the corrals past Stone Cottage would be a thoroughfare for another two hours. She did not want to sit indoors, acquainting herself with grief, listening to young voices. She went down the Cliff Trail.

Well below the rim, at the upper end of the cove where the trail crossed a crevice by means of a wooden bridge, she stopped, and leaned against its rail. From time to time, an exceptionally large wave thrust a geyser up the crevice and brushed her face with cool spray as it subsided. Her eyes were on the muted masts of the *Golden Hind*.

"Alrik, Alrik," she murmured, and did not know which Alrik she mourned. Was this one, too, to die, and yet live on?

While Miss Parelli was wending her way back down the trail from the Doghole, she saw three cars drive up the hairpin turns which would carry them to the top of the ridge and away from the school. The first was the chrome-armored coupé that Dr. Sterne had been driving for the past four months. Not two minutes after the three-o'clock rising bell, and before any of the boys had had time to get outside, Mr. Weber's prewar model came snorting around the turns. Not his free evening, if it was Mr. MacDowell's. Miss Parelli wondered whether he would get back in one piece, whether she would have to take his early classes again the next day. She didn't mind. She'd had a good time. Only perhaps tomorrow she wouldn't feel too bright herself—if she went into town with Mr. MacDowell. She decided she'd tell him she would go if he would come and pick her up at home. That would take him a long way around. Maybe he'd suggest that they go on into San Francisco. And finally came the yellow cab carrying the Señora Francisco de Herrera. It would be a good joke if she caught up with the doctor. Miss Parelli reached the southeast gate together with a couple of small boys. They had left the Doghole with a five-minute handicap, but Miss Parelli had not hurried. Douglas Cahill held the gate open for her. Although he was a puny little thing, the gesture carried authentic gallantry. She wished she could teach her little brothers to open doors.

Monsieur Trougnac was waiting for her in the Office. He looked less worried, but more suspicious. "Mademoiselle," he said, "it is necessary to make changes. In a short time, there will be someone here to take Miss Breckenridge's place. Until then, you will be alone."

"Miss Breckenridge!" exclaimed Miss Parelli, looking around the Office in amazement "Is Miss Breckenridge leaving?"

"I am recommending that your salary be increased as of the first of this month. Miss Breckenridge—Miss Breckenridge has been unable to adjust herself to the changes."

"Golly!" said Miss Parelli, sinking weakly into the chair that the Señora had lately occupied.

"It will not be for long that you are alone. Continue the bookkeeping, and for the rest, take messages for me. You, yourself, Mademoiselle, do not give information." He gazed at her sternly. "All, all, you refer to me."

Miss Parelli let her glance travel over the filing cabinets into which she had never looked, the door of the stores room to which she had no key, the safe for which she did not know the combination, the neat top and locked drawers of what, eternally in her mind, could only be "Miss Breckenridge's desk."

"Golly!" repeated Miss Parelli.

The telephone rang. Miss Parelli looked at Monsieur Trougnac and he nodded. She approached Miss Breckenridge's chair and sat down diffidently.

"Hello," she said faintly into the mouthpiece of the instrument. "Eh—this is Drake's Anchorage."

"Who is that speaking?" asked the voice of Mrs. Cnut-Sorenson from the other end of the line.

"This is Mary Parelli—the bookkeeper—"

"Oh yes." Mrs. Cnut-Sorenson sounded relieved. "This is Mrs. Cnut-Sorenson, Miss Parelli. Please tell Monsieur Trougnac that I got his message, and that I'll try to be there between seven and eight. I'm calling from the city. You have that straight? Between seven and eight

"Yes, Mrs. Cnut-Sorenson. You'll be here between seven and eight."

It wasn't going to be too bad. Miss Parelli hung up and turned to see whether Monsieur Trougnac had understood the message. She was startled by the intensity of his gaze.

"Mademoiselle, one thing I must be sure of, or you will have to go too. Not one word you say outside of what takes its place inside this Office. Have I your oath of that?" His face was almost touching hers, so much in earnest was he.

Miss Parelli leaned away from him. "Why yes, Monsieur, of course."

"*Bien!*"

Monsieur went out like a beagle, with his nose well in advance of his shoulders, and his shoulders in advance of his hips. He was fishing as he went in the pockets of his shorts, doubtless in search of his little black book. Miss Parelli was left in command of the Office.

As that Wednesday afternoon waned to its sudden brumal darkness, Nathaniel Vaughan lay passively in the gloom of the isolation room. He heard Peter Van Tassel apprehended and sternly dismissed by Miss Burtt when he had got up the infirmary corridor almost as far as Nat's door. Mr. Arbuthnot huddled over a fire in his study and poked persistently at the charring pages of a diary he was burning. In San Francisco, Mrs. Cnut-Sorenson had a cocktail with Mr. Josiah Pidgeon in his hotel and succeeded where all others had failed. She was granted an interview alone with his son. Mrs. Gordon Maxwell II sat in her hotel room under a pink bed lamp in a coral fluff of gently

waving marabou, composing letters to the school founders in black ink and a surprisingly bold hand. Mr. Weber
reached the mahogany haven of the '49 Club in San Rafael,
and Mr. MacDowell and Miss Parelli dined in Sausalito.

Not many miles away from any of them, as the crow
flies, limped one of the forgotten men. He was following
the coast road north, but he had no special destination. He
had had none for the last six years. In the summer of '41,
at the age of eighteen, he had been drafted into the army
out of a Cleveland filling station. Having developed arthritis in his knee during his basic-training period, he had
been beached from before Pearl Harbor until well after V-J
Day in one of the army's fields in Marin County. Hospi-
tals and agencies had conflicted in their diagnoses and in
their recommendations. He had been separated without a
medical discharge. Cleveland had seemed changed. He had
got back his old job, but he had not held it. The winter
had brought him back to California which might possibly
seem more like home. New Year's Eve had taken the last of
his cash. On this Wednesday evening, when he had gone
back to the field at which he had been stationed for five
years to ask somebody who might know, "What next?" he
hadn't been allowed to go through the gate. "You're not in
the army now, fellow," they had told him. He was cold, his
shoulder ached as well as his knee, and he had no money.
At nine o'clock, when a ride he had hitched dropped him
off at Stinson Beach, he entered Pop Bartello's Shrimp
Shop at the northern end of the town.

7

Miss Burtt: School Nurse

Miss Blossom opened her eyes on darkness and wondered what change in the restless outer night had wakened her. She was too cut off from the courtyards of the school for any sound to have reached her from within. There was the constant lament of the wind under the dank eaves above her windows and the monotonous thud of the surf below them. There was the faint raucous wail of the foghorn off Point Reyes. To these familiars of the night she should have been inured. She waited.

Then from within her own suite, her name was called. The voice was petitioning, but the empty hallway lent it an eerie echo.

"Miss Blossom?"

The realization that the wistful Mr. Arbuthnot was standing in her private corridor at—she consulted a luminous dial—at one o'clock in the morning was incongruously chilling. Never even in broad daylight had he heretofore approached her door. Had the impotent curiosity she had felt in his regard unhinged his reason and induced in him this extremity of bravado? Her door was not locked.

"What is it?" she questioned in as calm a voice as she could muster, and got out of bed to put on her bathrobe and slippers.

"Miss Blossom, can you come here, please?"

She went to her door and softly felt around the knob. Yes, it did have a lock. She hadn't, in her momentary panic, been sure. She kept her finger on the button in the center of the knob.

"Why? What's wrong?" she asked again.

"It's Miss Burtt," replied Mr. Arbuthnot, with a suggestion of panic in his own voice. "There seems to be something the matter with Miss Burtt. Can you come?"

Miss Burtt! That citadel of competence! Miss Blossom, the novitiate, was being called upon in the dead of the night to succor Miss Burtt! However startling these fresh tidings, they nevertheless appeared to explain the presence of Mr. Arbuthnot. Miss Blossom opened her door. Halfway down the corridor, a flashlight was pointed obsequiously at the floor.

"Why yes, of course." When she shut her door and went toward him, he turned and hurried down the hall ahead of her. "What's the matter with her?"

He led on along the rear passageway past the empty classrooms. "I don't know," he whispered over his shoulder. "You come and see."

He diagonaled almost at a trot across the north courtyard to round the corner by the Faculty Common Room. She was close at his heels. She had never been to the courtyards after the corner lights had been turned off. By his jogging light, the walls and posts seemed warped and twisted out of the positions in which she expected to encounter them, and she lost confidence in her sense of direction. In the entryway of the infirmary he stopped short and switched off his flash. She caught her breath. There was someone standing there in the darkness.

"Any more?" asked Mr. Arbuthnot in a low voice.

"No, sir," whispered the frightened voice of a boy.

"All right, Nat. Miss Blossom is here. You'd better go back to bed now."

"Not back *there!*" Nathaniel Vaughan beseeched him. "I *can't* go back in *there* again, sir!"

"No, you don't want to do that," Mr. Arbuthnot agreed. "You'd better go to your own room. Can you make it all right now? I'll look in on you later."

"Yes sir, thank you sir," replied Nat fervently, "I'll be all right." He was gone immediately.

Miss Blossom waited, and Mr. Arbuthnot waited. Finally, the latter suggested, "You look, Miss Blossom." When she still hesitated, ill-prepared to challenge the unknown before which both Nat and Mr. Arbuthnot had quailed, he added faintly, "In the living room—I think."

Miss Blossom forced herself to advance past the dark door of the dispensary to the entrance of Miss Burtt's living room. The door was open. She could hear nothing. Yet something seemed to be waiting there too in the darkness. She felt inside the door and found a light switch and flooded the room with light.

In the middle of the living room, halfway between her bedroom door and the door which opened directly into the dispensary from her living room, Miss Burtt was crawling on her hands and knees, clad only in an inadequate nightgown. Her heavy hair hung down in two disheveled braids to catch under her hands as she placed them flat on the floor. Miss Burtt interrupted her labored progress to glance over her shoulder around one of her braids at Miss Blossom, transfixed in the doorway. Her face broke into what could momentarily pass for the professionally cheery smile with which she approached little boys with a throat swab. But there was a glitter in the wide eyes, and a strain in the lines around them and around the mouth as it stretched on back and back from her teeth in a slow grimace. From her throat came a long high howl like a coyote's. With little pants, and still grinning, she shifted her hands as if to crawl toward Miss Blossom. Almost swooning with terror, Miss Blossom backed out of Miss Burtt's line of vision. But that location was even worse. Now she couldn't see Miss Burtt either, nor know whether she was coming on. Miss Blossom ran back to fling herself into the timorous arms of Mr. Arbuthnot.

"That's the third time she's done that," quavered Mr. Arbuthnot, so completely deranged that he did not immediately notice his unaccustomed position. "She woke Nat up with the first one. He called me, and when I— knocked—" He gulped. "When I—looked in, she did it again!" He disengaged himself jerkily from Miss Blossom's clutch. Then he waited again for Miss Blossom to take the initiative.

Miss Blossom stared back at the illumined doorway. Nothing appeared in it, and from it issued only an urgent silence. She began to be able to reason. "It must have something to do with her diabetes," she said.

Her relief at having hit upon a natural explanation for the shockingly unnatural was short-lived. Who among them, at Drake's Anchorage, could shoulder the crisis when the nurse, herself, was the patient? "You'd better call Dr. Sterne," she added feebly.

"My heavens," replied Mr. Arbuthnot. "He's thirty-five miles away. Something should be done now!"

"Well, call him anyway, and he can tell us what to do till he comes."

The light from the living room shone through the open doors of the dispensary where the telephone was. "You'd better do it," said Mr. Arbuthnot.

Little Miss Blossom called up her reserves of strength. There was a human being inside that animal that was somehow doubly awesome on account of the demeanor one expected in Miss Burtt. She went into the dispensary to the telephone which was on a desk behind the door that gave on the living room. She had to cross before that door. As she did so, Miss Burtt howled again.

It seemed to Miss Blossom that it took her forever to locate the Ross number in the nurse's directory, to get the operator, and to hear the connection put through. Then it seemed to her that Dr. Sterne took forever to answer.

"Hello," a sleepy voice said gruffly at last. "Dr. Sterne here."

"Oh, Dr. Sterne!" Miss Blossom attempted to describe their predicament.

Dr. Sterne asked a number of questions sharply that Miss Blossom considered irrelevant. "An insulin reaction—" he decided in a strange voice, and was silent. The line was so silent that she was afraid the connection had been broken.

"What should I do, Dr. Sterne, until you get here?" she asked.

"She needs sugar—" he said, "sugar dissolved in hot water—not too hot, but hot enough to melt the sugar. Get her back in bed and feed her sugar immediately. That's all there is to it."

"You—you're going to come out, aren't you?"

"No, it won't be necessary for me to go out there now. Tell her, if she asks, that I'll be there first thing in the morning. Er—call me again if you run into any trouble," he added as a reluctant afterthought, and hung up.

"Bed—sugar—hot water—" breathed Miss Blossom to her still wildly pumping heart. It all seemed so simple to Dr. Sterne!

"Mr. Arbuthnot," she called, from her comparative security behind the door, "help me get her back to bed. The doctor says she has to get back in bed and take sugar." She took a deep breath. "He isn't coming. We'll have to do it alone."

Mr. Arbuthnot came slowly through the dispensary door and advanced far enough to look into the living room. "Oh, no," He backed out into the hall again. "I—I—I'll fetch Mrs. Bjornstrom to help you," he said, and bolted. Before she could remonstrate, he was gone with the flashlight.

Miss Blossom wrung her hands. She couldn't expect reinforcements for at least twenty minutes, if then, and the doctor had said "immediately." She had a vague idea that a diabetic person, suspended between "sugar" and "insulin," was something like a nicely poised chemical experiment with acids and alkalis, and that any deviation from the neutral state could be rapidly fatal. "Sugar," she said to herself again. Miss Burtt must have some around if she was liable to need it like this. She had been crawling toward this room. There must be some somewhere in the dispensary. For a few minutes she examined the bottles and containers that lined the shelves. There were so many of them! She plucked up courage to peer around the door into the living room. Miss Burtt was now lying flat on the floor. Perhaps the nurse was dying while she fumbled!

Terror threw Miss Blossom into action. She rushed out of the infirmary and down the front passageway toward the dining room. She was without a light and the way was dark. She didn't know where the light switches were. She rather thought there was a central control board somewhere. In the Office? She was at that moment passing the Office door and she flung herself against it. It was locked. "I didn't know they locked this at night," she thought. She came back to the north windows of the Office. They were very dark, but was it her imagination that placed a soft glow along the edge of the one farthest up the court? Could someone be in there at this hour with the blinds down? Could Miss Breckenridge be working now? Could Monsieur have his long nose in the records of the school?

She went back to the door, thinking to knock, but was struck with the idea that if there were anyone in there willing to be discovered, he would have heard her and long since opened the door. The unexplained undercurrents of conflict she had sensed in the school since the disappearance of the headmaster had been supplying a menacing backdrop for her alarms ever since she had been awakened by Mr. Arbuthnot's call. She backed away from the Office, and her imagination peopled the night with malevolent beings behind every closed door.

"Sugar," she reminded herself through chattering teeth, and stumbled through the Great Hall and into the dining room to bump into a table. She ran her hands back and forth over it. No sugar bowl. Now where? A sideboard somewhere? She couldn't remember. Scattering chairs and tables, she got to the other end of the dining room and into the passageway again. She found the corridor that led toward the kitchen and felt along its wall. Still no light switches, but she came upon a door. It opened to the pressure of her hand. Somewhere along here there was a pantry. This must be it. She paused inside and the door swung shut. She fingered the wall by its frame fruitlessly. She had never been in here before. Once again she was overcome by the suspicion that she was not alone in the room. She felt as if the glowing numerals on the face of her wrist watch provided a beacon to determine her location. She covered it with her other hand and held her breath, but she could hear no other breathing. This was madness! There couldn't be people everywhere she went! She tried to swallow the terror that threatened to engulf her. She managed a little anger at the complex of circumstances into which she had been thrust. This certainly had not been in the contract she had signed so proudly just a month after graduating from Teachers' College. The headmaster had been so superbly impressive there in the employment office, but he had abandoned her to this. Even Miss Burtt's incomprehensible collapse seemed somehow the result of his departure. Miss Burtt! She must get back quickly to Miss Burtt!

She found a zinc-covered shelf under her hand and began to feel her way along it, reaching back and forth across its cool expanse. She came upon a huddle of salt and pepper shakers, and then her searching hand cupped a larger rounded glass object. She stuck her fingers into the top of it and was rewarded by the feel of something gritty between them. She tasted a pinch. Sugar at last!

Now further practical considerations floored her momentarily. It should be dissolved in hot water. Pan? Spoon? Stove? Cup? This was the pantry, not the kitchen, and always time was slipping by. She seized a bowl of sugar in each hand and set out for the dispensary, which was lighted, and must have a hot-water faucet. The nicer features of the service could be dispensed with.

She bumped her left elbow along the wall of the passageway for guidance. Thicker darkness told her she was opposite the Office again. She looked back when she felt that she had passed it. She could perceive no glow where the windows should be, but down in the center of the block of rooms behind it, a fan of light spread out from under a door. Mr. MacDowell must be still up. She hesitated. Miss Burtt had to be got back to bed. She consulted her watch. One-thirty. How soon could she count on Mrs. Bjornstrom's arriving? She went up to the door, set one of her bowls of sugar down by her foot, and knocked. There was movement in the room, but no answer.

"Mr. MacDowell! It's me. Miss Blossom," she whispered with her lips against the edge of the door.

The fight was extinguished and the door thrown open and she found her nose in Mr. MacDowell's chest.

"What the hell?" inquired Mr. MacDowell with some reason, but put his arms around her cooperatively. She backed away, kicked the sugar bowl, and stooped to rescue it with a little mew of consternation. It was on its side and half the sugar spilled out. Striving to keep level the other bowl, out of which she had probably also lost some during her collision with Mr. MacDowell, she picked it up lovingly.

"Help me get Miss Burtt back to bed," she entreated Mr. MacDowell. "She's unconscious—maybe dead."

"Good God!" said Mr. MacDowell, stepping out into the courtyard and closing his door behind him carefully. "Now begin again. What are you babbling about?"

"Hurry!" said Miss Blossom. "Only hurry! Come with me and I'll tell you." She started again for the dispensary. "Look out for the sugar!" she added warningly when he took hold of her elbow.

"Clarity is not your long suit," said Mr. MacDowell. "What are we doing with sugar?"

"Diabetes," explained Miss Blossom, moving faster when she was able to orient herself by the glow seeping out through the entryway of the infirmary. "She's got an insulin reaction on the floor and she has to be put back in bed and fed sugar. Mr. Arbuthnot went for Mrs. Bjornstrom, but I don't know what's happened to them."

Miss Burtt was still lying face down on the floor. Mr. MacDowell was not appalled by the spectacle of her bare legs. He reached for her pulse, and appeared a little surprised. "Seems to be all right," he said. Miss Burtt stirred and half opened her eyes. "Well, let's get her in bed."

He took hold of her under the arms, and Miss Burtt gave a little groping cooperation to the business of getting on her feet. Supported on either side by Mr. MacDowell and Miss Blossom she took stumbling steps to her bed and subsided in it. Her eyes were again closed. Miss Blossom pulled the covers up over her with a sigh of relief and sped

back to where she had set down the sugar. Mr. MacDowell stood over Miss Burtt thoughtfully for a moment, and
then followed Miss Blossom.

In the dispensary, Miss Blossom was letting two faucets
flow strongly until the water from one of them should run
hot. "Do you see a spoon and a glass?" she asked.

Mr. MacDowell shifted bottles and containers and turned
up at her side with an enamel cup and a throat swab from
which he had removed the cotton. "Use these," he said.

Mr. Arbuthnot appeared in the doorway, breathing rapidly. His bathrobe was furled behind him, and his light
hair stood on end. "Mrs. Bjornstrom's coming," he assured
them between pants. "She's dressing."

"Too late, fellow," said Mr. MacDowell. "The emergency
has been met. You'd better run back up and tell her not to
come."

Mr. Arbuthnot's nearsighted eyes focused on Mr. Mac-
Dowell, impeccably attired, in cozy proximity to Miss Blossom. He pulled his bathrobe around his rumpled pajamas.

"How did *you* get here?" he inquired suspiciously. "How
come you're dressed at this time of night?"

"Night life," explained Mr. MacDowell easily. "Well,
everything under control, Miss Blossom? I'll toddle along
and get my beauty sleep."

Miss Blossom, her potion mixed, had rushed back to
her patient's bedside.

Mr. MacDowell smiled quizzically at Mr. Arbuthnot as
he went out the door. "All yours," he said generously. "Make
what you can of it. I'll head off Mrs. Bjornstrom for you."

In the other room, Miss Burtt was meekly imbibing the
half-dissolved sugar. A good deal of the mixture spilled on
the sheets. "'Nough," murmured Miss Burtt, and lapsed into
inertia.

Miss Blossom's sorely tried equilibrium was threatened
once again as a new question occurred to her. How much

sugar? Had she erred now on the other side? How much
had she already fed the nurse? She returned unhappily to
the dispensary and Mr. Arbuthnot.

"Now I don't know how much to give her," she said to
him. "Where's Mr. MacDowell? Maybe he knows."

"He's gone to the Doghole— But he wouldn't know any
more than I do!"

"Well, do you know?"

"No."

Miss Blossom put her hand out for the telephone. "I
guess I'll have to call the doctor again," she said dejected-
ly. While she was waiting for the call to be put through,
she glanced at her watch. It wasn't yet two o'clock. A lot
could happen in an hour, she reflected.

"Yes?" came Dr. Sterne's voice, as sleepily as before.

"Dr. Sterne, how much sugar?"

Dr. Sterne sounded as if he thought he shouldn't have
been disturbed. "Oh, you can't give her too much. Give
her all she'll take. Have you got any in her yet?"

"Yes, but I don't know how much."

"Well, feed her all she'll take, and then go along to
bed. She'll sleep it off. Be sure she's warm enough. Did
you tell her I'd be out early in the morning?"

"She's unconscious."

"She's probably coming out of it now. Tell her I'll be
along, and then she won't worry."

"Thank you," said Miss Blossom, experiencing the rid-
icule of anticlimax.

She went back and offered the cup again to Miss Burtt's
lips, but got no response. "The doctor's coming out early
in the morning," she said loudly. "Everything's all right."
Miss Burtt appeared already to have sunk into heavy slum-
ber. Miss Blossom spread another blanket over her and
turned out the lights.

"Well, that's that, Mr. Arbuthnot," she said into the hallway. "Where are you? We have to see about Nathaniel Vaughan yet."

Mr. Arbuthnot winked his flashlight. "Here," he said, hoarse with courage, and once more waited for Miss Blossom to take the initiative.

Miss Blossom walked by him, a little tired, and insensitive to briefly knocking opportunity.

"Where's his room? Why don't you keep your light on?"

Mr. Arbuthnot followed after in mingled relief and dejection.

"Over here," he answered, switching on his light, "next to Mr. Weber."

He found the door, opened it, flashed the beam of his torch across the bed. It had not been disturbed.

"Oh dear," exclaimed Miss Blossom. "That poor child with his bad heart! We shouldn't have forgotten him for so long. Where could he be? Do you suppose *he's* fainted somewhere now? Where's the nearest washroom?"

Mr. Arbuthnot closed the door again. "You go on back to bed," he said urgently. "I'll look after Nat."

"But I want to know he's all right first."

"No!" Mr. Arbuthnot was suddenly petulant. "I tell you I can take care of him. You go away now."

His desire to get rid of her was ungrateful. He was rude. He was furtive. He was unpleasant. She didn't like him. She was tired. "Oh, all *right!*" she said, and switched off in a huff to traverse the silent school to her own distant corner. Let him *take* a little responsibility for a change!

But as she went, she couldn't help worrying. What could have happened to the poor child in the hour since he had listened to Miss Burtt's three bloodcurdling howls? They had been enough to interrupt the beats of stronger hearts than Nat's.

8

Mr. Pyke: History

When Mr. Pyke reached the dining-room doors at seven twenty-nine on Thursday morning, the only members of the staff to have arrived ahead of him in the Great Hall were the Bjornstroms. Mrs. Bjornstrom was in the act of banishing Juan de Herrera to secure a bustle of flannel shirt that hung out behind over his belt. Mr. Bjornstrom had separated himself from the domestic scene and was abstractedly fondling an empty pipe. Mr. Pyke walked to the door to inspect the weather which he found to be non-committally pale gray. It was, though he didn't consciously make the comparison, a fitting accompaniment for the mood in which he had regarded his job ever since the Head had left the school. When the doors had been opened into the dining room and a crowd of hungry boys had collected before them, Mr. Pyke wandered over to join Mr. Bjornstrom.

"Where the hell is everybody?" he asked in an aggrieved undertone.

Mr. Bjornstrom came out of his brown study with a start and looked around. "Don't know," he replied. "Isn't Frenchy in the Office?"

Mr. Pyke craned his neck to look out across the passageway at the Office door. When Monsieur Trougnac had not appeared after a decent interval, he crossed over to the door and tried to open it. He found it locked, one more disagreeable jar, typical of the way things were going at the school.

He knocked. "Monsieur, are you in there?"

"Yes, yes," came the answer impatiently. "Do not disturb me now. I make an important call."

"Well, the doors are open."

"Then go in. Do not wait for me."

Mr. Pyke returned to Mr. Bjornstrom. "We may as well go ahead. He's hugging the phone in there."

"What about?" asked Mr. Bjornstrom. "Has something happened?"

"It's by me. Maybe everybody else has quit and he's hunting up a new set of teachers." He sighed. "Well, come on. Let's get going. You handle the blessing."

When the boys had settled themselves at a table, Lester DeVries spoke importantly over the lip of his glass of orange juice. "Sir, there were wolves around the school last night. I heard them howling."

"Nuts!" said Ralph Johnstone with the wide wisdom of the tenth grade, "There aren't any wolves in this whole county. You were dreaming."

"No, I wasn't," insisted Lester. "Spencer Kydd says he heard them too."

"I didn't hear any howls," volunteered Herbert Dow who was in the ninth grade, "but I heard people walking around and talking."

"Maybe they were out looking for the wolves," suggested Lester.

Neil Truesdale, at the other end of the table, became interested. "Were the people inside or outside? What time did you hear them?"

"Oh, late. I don't know how late. They woke me up walking around in the courtyard. Until I remembered, I thought—" Herbert Dow stopped speaking to take a large bite of toast.

An argument over whether anyone could know for sure that there weren't any wolves anywhere in Marin County claimed the attention of the table, and Mr. Pyke noticed that Herbert was satisfied not to complete his sentence. He had probably been going to say that he'd thought he heard the headmaster. For the past few days, the boys had refrained from all reference to the headmaster, at least in the presence of their elders, and it had been impossible to gauge what they thought or felt or knew. Mr. Pyke approved of this attitude. It was also his own. He had avoided Mr. Dingle, and listened in silence to the exhortations of Monsieur Trougnac and Miss Breckenridge, but there was a limit to his dogged endurance and he felt that he was nearing it this morning. He looked around at the other tables, still, except for the Bjornstroms, without heads, and his sense of injury deepened. He gulped down the last of his coffee and rose to go.

Neil Truesdale interrupted his departure. "Sir, will it be all right if I call for trail work today? We haven't been out yet this term."

"All right with me," agreed Mr. Pyke indifferently.

"Oh, but you said the seventh and eighth grades could have their match today, if it didn't rain," exclaimed Gellion Chevalier. "We've got to have Neil!"

"I guess I did, at that. Better make it tomorrow, Neil."

"O.K., sir," Neil accepted the suggestion with his usual courtesy. "I just thought— We don't want to let it go too long." His eyes added a determination not to let the Head down.

"You'll have better luck getting a crew of the older boys together tomorrow. I've promised the Doghole gang they can play the sixth grade."

"Jeepers! Tomorrow *is* Friday," said Lester DeVries, "and my new English saddle hasn't come yet. May I phone Mother before class, Mr. Pyke?"

"See Mr. Arbuthnot after he's checked your room," said Mr. Pyke, and escaped.

When the room was practically cleared of boys, Mr. Arbuthnot appeared, his eyes pink-rimmed with recent sleep. He made for the table nearest the kitchen passageway and petitioned humbly for coffee. He was joined shortly by Mr. MacDowell who came by his own table to pick up his glass of orange juice and increased Mr. Arbuthnot's order to include fresh toast and scrambled eggs. The waiter grumbled, but brought them, and a pot of coffee.

"Skoal!" said Mr. MacDowell, quaffing his juice. "I trust last night's adventure ended on a note of triumph?" Mr. Arbuthnot helped himself to a piece of cold toast. "Ah, there's the lady now." Mr. MacDowell called cheerfully to Miss Blossom who was standing uncertainly in the dining-room door, "Grab your orange juice, and come down here and join us."

"I didn't even *hear* the bell," said Miss Blossom when she had followed his suggestion. "When the children were going back to the Doghole, I thought they were coming down. How's Nat? Where did you find him?"

"He's none the worse," replied Mr. Arbuthnot stiffly. "He'd gone into the older boys' suite for company. I put him back in his own room and told him not to get up this morning. That reminds me— Oh, waiter!"

"And your patient?" Mr. MacDowell inquired of Miss Blossom as Mr. Arbuthnot rerouted Nathaniel's breakfast tray. "How's she this morning? Or don't you know yet?"

"I looked in but she was still sound asleep. I wonder what the doctor calls early. I wonder whether I should wait around for him. Have you told Monsieur about the nurse, Mr. Arbuthnot?"

"Haven't seen Monsieur. You tell Monsieur. It sounds better coming from you."

Mr. Weber entered the dining room by the rear door and sat wearily down at the table with them, dabbing with his handkerchief at a small cut on his recently shaven lip. Another waiter followed him with another pot of coffee and a cup. Mr. Weber seemed hardly aware that he had company. He poured out half a cup with one trembling hand, while he held his head with the other. The trio at the other end of the table watched him try to drink the hot liquid in not unsympathetic silence.

"Have some eggs, Mr. Weber," said Miss Blossom, shoving the platter down his way.

Mr. Weber shuddered. "No. No. I thank you. Just coffee."

"You must learn to be more discerning than that, Miss Blossom," Mr. MacDowell admonished her. "Mr. Weber shows evidences of having come through a night more debilitating even than yours—though certainly not more praiseworthy. Did you know, Mr. Weber, that our shy little Blossom came to the nurse's rescue in a sudden emergency last night, and possibly saved her life?"

"Indeed?" Mr. Weber relaxed his grip on his coffee cup and looked up with almost a normal display of incredulity. "Miss Burtt? To what emergency was Miss Burtt unequal?"

"Oh, I did nothing, really," said Miss Blossom. "It's just that it was scary and we lost a lot of sleep. She had an attack and called for help, and Mr. Arbuthnot called me, and I called the doctor and he told me what to do. Mr. MacDowell came along and helped too."

"You underrate yourself, Miss Blossom," said Mr. MacDowell. "I understand from a couple of boys who heard, but did not budge from their beds, that she howled like a hyena."

"I hope you told them not to talk about it," exclaimed Miss Blossom.

"I did, but that won't stop them. It's too good a story—especially about Miss Burtt. From what I'm told, it's a wonder she didn't wake even you up, Mr. Weber."

"He wasn't in his room," said Mr. Arbuthnot. "At two o'clock, he wasn't. I looked in when I was hunting for Nathaniel Vaughan."

"What ho!" said Mr. MacDowell. "Did you make a night of it? Were you in town?"

"Young men," said Mr. Weber, assuming an air of virtue, "it should be enough that I am here now. My nights are my own."

"When *did* you get back?" inquired Mr. MacDowell, unsubdued.

Mr. Weber's bleary little eyes brightened with a recollection. "With the dawn," he admitted. "And I wasn't the only one out at that time. I could a tale unfold beside which yours would pale." Revived by his coffee, Mr. Weber appeared to be giving himself over to private enjoyment of a scene recently witnessed and only now appreciated. His belly shook in silent mirth, till he clapped a hand to his wobbly head and again subsided.

"May I join this charming circle? Miss Blossom, with your permission? Waiter, some fresh coffee."

Mr. Dingle, whose approach upon crepe soles had gone unnoticed, sat down in one of the remaining chairs. His arrival dispelled the modicum of fellow feeling which had been holding the group together. Miss Blossom, when his pale eyes turned upon her, felt gauche. She saw Mr. Arbuthnot's face become resentful. Mr. MacDowell slid his willowy backbone down almost into the seat of his chair, stuck his thumbs in his belt, and gazed at the ceiling.

The quality of his tones became more markedly Southern. "What happened to *you* last night, Dingle? What earthquake has thrown you off schedule?"

Mr. Dingle put sugar and cream in his coffee, stirred it, and removed the spoon neatly, before replying. Miss Blossom, watching him, found herself able for the first time to get her concept of Mr. Dingle into a clear focus. What she apprehended surprised her. His body and mind and sentiments were so groomed by a profundity of implied experience that heretofore she had been subdued by his mere presence into accepting him as a master spirit. While she waited for him to answer Mr. MacDowell, a comment whose meaning did not reach her until the words had completed themselves crystallized in her mind: "He's a beautiful vessel that contains nothing. He's a cold weak fish!" Digesting this, she made a further observation: "He's had a shock. The way I'm seeing him is the way he's seeing himself."

"Nothing happened," replied Mr. Dingle. "I'm merely—unwell." He did not look well. Miss Blossom noticed now that his skin was pale and moist.

"All passion spent?" inquired Mr. MacDowell.

"Flat unprofitable years," Mr. Weber quoted loosely. "His way of life has fallen into the sere and yellow leaf."

Miss Blossom glanced at Mr. Arbuthnot to see whether he was experiencing the prevailing reaction. He looked puzzled, but an expression of satisfaction was making a guarded appearance on his face when his lifted eyes encountered some vision at the other end of the room, and he scrambled guiltily to his feet. The others turned to see what had startled him, and discovered Monsieur Trougnac advancing toward, them with long strides, pink flags on his cheekbones.

"What is the meaning of this? This is insubordination. This I will not have! Why are you not in your corridors? Inspecting the rooms? Watching the boys? Go! Go! Go! I tell you again, this I will not tolerate!"

He might have been a buzz fly. Mr. Weber appeared oblivious; Mr. Dingle caught Monsieur Trougnac's glittering black eyes with his contemptuous blue ones, and held them; Mr. MacDowell laughed.

"Your patrol, Monsieur," said Mr. MacDowell, "is more demoralized than your prisoners. You'd better work up some system of counterespionage. Maybe the Doghole boys are uncontaminated. Try them."

Monsieur dragged his gaze away from Mr. Dingle. "You will not joke on such subjects, Mr. MacDowell," he said angrily. "Pay attention that I have authority. Without hesitation I use it. Who I find derelict from duty I dismiss. This is not words. This is fact." He moistened his lips and spoke more slowly. "I have found it necessary in the interests of the school to discharge Miss Breckenridge."

Amusement was wiped off Mr. MacDowell's face. He pulled himself slowly to his feet. He faced Monsieur Trougnac for a long moment and then walked out of the room without a word. Mr. Arbuthnot trailed after him. Although she had no corridor calling her, Miss Blossom wished, too late, that she had taken that opportunity to get away too. But now she did not want to break the silence that had followed Monsieur Trougnac's announcement by getting up. There was too much in it that she didn't understand. First the headmaster. Now Miss Breckenridge. What was happening to the school? What did the men know that she did not know? Miss Breckenridge had known. Were Mr. Weber and Mr. Dingle glad or sorry that Monsieur Trougnac had sent her away? Miss Blossom couldn't read their expressions.

"So," said Mr. Weber finally.

He pushed back his chair and left the table. Miss Blossom made haste to follow. When she reached the dining-room door she did not look back, but she felt that neither

Monsieur Trougnac nor Mr. Dingle had yet moved or
spoken.

Monsieur Trougnac met Miss Burtt in a passageway toward the end of the milk-lunch recess.

"Ah, Miss Burtt. Miss Blossom has just informed me
that you are ill. What—"

"The circumstances of the past week, Monsieur, the
new term—I expended more energy than I realized and
failed to reduce my insulin."

"I understood from her that you were confined to your
bed."

"Not at all. A good sleep was all I needed to put me
right again. I thought it best to take two extra hours to
escape the nausea which sometimes results, but I am quite
able to be about now."

"Sometimes? You are subject to these attacks often? I
do not like that."

"Very rarely, Monsieur. I understand my condition, and
take precautions. You may be sure that I am sufficiently
exasperated with myself not to allow such a thing to happen again. I am quite dependable."

"I shall consult Dr. Sterne."

"As you wish, Monsieur. You will find that his opinion
supports mine."

Sounds of struggle reached Mr. Arbuthnot through the
walls of his room during rest hour. He went to the door
of the washroom which lay next to his quarters and heard
more cracks and thuds and stertorous breathing. He had
pushed the door half open when a body hurtled against the
other side of it and Peter Van Tassel's head came around to
obstruct Mr. Arbuthnot's brief glimpse of two boys locked
in combat on the stone floor of the washroom.

"Oh, sorry, sir," said Van, but did not look sorry. "I can't let you in just now!" He engaged without hesitation in a contest in brute strength with the master and succeeded in closing the door upon Mr. Arbuthnot's amazed and discomfited face. Mr. Arbuthnot, blushing even in solitude for his predicament, miserably longing for the authority of Mr. Pyke's fists, hovered in the corridor, listening. There was a muffled howl and the thuds ceased. Then there were voices, too low to be overheard. Mr. Arbuthnot pressed on the door again, but it didn't move freely, and he didn't propose to start anything else he couldn't finish. He waited bitterly.

Van opened the door. His golden eyes were carefree and oblivious of sin. "It's all right, Mr. Arbuthnot, honestly. All over. They're getting washed up."

"Go to your room," said Mr. Arbuthnot feebly.

"Yes, sir." Van departed like a well-trained bird dog.

Mr. Arbuthnot entered the washroom. At the left wall, Wyman Gould leaned over one basin, and Neil Truesdale over another behind him. Bright red drops were spattering from the noses of both boys, but the basin of Wyman looked the more gory. There was also a lump on his temple that seemed to be elevating the hairs of his head as Mr. Arbuthnot watched.

"Five demerits each," said Mr. Arbuthnot.

They did not look up from their pursuits. After a speculative pause, Mr. Arbuthnot went into a cubbyhole and brought them each a batch of toilet paper.

"You'd better go and see the nurse."

They received both the paper and the suggestion in silence. It was apparent to Mr. Arbuthnot that the incident was closed and not open to discussion. He faded away, relegated as usual to the periphery of events.

Mrs. Bjornstrom presided over the tea-table. She wore gray alpaca and a white fichu but her resemblance to Whistler's mother ended there. She was broad rather than long, rather complacent than benign. Her plump red hands deployed themselves possessively amid the cups and saucers. When she had served the half dozen who were gathered there, and the interchanges concerning sugar and cream and cakes and chairs had been concluded, there was a quiet interval which threatened to lengthen into the proportions and atmosphere of a wake.

Miss Blossom was searching her mind for a safe subject, wondering at the same time why she bothered, when Mr. Dingle filled the breach.

"Is it possible that her recent indisposition has had a humanizing effect upon Miss Burtt? This is the first time, I believe, that she has stopped in for tea."

Miss Burtt frowned. Miss Blossom found that she could look at her. It was her smile that was uncomfortably reminiscent.

"I feel that I owe an apology and I have come to make it," said Miss Burtt. "I want to assure you that I will do nothing so upsetting again."

"Skip the apologies, Miss Burtt," said Mr. MacDowell. "We are none of us without our peccadilloes."

"And the day after," commented Mr. Dingle, "when all is dust and ashes, we make resolutions. Here, for example, is Mr. Weber, mildly taking a dish of tea. I gaze upon the homely sight and know not whether to laugh or weep."

"Incongruity is the essence of humor," said Mr. Weber, without rancor. "You're welcome to what amusement I may afford you. For chivalry has obliged me to withhold something much more titillating."

"Oh yes, what *was* it you saw early this morning that amused you so?" Miss Blossom asked.

"Lovebirds," said Mr. Weber. "More than that I will not say."

There was an odd hush. Miss Blossom was wondering whether her contribution had after all been ill-chosen when Monsieur Trougnac arrived to claim the center of attention. It had already been borne in upon Miss Blossom that in his new role Monsieur was subject to tantrums whose periodicity was accelerating, but his previous seizures had been temperate compared to the emotion that possessed him now. It was novel in that it appeared to have carried him beyond garrulity, and even to have stabilized his English idiom.

"Mr. MacDowell," he asked in a low furious voice, "did you bring anyone with you into this school last night?"

Mr. MacDowell was not ready with an answer. He hedged. "Why do you ask a question like that?"

"Because the police are here asking it. There is a man in the uniform of the law in the Office demanding to see you. Answer my question yes or no. Did you bring anyone into this school last night?"

"Have we flushed the lovebirds?" murmured Mr. Dingle.

"It wasn't a woman," said Mr. MacDowell impulsively. "It was a man."

Monsieur's voice was almost a hiss. "A man. Yes. A *man!* What did you do with him? Where is he?"

"He slept in my room, and when I woke up he was gone. I have no idea where he is."

Monsieur's heat exploded into flame. He looked as if he were on the point of attacking Mr. MacDowell physically. "At a time like this! At a time like *this!* You bring a man into your bedroom for the night! It is criminal! You are no mentor for children! Your irresponsibility here is finished!" Monsieur Trougnac paused to emphasize his ultimatum. Mr. MacDowell returned his look but said nothing. "I will not tolerate conduct unbecoming to a master in any member of the staff!"

"Not even in Miss Blossom?" Mr. Dingle pricked him.

Perhaps Monsieur did not notice the interjection; perhaps it was the final small threat to his authority that pushed him into a commitment. At any rate, he continued in a thin voice to Mr. MacDowell, "When the police are through with you, pack and get out before night falls. I discharge you. It is effective immediately."

Mr. MacDowell's lip curled in what might have been either contempt or bravado. "You've gone mad," he said.

Miss Blossom watched him stride from the room. "Three down," she counted to herself. Her expectancy was intense but dreamlike. It was as if she were again the child who had watched, in otherworldly suspense, while Peter Pan knocked off the Pirates.

9

Walter Huggins: Cowboy

Sheriff's Deputy Frank Zanetti relaxed his professional facade when the Office door had closed on Monsieur Trougnac's rigid back, and favored Miss Parelli with an everyday smile. He and her oldest brother had been contemporaries in high school, but she had not seen him since the war, and she had not known while he was talking to Monsieur whether he had recognized her. She returned his smile with enthusiasm. This first day without Miss Breckenridge, capped by an unbroken afternoon with Monsieur Trougnac, had been getting her down. Frank Zanetti, though almost a stranger and dignified by the regimentals of his calling, seemed like a breath of home.

"Well, Mary, I heard you were working out here, but I hadn't realized you were holding down an office all by yourself. Ought to be a good job. How's Alfred?"

"He's swell. He's working the ranch with Pop. Why don't you drop in when you're over that way?"

"I sure will!" He found her spontaneous invitation a pleasing contrast to Monsieur Trougnac's hostility. Al's little sister had grown up into something very pleasant to look at. "Might even make it tonight. I was down as far as Stinson Beach this morning, and I may be going back— If I can get a line on the guy I'm looking for from this teacher the Frenchman has gone to bring in." His mind returned to official channels. "What sort of a fellow is this MacDowell? You know him pretty well?"

Miss Parelli felt the first stirrings of a sensation with which she was destined to become increasingly familiar over the weekend. She had been living quite easily in two worlds—the one, the Marin County she had known all her life, the other, the school. Until now, they had not overlapped. It had not occurred to her that situations might arise in which she could not be loyal to both. It had not occurred to her to consider the subject of loyalty at all. She was not given to examining ethical concepts. But down in the dim area from whence stemmed her impulses, the deputy's question set up a conflict.

"Not very well," she said uncomfortably. "What happened at Stinson Beach? I didn't see any wrecks as I came through this morning, except—" She got another red light from her subconscious and made a quick substitution. "Except that old Buick without any wheels that's been in front of Luigi's barn ever since I can remember."

"It wasn't a wreck that took me over there. Pop Bartello got conked on the head last night, and had about $40 taken from his till."

"Oh! Well, my goodness, you don't think Mr. MacDowell had anything to do with that, do you?"

"No, but it looks as if he picked up the man who did do it and brought him up here."

"Up here? What makes you think that?"

"I've found a man in Olema who says he saw him do it. By the time Pop had phoned his complaint into San Rafael, and the deputy who answered his call had got out to Stinson Beach, heard Pop's story and looked at his head, it was after midnight and too late to check on anything in the neighborhood. So I've been back down there today, hunting around for a lead. Just an hour ago, I had the luck to find out that Ed Lemon had been going home from

Stinson Beach to Olema about the time I figured he might have seen something. And sure enough, he had!" Frank looked pleased with himself and seemed to expect her to share his approval. "He'd passed a convertible that he recognized as belonging to someone at this school drawn up beside the road three miles north of Stinson Beach. A man that fitted Pop Bartello's description of his assailant was getting into it."

Miss Parelli still wasn't convinced. "Mr. MacDowell might give a man a lift, but why would he bring him up here?"

"Beats me," Frank said cheerfully, "but Ed Lemon says he did. He says the car started up as he was going by it, followed him along the lagoon and up those turns through the eucalyptus grove, passed him in the straightaway along the valley, and turned up the road to Drake's Anchorage without ever stopping again."

"Well, that doesn't make sense. Ed Lemon must have got two cars mixed." Miss Parelli's vague uneasiness had subsided and she was eager for details. "How's Pop Bartello's head? Was he badly hurt? How'd it happen, or aren't you supposed to say?"

Frank seated himself comfortably beside her desk. "Oh, there's no secret about it. The way Pop tells it, the guy came in late, ordered a hamburger and coffee, and went on sitting at the end of the counter with a newspaper in front of him after he'd finished and Pop had taken his cup and plate away. Pop didn't pay any attention to him because he was chewing the rag with a friend who eats there regularly, Jim Fallon."

"Oh, sure," Miss Parelli interrupted. "I know Jim Fallon."

"Well, Fallon stayed till ten o'clock, the time Pop generally closes up on week nights, and then went home. He hadn't noticed anything out of the ordinary about the other fellow either. Fallon had given Pop just the right change to pay for his meal, so Pop still had his cash in his hand when he stopped to tell the guy at the counter he wanted to close up."

"Didn't Pop notice anything funny about him even then?"

"Seems not. Pop thinks he said 'All right,' and that he was folding up his newspaper when Pop turned around to ring up Fallon's money. And that's the last thing Pop remembers till he came to with a bump on his head to find his cash drawer open and no money in it."

"The poor old guy! What about his head?"

"Pop wouldn't see a doctor. But I guess he's more angry than hurt. He knows he was a fool to turn his back on a stranger."

"Well, you don't expect a thing like that to happen in Stinson Beach," Miss Parelli excused Pop Bartello.

"It'll be a lesson to him. His joint is set off a good piece from the rest of the town. He could have been badly hurt and lain there all night, and chances are no one would have known the difference."

"Imagine!" Miss Parelli registered suitable horror. "I wonder where the man came from."

"I wonder where he *went*," Frank said ruefully. "He hasn't been spotted on any of the roads leading out of here." He got up to walk restlessly over to the windows through which he could only see the courtyard. "There's not much more daylight. What's taking that Frenchman so long to bring MacDowell?" he asked impatiently. "What's eating him anyway? When I was questioning him, he looked as shocked as if I'd accused the man of murder. Why? Aren't the teachers allowed out nights?"

For several unformulated reasons, Miss Parelli found this difficult to reply to. Deputy Frank Zanetti felt her constraint and turned away from the window to look at her. Meeting his eyes, Mary essayed a laugh, but it was self-conscious.

"I'll bet you were out with him yourself!" said Zanetti. He saw that his chance shot had been a bull's-eye. "He took you home!"

"Well, what's wrong with that?"

"Not a thing, so far as I know," replied Zanetti, manfully ignoring the personal angle. "He left you—when? About eleven, or a little after?"

"Um-hum. I guess so."

Zanetti thought back. "What made you say you didn't know him very well?"

"I *don't* know him very well. Last night was the first time I'd ever been out with him."

Seemed reasonable enough. But Zanetti was remembering also the way the man up at the corrals had acted when he'd stopped there on the way in. Walter Huggins was a man he'd run into several times in San Rafael. He'd impressed him as being a placid easygoing fellow, not one to be thrown out of countenance by the mere sight of a uniform. But this afternoon Huggins had answered his questions guardedly. He had indeed identified the car Zanetti had described to him as MacDowell's. But he had been too careful and too courteous. A contrast to Monsieur Trougnac. Monsieur Trougnac had erred in the other direction. He had seemed to take the position that the sheriff's deputy was the criminal, if only for having inflicted his presence upon the innocent children of Drake's Anchorage.

These people wouldn't knowingly have been in league with the perpetrator of a $40 holdup, but if they hadn't known about the holdup and had helped the man, supposing him to be a tramp, they wouldn't act like this. Was there something else, not at all connected with the fugitive, that was making them all uneasy? Zanetti didn't get it, but Mr. MacDowell's arrival interrupted his pondering.

"I understand you want to know about the man I picked up last night," he said immediately. Zanetti automatically made a quick inventory. Dark hair and eyes, regular features, medium height and light weight. He put them at five eight and 150. Age about 30. Pale and nervy.

"Yes. I'd like to have any information you can give me about him. Was he a stranger to you?"

"That's right."

"But you brought him up here with you?"

"Yes, I did." Zanetti got the impression that the question angered him. "It was almost midnight when I picked him up. I wasn't going into town, and I was pretty certain there wouldn't be anyone else coming along that road who would be. I don't see anything unreasonable about bringing him up and giving him a bed for the rest of the night."

Zanetti filed his impression away with his others and equally pursued his inquiry. "And where is he now? What happened to him?"

"I don't know. I bedded him down on the couch in my study. At two in the morning, he was still there. When I woke up at eight o'clock, he was gone."

"Will you describe him, please? Did he tell you anything about himself?"

"No, nothing. He didn't talk. I didn't see him in a good light, and I didn't notice much about him."

"Didn't you notice that he was an unusually large man?" Zanetti asked blandly.

"Well, yes, I guess he was."

"And blond?"

"Er, yes," said MacDowell with what seemed like a growing reluctance. "Look here! What's it to you? What do you want to know about him for?"

"I'm looking for a man who committed assault and robbery in Stinson Beach last night," said Zanetti, watching him closely.

MacDowell looked genuinely surprised. "I say! Was it much of a bust-up?"

"The man wasn't seriously injured, and the amount stolen was only $40, but that doesn't make us any less interested in finding the person who did it."

An expression of amusement flickered across Mr. Mac-Dowell's features and was immediately repressed. "I'm sorry I can't be of more help to you," he said. "May I be getting along now? I have a spot of business of my own to attend to."

"Just a couple more questions. What was the man wearing?"

"Some sort of working clothes," said Mr. MacDowell vaguely.

"Sweat shirt, windbreaker, probably government issue, and jeans?" Zanetti pursued him.

Mr. MacDowell turned his head sidewise to run a quick hand through his hair. Zanetti noticed that he took this opportunity to let his glance rest briefly on Mary Parelli's face. Zanetti looked at her too, but saw nothing in her expression but lively spectator interest.

"That sounds about right," admitted Mr. MacDowell.

"And did you get the impression that he might be a veteran?"

"He could be," MacDowell admitted remotely, and then gave him a square glance and added quickly, "Aren't we all?"

"We're all citizens too," Zanetti caught himself saying unctuously. "We can't let anybody who breaks the law go unpunished just because he's a veteran." He was immediately angry that he had allowed himself to be put on the defensive.

"Quite," said Mr. MacDowell.

"You can remember nothing that might give me a line on where he came from, or where he might have gone?"

"Not a thing."

"All right then. That's all, thank you."

When Mr. MacDowell had gone, the deputy turned to Miss Parelli.

"The fellow was here all right. And I don't think he's got far away. The roads are too well patrolled. He could be anywhere in these damned woods, but the chances are he's hiding out near where he can get something to eat. I'd like to take a look at the outbuildings around here, and I'd better speak to the man that runs the place first. Can you find him for me?"

As Zanetti spoke to Mary her back was toward him. She was busying herself stacking up large books and veiling the typewriter and the adding machine. "Are you leaving?" he asked.

"Past closing time," she answered without turning around. "But I'll hunt up Monsieur for you before I go."

"I'd rather see the head man—the one with the Scandinavian name—whatever it is."

"He's away," said Mary. She seemed suddenly to be in a great hurry.

"What do you mean by 'away'?"

"Chicago," said Mary, and threw on her coat and grabbed her bag. "You wait here. I'll send Monsieur."

"I'll wait out in front," he called after her.

Zanetti walked through the Great Hall, gloomy and completely empty, and out to the terrace. He saw the broad panorama spread out at his feet in terms of his prey. The man would not be likely to have gone in this direction. The grassy slope careened down to jagged bushes in small ravines, to sheer cliffs on the promontories. Far below lay the leaden sea. When several minutes had passed and no one had appeared, he walked to the northern end of the terrace, and from there he could see the breakers racing through the narrows. The only possible refuge was the little ship riding at anchor in the lee of the opposite point. His glance traveled along what he could see of the trail that appeared to lead down to it. It was several feet wide and well graded. A stranger, with care, could get down it safely in the dark. But the place was a cul-de-sac. It wouldn't be the sort of retreat he would pick. Yet something seemed to be drawing him into the cove. He was about to start down the trail when someone came out of a door behind him. He turned to find Monsieur Trougnac coming toward him, his brows, if that were possible, more beetling than when he had talked to him in the Office.

"Mr. MacDowell has told you that the stranger he so unwisely brought into the school has not been seen since early this morning," said Monsieur. "I must ask you to leave immediately."

"Miss Parelli didn't find you?" Zanetti tried to keep the irritation out of his voice. "I explained to her that the man must be still hanging around this locality. I'd like to look around a little."

"He is not here," said Monsieur Trougnac positively. "If he comes back, of course I shall let you know. I insist that you go away now before the boys return from the sports. It is not good that they see a policeman in the school."

Zanetti bristled at the title. "It would not be good if they ran up against this fellow and got conked on the head either. If you force me to, I'll get a search warrant and come back with enough men to cover the place after dark. If you let me go ahead now, it will be a lot less conspicuous. Have I your permission?"

Monsieur Trougnac stared at him sharply until he had decided that he meant what he said. "Very well," he said, "You may search, but he is not here. Where will you search?"

Zanetti looked down at the *Golden Hind*. Monsieur Trougnac took two casual steps that placed him between the deputy and the head of the Cliff Trail. Zanetti saw the little skiff drawn up on the beach well above the high-tide line. The fellow could have swum out but it was highly unlikely that he had done so.

"Is there food on that boat?" asked Zanetti.

"No," replied Monsieur. "No food is kept on the boat."

The answer was in a more civil voice than any he had yet used. Zanetti turned away from the Cliff Trail and looked up toward the higher land behind the school where he could see several other buildings. A small dissatisfaction tugged at the back of his mind, but it seemed more logical, in the time that was left before dark, to look into them, than to take the long trail down to the boat.

"I'll take a look in those sheds up there," said Zanetti.

Having secured from Monsieur the assurance that his entire staff, especially those in the kitchen end, would be alerted, Zanetti went past the parking area toward the trail that went up the hill behind the school. Back along the rear of the school he saw what appeared to be a wood-shed, but he decided that it was too small, and too near the main building, to afford a refuge. He went on up the trail.

In five minutes, puffing slightly, for the trail was steep and he had hurried, he stood before Stone Cottage. He knocked on the door. The door, which had not been closed tightly enough for the old-fashioned latch to catch, opened under his hand, and swung inward with a protesting squeak.

"Hello," he said. "Anyone here?"

When there was no answer, he stepped inside. There was only one large room. The doors opened into closets and a bath and he ascertained quickly that no one was behind them. He wanted to get on to those rambling buildings he had noted from the road as he was driving in, but as he was about to leave he hesitated. There was something

about the cold dim room that was unusual. He looked
around again. It was neat, old-fashioned, the living quarters, evidently, of an elderly woman. There were only two
windows. Both were raised wide open to the damp evening
air. Before a large blackened fireplace that looked as if it
had been used for cooking in early days stood a round oil
stove. He got it! The incongruity that had bothered him
was the faint odor that in spite of the open windows clung
to the room. It was not kerosene. It was—ether.

"So what?" he demanded of his speculative nose. "The
old woman's been taking spots off her bib." He adjusted
the door as he had found it and took off along a compar-
atively level trail that would take him toward the sheds
which he had felt from the beginning were his best bet.

He entered first a long narrow frame building that was
little more than a lean-to. A quiet once-over of the gar-
dening and road-mending equipment assured him that no
one was concealed there, and he was about to pass through
a door in the center of it into a larger building behind,
when a soft tap-tap reached his ears. It was coming from
the room he had been about to enter. He looked through
the door, which was ajar, at the end of the room that was
visible. He saw workbenches, a small lathe, a drill press,
and some other metal-working tools, but not the source
of the tapping. He thrust his head far enough around the
door to look into the other half of the room. It seemed
to be a carpentry shop. At the end farthest from him, just
inside some open double doors, a circular saw was set up
for sectioning logs. Above the saw, a chain hung from a
wheel trolley. A truck, half loaded with logs, was backed
into the doorway. On the tail gate of the truck a little
old man was sitting dangling his legs. In his right hand
he held what Zanetti made out to be a pipe. The curious
noise was the sound he made as he plopped the bowl of his
pipe into the palm of his other hand. He had the regularity

of a grandfather's clock. Zanetti suppressed an impulse to remain concealed and begin counting the strokes.

"Good evening," he said, and moved past a line of tool cabinets toward the old man, "Have you seen a stranger around here today?"

The old man dropped his pipe and gripped the floor of the truck. Zanetti picked up the pipe and returned it to him.

"Sorry to startle you. I came in from the other side. Have you been here long?"

"Yes," said the old man, peering at Zanetti in the fading light. "Yes, I've been here—a long time. Who are you?"

"My names Zanetti. I'm from the sheriff's office. And what's your name?"

The old man laughed, "They call me *Mr.* Bjornstrom these days!" Then his manner changed. "Who are you looking for?"

"A big, light-haired fellow. He spent the night here, but he hasn't been seen since early this morning. I thought he might be hiding out in one of these sheds."

Mr. Bjornstrom became still more exacting. "*What* big, light-haired fellow? What do you want with him?"

"I don't know what his name is," explained Zanetti patiently. The old man seemed a little childish. "That's the description I've been given of him. He robbed a lunch counter over in Stinson Beach last night, and hitched a ride up this far with one of the teachers here. Have you seen anyone like that today—or any stranger?"

Mr. Bjornstrom began to shake his head, and to knock his pipe again. The two motions were in counterpoint. "No. No. I haven't seen any stranger. Strange things I've seen," he murmured, "but no stranger."

Zanetti shook his own head irritably. Everybody in this damned school was balmy. A bell rang, and Mr. Bjornstrom mercifully stopped his tapping to climb down off the truck. "What's that for?" asked Zanetti.

"Five thirty," said Mr. Bjornstrom gravely. "I've got to dress for dinner."

Zanetti followed him around the side of the truck and gave up. "Well, all right, thanks! And keep an eye out for him, will you? If you see anyone who doesn't belong here report it to Monsieur Trougnac."

Mr. Bjornstrom began limping along the continuation of the trail Zanetti had come up. "Monsieur Trougnac!" was wafted back over his shoulder in scornful tones. "Humph!"

Zanetti followed the truck lane and it brought him out on the upper road not far from the corrals and the buildings adjoining them. Boys flitted across it, like shadows in the half-light, and down the trail that led back to the school. By the time Zanetti reached the corrals, the place appeared to be deserted except for Walter and the horses. Walter was tossing pitchforks of hay into a line of mangers under a lean-to against the barn. Horses were hanging their necks over fences, watching him. There must have been about fifty of them, heads all turned the same way.

"See anybody since I've been gone?" asked Zanetti.

"Nope," said Walter. The politeness which had distinguished him earlier in the afternoon had evaporated.

"I'd like to go through your barn, if you don't mind, just on the off chance."

"I *do* mind."

"Why? Monsieur Trougnac has given me permission."

"Monsieur Trougnac!" said Walter. "Humph!" The reaction seemed to be widespread. Zanetti wondered how long the head of the school was to be away. He decided to go into the barn anyway, without more words.

In the interior of the barn, lit by one yellow electric light, he found a row of stalls, in three of which were horses.

"That there stallion will bite you," Walter called to him from outside.

Zanetti gave all three horses a wide berth and approached a ladder at the far end of the barn. This he ascended. The loft above was pitch black. He stopped with head and shoulders through the hole. He had left his large flashlight in his patrol car, but he pulled a small emergency one out of his pocket and cast its tiny beams around him. A cat's eyes caught and reflected the light and then disappeared. He climbed through onto the soft hay and followed the cat around a mound of the stuff. There was a hollow there, and in the hollow was a blanket. In the middle of the blanket was the cat and four kittens. She spat at the flashlight. He turned the light from her and threw it along the near wall. On a cross support, between two studs, he spotted something white, and moved closer to inspect it. It was a heavy porcelain cup. Inside, there was coffee sediment, and it was still wet. Rapidly he crossed and crisscrossed the loft with his small beam, cursing himself for not having brought his powerful torch. He kicked through the mound of hay, and tramped back and forth around the entire loft, but he could find no one concealed there.

"Hey!" Walter's outraged voice came from inside the barn below. "Quit walking around up there breaking down my hay. What do you think you're doing?"

Zanetti picked up the cup with his handkerchief and came angrily down the ladder.

"What do you think you're doing? You put that man up here today," he accused Walter. "He was probably up there all the time I was talking to you!"

Walter hung a nose bag on one of the horses.

"Answer me! Was there a man hiding here?"

Walter stepped outside and spat. When he came back in, Zanetti held the cup out for him to see. "You might have given them a blanket, but you don't take coffee up to those kittens!"

Walter raised his eyes from the cup to Zanetti's face. "Well," he said deliberately, "now that you ask me, he may have been up there when you stopped by. Maybe he heard you talking. I been too busy to look since. Guess he lit right out. I would, if I was him."

Zanetti swelled with the effort it took to crowd back unprintable words. He knew it was partly his own fault. He had been in too great a hurry to get to MacDowell, He had not actually asked Huggins for information about anybody but MacDowell. "Got a phone?" he asked, when he could trust himself to speak.

"Nope," said Walter, and allowed a glint of admiration to appear briefly in his eyes. "It's down in the Office."

Zanetti went out of the barn and down the most direct trail to the school as rapidly as he could manage it with his weak light. The man had had over an hour's start, but it was three miles from Drake's Anchorage to the coast road. If he could contact another patrol car near at hand, they still ought to be able to close in on him. He cursed his luck and his stupidity and all the inhabitants of Drake's Anchorage and stumbled down the rocky trail.

10

Mr. Bjornstrom: Superintendent of Buildings

On Friday, the last day of the school week, there was no evening study hall, and the afternoon rest hour was omitted. "Friday afternoon" was a term fraught with high romance. It carried with it memories of smoke redolent with bay and eucalyptus, and hot dogs charred on one side and oozing on the other; it called up still-life vignettes of heady violence, of a rail awash in a close tack, of taut lines biting into numb red heroic hands; it held out promise of a future when one would be mature enough to carry a sleeping bag to the summit of Tamalpais. This Friday afternoon was polished bright with cold and sun. And although there were no privileged groups in the pantry, fortifying themselves against the rigors of prospective adventure, the fourth and fifth grades had challenged the sixth grade to a polo match, so the youngest boys, at least, were happily fired with a spirit proper to the day.

Mr. Bjornstrom, caught up in Doghole loyalties, accompanied the fourth and fifth graders to the corrals. He joined Walter and Mr. Pyke in leaning against the fence. The boys went into the tack room and then, tie ropes in hand, slid through a gate into the corral where the horses were. The horses, looking absent-minded, bunched and began to meander.

"Heck, Jarvis!" Dinwoodie Magill called out impatient-ly. *"Don't* stick your rope out in front of you like that! Can't you see you're starting them to mill around?" Din-woodie, a sixth grader, was barred by custom from enter-ing the corral until the younger boys had come out. This order of precedence was not always adhered to when adults were not at hand, but with Mr. Pyke present it was strictly observed.

The turned-up cuffs of Jarvis Ewing's jeans extended above his knees, and collided with the corrugations below his belt that outlined buried layers of surplus flannel shirt. He could almost pass underneath the bellies of the horses. "Like this?" he chirped cheerfully. Putting his short arms behind him, he dragged his rope on the ground and disap-peared between the legs of the shaggy beasts.

Robert Wintringham was the first to secure his mount and lead him into the saddling corral. Douglas Cahill fol-lowed, but he was discovered to have Juan de Herrera's horse and so had to go back for his own. There were hoots from the sixth graders, perched condescendingly on the fence.

"Look at him!" groaned Lester DeVries. "Doesn't even know his own horse!"

The two elderly, winter-coated bays exhibited, in truth, so little personality that the mistake was understandable, but no one mentioned this. It was an unbreakable law that no man spoke disparagingly of another man's horse. Juan de Herrera, having had the good fortune to be shunted past one hurdle, approached his nag with bit and bridle and unlightened heart. He knew it wasn't going to open its mouth. In contrast, the will of Juan's little brother Alonzo seemed so inevitable to his horse that, having dropped his tie rope, Alonzo was at that moment leading her out by her mane. From the ground, Alonzo could not reach up to her ears nor even to her back, so he tied her to the fence on which he had hung his gear and stationed himself on the top rail for business.

After the fourth and fifth graders, the sixth graders brought out their horses. While the saddling up was being completed, several older boys arrived at the corrals.

"Van," said Mr. Pyke, "would you and Fitz like to referee the match?"

"Gosh, I'd like to, sir," replied Van, "but I've told Neil I'll mend trail this afternoon. I think I'll stay with it. What about you, Fitz?"

"Oh, you come, Fitz!" shouted Rab who was already up on his horse and standing out in the road. He swung his mallet with careless rapture and his horse shied.

"Rab!" said Mr. Pyke sternly. "You know better than that!"

"Sorry, sir," said Rab, quickly meek. One didn't take chances with Mr. Pyke. Penalties, when they were levied by him, were severe and not open to review.

"I came out for trail work," said Fitz. "I'll go ahead with it."

"Another time, then," said Mr. Pyke, not misled by Fitz's apparent lack of enthusiasm. "Any of you others want to?"

"What about us, sir?" said Ralph Johnstone, indicating himself and Langdon Beaumont.

"Oh, I say, fellows," remonstrated Neil.

"I want two men from the first team to have that practice, Neil," said Mr. Pyke. "You've a decent crew without them."

"Owwwww! He's on my foot!" The howl came from under Beattie Eberheart's horse.

"Grab his fetlock," said Walter without unfolding his arms. "Next time, go around." Beattie extricated himself without assistance, and tightened up his saddle girth, emitting occasional unheeded sniffs. Alonzo de Herrera descended for the fourth time to push his horse over to where he could reach her from the top of the fence. As he climbed back up, the mare once more drifted away. At a nod from Mr. Pyke, Ralph Johnstone went over and held the horse parallel to the fence while Alonzo saddled. Walter and Mr. Pyke finished up for the three or four others who were still in difficulties, and checked saddle girths. Then the two teams were ready, and they plunged out into the road in a swirl of white helmets and mallets. Mr. Pyke yelled. They slowed to a dogtrot and moved sedately up the road.

When the older boys and Mr. Pyke had saddled up and ridden off in two groups, the one heading south toward the polo field, the other north, equipped with a pick, an ax, a spade, and a canteen of water, Mr. Bjornstrom followed Walter into the barn. Walter set about adjusting the bandage on the leg of a lamed horse. Mr. Bjornstrom walked the length of the barn, paused before an empty stall, and came back to stare at Walter.

"Where's Twinkletoes?" he asked. Twinkletoes, a great black hunter with powerful shoulders and hindquarters, had four white ankles. His present owner, the headmaster, had allowed that he had probably been a cute colt and refused to change his name.

"Out to pasture," said Walter, seemingly intent on a neat rewinding of the bandage.

"He was here yesterday," Mr. Bjornstrom said pointedly.

"Gol darn you, Eloise," said Walter. "Lean the other way."

"Kind of rushing the season, aren't you?" Mr. Bjornstrom persisted.

Walter tucked in the end of the bandage, set down the foot, and smacked Eloise on the rump. "Yep."

Above the diapason of boy and horse noises that had continued outside, soared a female voice. "No thank you, Grover. I'd rather get him out myself."

Walter went to the door of the barn with Mr. Bjorn-strom still at his heels. Miss Blossom was in the corral, se-ducing her horse. "Hello, honey child," she cooed. "How's the sweet old thing?" Her dulcet tones continued until she had a rope around his neck.

"Nice day for a ride," remarked Mr. Bjornstrom as she led her horse past them to where she had left her saddle.

"Yes, isn't it?" Miss Blossom smiled at them a little mournfully. She was going out with no plan but to get away from the depression that hung over the school. Even though blessed by sun, the high wind-swept hills looked lonely, and she did not feel that the companionship of her horse, who was tolerant rather than interested, would be adequate. But to whom else could she turn? "Not going out after any stock, are you, Walter?"

"Nope."

"Say howdy to Twinkletoes, if you run across him," said Mr. Bjornstrom with a side glance at Walter.

"Is he out by himself?" asked Miss Blossom, patting a saddle blanket into place and stepping back to survey with an anxious eye its relation to the withers of her horse. She threw on the saddle and inspected the symmetry of the whole before she cinched up the girth. "I should think he'd be lonesome."

"There's always the steers," said Mr. Bjornstrom, still addressing Walter. Walter had business that took him back in the barn.

Mr. Bjornstrom held open the gate for her, and Miss Blossom rode out onto the road. She followed it until it turned east and there left it for the open fields. Her gen-eral intention was to keep going up, to keep in the sun, and to keep off trails. In this way she could be most com-fortable, put herself in the way of encountering novelty, and enliven her horse. Parson became willing and his gaits smoothed out whenever he thought he was out on business.

She had found she could give him this impression by sending him from time to time to the top of little rises and sighting in all directions as if hunting for stock. A sudden dig would then send him plunging down the slope to scramble enthusiastically in any direction she indicated so long as she kept up the game. So they played along a northeasterly course until they were on the crest of the highest ridge between the school and the valley of the Olema Creek and there was consequently no more "up."

Here, where they encountered the old Ridge Trail, Miss Blossom paused to consider. The trail offered a route home over territory they had not covered coming out, but it would put her back at the school in not more than half an hour, and it was not yet four o'clock. Deciding to keep on as far as the old Lime Kilns, she pretended to discover the red back of a steer in the manzanita thickets that encroached on the trail ahead, and leaned forward.

"Sick 'em, Parson," she urged.

The trail dipped below the summit of the ridge, but on the seaward side, so that so long as they were in open country they still had the sun with them. But the Kilns were in a dell under live oaks and evergreens and the air there was like the inside of an icebox, so she didn't pause long to savor the *Urne-Buriall* melancholy of their moss-covered masonry. She encouraged Parson to clatter on across the rocky bed of the stream below the spring and up into the sunlight on the other side. While she was lost in wondering once more who had built the Kilns and why, so far away from anything else, and so long ago that a foot-thick fir had grown up through the center of the middle one, they entered the edge of the Burned Area.

In this section of it there were no dead trees, but only a wide graveyard of manzanita. Black twisted prongs, transfixed in attitudes of agony, rose out of the barren ground. Two years before, these same convolutions, then satiny maroon and amber and intermittently displayed through green leaves, had had a sensuous, almost fleshly grace. But the flame that had swept inland for three days and nights had stripped off the beauty and left these indecent sticks. They were thin and lamenting against the sky line on her right. Down the slope on her left, they were a thicket of malicious swords against which she should not put her horse. The trail was sandy and its dips were gentle. She quickened Parson's lope and they fled with increasing speed through the avenue of ghosts. On ahead, she hoped, they would find a draw, down which they could make their way to another trail that she knew lay below them.

On the top of a rise, she tugged him to a halt, for she could see from there that the next dip would lead them up to and over the summit of the main ridge and into a dead-end labyrinth of burned trees on the other side. That was as far as the old Ridge Trail had been cleared. She was considering whether she could conscientiously lead her horse through the manzanita barbs down to the other trail a half mile below or whether she must ignominiously backtrack, when, in the gap on the ridge to the east, a flash of red really did catch her eye. She stared fixedly at the spot, and with another movement the animal outlined itself in the brush. Long body, long neck— It wasn't a steer, but a saddled horse. Who could be afoot over there so late in the day, so far from the school? Eventually a new trail would be cut through there to connect with the logging road, but now the area was out of bounds for boys unless they were under the supervision of the headmaster. She herself had been warned away from it. She knew that Walter, Mr. Bjornstrom, and Mr. Pyke were not out; the headmaster and Mr. MacDowell were gone; the other masters didn't ride. So there must be boys adventuring alone in that uncertain region and Miss Blossom considered that it was her business to get them out of it.

Taking color from her mood, Parson bridled, impatient to be off. She gave him free rein and he catapulted forward into the hollow and up the rising ground beyond. Arrived on the ridge, Parson pulled up of his own accord beside the three horses that stood there, two with divided reins dragging, one with his tie rope twisted around the trunk of a small dead tree. Miss Blossom got down and tied Parson to another tree. He was trained to stand, but she wasn't quite sure of him. She listened for the sound of voices. The four horses stared at her in that detached way animals have of putting you on your own. Following the turbulence of her arrival, the stillness seemed absolute. Life had begun to creep back into the devastated area, but only in little ways. There were no human sounds. Aside from the waiting horses, the only evidence that people had passed that way lay in the trail route blazed down the east side of the gap by three scraps of white cloth that she could see tied in the dead brush. She began to follow down the course they indicated.

The draw deepened quickly into a canyon cut by a stream that must be fed by springs on the ridge. Logs crisscrossed it thickly and many trees still stood. They had been live oaks, and their long heavy branches were again festooned with the hanging moss that told of the continuous drift of fog. In just a few minutes she was in a gloomy twilight. As the sky too was gray, she knew that the sun must have set, or at least retired behind the ocean mists which at this season often claimed it before it touched the horizon. The declivity of the canyon became so sharp that the rudimentary trail began to zigzag, directed in its course by the white markers. Heavy logs lay across it and limbs that would catch a saddle horn spread above it. She sat down to slide over a six-foot drop of almost perpendicular shale.

She remained seated at the end of her slide and looked around. It would be a tough job to fix that up for a horse, but if the trail was to keep to this canyon, there was no better route. She looked up to discover that she was directly under a tall black shell that leaned. She crawled forward quickly and stood up. She was cold, muddy, and smudged with charcoal. This was a heck of a place! Where had those boys got to? At the foot of the third place that was so steep that she had to crawl, she found their tools abandoned. Evidently their own doubt of the feasibility of the route had crystallized at that point. She listened without reward for some sound of them. Not even a whisper from the sea penetrated the ruined cathedral of trees.

Miss Blossom's impatience gave way to a presentiment that those whom she had been following were close by, in the gloom below her, as motionless as she. A formless dread rolled up to her from the silence, calling on her to hurry. They were trapped! Pinned under some heavy weight! In pain! Why were they so quiet?

There were fewer live oaks in the canyon now, and more redwoods. Their trunks were charred but most of their tops were green. The floor of the canyon flattened out and the trail was straighter and the ground softer, but it was so dark under the redwoods that she had difficulty finding the markers. Now much of the underbrush bore leaves. She was nearing country which had not been burned over. She paused with her hand on a branch to which a rag was tied, sighting for the one beyond. What she made out first in the glade ahead was a pile of logs. Hastening toward it, she stumbled over ruts that must have been roiled up in the mud by turning trucks. She was running because from behind the logs there came the sound of choked retching.

On the other side of the logs, Neil Truesdale was kneeling, clinging to a stump for support, being violently sick.

She knelt beside him and put her arm around him, hunting for a handkerchief with her free hand.

"Neil, honey! What's the matter with you? Is it the asthma come back?" It was lighter here at the edge of the clearing. Another canyon came down from the north to join and widen out the one she had been descending, but she could see no one in it. Fear gripped her anew. "Who's with you? Where are the other boys?"

Neil accepted the handkerchief, retched once more, and stood up to turn his back to her while he wiped his face. He tried to speak, but could only wheeze, and this started him to cough again. She espied a trail marker up the other canyon. Maybe they were all right. Just up there searching for another route.

"Yoo-hoo, up there, whoever you are!" she called hopefully. "Come on back. It's time to go home."

Fitzsimmons Eubank materialized out of the bushes only a few paces away from her. "Well, for heaven's sake," she exclaimed. "What are you doing? Playing hide and seek? Where's the third one?"

She couldn't see Fitz's face, and his steps lagged as he closed the gap between them. "He'll be along in a minute," he answered.

"Let's start on," croaked Neil.

He began to walk back the way she had come. When she did not follow, he paused and looked back at her. Fitz had stopped, too, while still ten feet away. They made a silent triangle.

"What are you two trying to keep me from finding out?" demanded Miss Blossom. "Who's the other one with you and why doesn't he come?"

"It's Van," said Fitz. He hadn't just been coughing, but his voice, too, was unnatural.

"Van? What's happened to Van?" She started to run past Fitz. "Something's fallen on him!"

Fitz caught her arm and pulled her to a halt. "Don't go back there," he commanded her.

She freed her arm. "You forget yourself, Fitz!"

When she started to go on, Van rose up above the same bushes from which Fitz had come. He seemed to be standing in a hollow behind a log, for he was visible only from the waist up. She was near enough now to see the tears on his cheeks. "I'm all right, Miss Blossom. *Please* go," he beseeched her.

She moved slowly toward him through the green gloaming. The other two followed. With a boy on either side, she rounded the end of the log, and froze. At Van's feet, Miss Breckenridge's Paisley shawl was spread over something bumpy.

"What is—under there?" she whispered.

Van's lip trembled, but he couldn't get the words out. Grim anger had closed down over Fitz's face. Neil looked as if he were dizzy with nausea. Miss Blossom reminded herself that they were children, and she was twenty-two years old. They were schoolboys, and she the teacher. She stretched a hand toward a corner of the shawl.

"Don't!" Van burst out. "She's dead! She's dead!"

"Go back—down the trail." Miss Blossom had kept her voice controlled. Then she screamed. As she had lifted the shawl, her hand had brushed against flesh colder than any she had ever known, and her convulsive start had bared an old white foot raised stiffly in the air. She dropped the shawl back on the foot and sank to the ground with her face in her hands. The world seemed to be turning with her head as its pivot. Thrown out from the axis, the reds and yellows of the Paisley rippled in sickening, suffocating whorls. The colors rocked back and forth to a halt, and she thought she was going to be sick. When she wasn't she lowered her hands and looked at the real Paisley. It was true—that which her eyes had registered immediately but her mind had refused to credit. The shape under the shawl was that of a person lying sidewise, and jackknifed as if sitting in a chair, only there was no chair. It was like a figure that has been taken down out of a clothing-store window that is to be redecorated. A pink, defenseless mannequin. This foot had been chalky white. But—what about—the clothes? Where had the Paisley shawl been when the children had come upon it?

She raised her eyes to them pityingly, and discovered that a change had come over them. They had drawn closer together, and their glances were hostile. Fitz spoke for them. "Leave everything as it is, Miss Blossom."

She wobbled to her feet to go to the end that must be the head of the thing. Fitz got there before her and prevented her from touching it.

"I've got—to know—who it is," she whispered.

His grip on her shoulder tightened. "No. You don't. You haven't seen anything, and you're not going to. Come away."

11

Fitzsimmons Eubank: Disciple

"Come on," said Neil. "We've got to get out of here. The light's going."

Fitz piloted Miss Blossom firmly around the body and down to the log pile. Neil went ahead and Van followed. Already, Miss Blossom thought, it must be too dark for Neil to find the trail markers.

"We'd better go down to the main road," she said. "Somebody will pick us up, and we can phone for the police."

"No," said Fitz, and pushed her along after Neil.

The situation was in masculine hands. Miss Blossom had been shocked into a role that was actually more congenial to one of her temperament than that of preceptress. She allowed herself to be led.

"Look out for this branch," said Neil.

"Duck, Miss Blossom," said Fitz.

As the balance and soundness of the timbers that choked the canyon were unknown quantities, it would have been hazardous to follow the simplest expedient of letting the creek bed guide them to the top. Fitz went on ahead to help Neil. They shouted back and forth to each other from marker to marker. Van stayed to assist Miss Blossom up the steep places. Miss Blossom left the choice of route to the boys and addressed herself to reestablishing some coherence in her whirling thoughts.

Hidden behind a log, some fifty feet from the head of the logging road, lay a human body. She realized that she had been maneuvered away from it before she had actually established its identity. She hadn't even consciously checked on whether it was dead, but surely that hadn't been necessary. She rubbed her little finger savagely against her jeans. As to how it had met its death, she hadn't the vaguest idea. And how—and why—and by whom—had it been brought to that spot? As her abhorrence for the object itself loosened its grip on her senses, her horror changed qualitatively to include more rationally based fears.

Who was it? Who was it lying there in that remote dank hollow under Miss Breckenridge's shawl? To be nearly yet not quite certain was horrible! She should have insisted on looking. If it was Miss Breckenridge? It must be Miss Breckenridge! Then—what followed from that?

Memory brought up a picture of Miss Breckenridge's fierce features played upon by the leaping lights and shadows thrown up from the hearth in the Common Room. Miss Blossom supposed she must have seen her since that evening, but she could remember nothing later than the moment of that exit, when Miss Breckenridge's vitality had reduced a roomful of people to propitiatory silence. From that—to the thing under the shawl! Could the personality of Miss Breckenridge have shrunk to the mute limits of that helpless grotesque?

This, then, was death.

But the disaster was crouched to spring with more than this lesson upon little Miss Blossom. Memory rounded out to include the rest of that firelit room. Lurking in the shadows with the enigmatic figures of those people who had listened to Miss Breckenridge's denunciation now gleamed a malevolent purpose. Miss Blossom tried not to admit to herself that she saw it. Her mind fled now from the conclusion it forced on her as that night she had fled from the intimation of its presence.

What day was it that she had rushed out into the darkness seeking sanctuary with Miss Breckenridge from a presentiment of evil? Wednesday? No, Tuesday, the first day of the term, the day the headmaster had disappeared. And when had Miss Breckenridge left the school—been supposed to leave the school? She *left* the school Monsieur had said— That was at breakfast, after the nurse— When was that? Not last night because Mr. MacDowell had still been here. One by one, during the past week, the props had been knocked out from under concepts and persons whose permanence had been the precondition of her ordered world. She had been numbed by the successive shocks into a false passivity, and now the week was a jumble in her memory. She let it remain so. She clung heavily to Van's arm and let him drag her up the last incline almost without assistance from her.

They came, finally, up out of the valley of death, two by two along a straight trail.

A horse whinnied a relieved welcome. "Here I am, Jenny," called Neil. "Come back over here." The black silhouette of the horse jerked a lowered head and tried to back. "No! Hold on! Whoa, girl." Neil dropped the tools and ran to disentangle his horse, before she should break the reins, from the manzanita prongs in which she had involved herself.

Van's sorrel mare stood quietly while he hitched the canteen to a thong on his saddle. Fitz untied his own horse and then Miss Blossom's.

"Wait a minute, Miss Blossom," said Fitz as she put a foot in a stirrup and took a weak grip on the saddle that seemed very high above her. "Before we start, we'll have to have your word that you'll say nothing to anybody about our having found anything in the canyon."

His words registered slowly, and she leaned wearily against Parson's solid warmth. It was too much. Why did he have to be like this now, when she was too tired to be patient, or even to make sense?

"You don't really know anything, you know, Miss Blossom," said Van. "So you won't be lying if you just keep still."

Miss Blossom straightened up and dragged herself back to an awareness of responsibility. "Boys, this is a horrible thing—for all of us. There's exactly one thing for us to do about it, and I have to do that as soon as I possibly can. That's notify the police. Put any other idea out of your minds."

"No," said Fitz implacably.

"We won't argue about it," said Miss Blossom, and essayed again to get on her horse. This time Fitz helped her, which was fortunate, for her legs were like noodles. If she had to say one more thing, she'd be weeping.

When they rode down the trail through the acres of dead, uplifted arms, Van took the lead and Fitz closed in behind her. Each of the boys carried a tool, upright in his free hand, Van the ax, Fitz the shovel, Neil in the rear with the pick. She felt like a prisoner in a Salvador Dali landscape. Though they were silent, she knew they hadn't accepted her decision. They had some mad scheme of private revenge. Revenge? She caught her breath as the word punctured the cocoon of lethargy she had allowed to fold around her. Then they thought it was murder? Of course they thought it was murder and so did she. Monsieur! Monsieur's strangely cold voice extinguishing the frothy crosscurrents of the breakfast table, "I have discharged Miss Breckenridge."

It was unthinkable that anyone at the school was a murderer. Yet she knew that was what the children believed. And Fitz was going to make sure that she did not prevent them from doing whatever it was they were planning. What if it were true? What if the whole staff was in it together? Miss Breckenridge had threatened them. She had said they were wicked. They had feared her. They had killed her. She must get help quickly, and from outside the school. She must get it before the boys had had time to endanger themselves.

"Van!" she cried out. "Van, I've got to hurry. Let me go ahead of you."

She kicked Parson into a run and tried to rein him around the horse in front. Van turned his horse sidewise in the trail, and Fitz came up beside her, caught her reins, and pulled Parson to a halt.

"Listen to me, Miss Blossom," said Fitz. "You've got to do as we say! You've got to give us your oath that you leave everything to us, or we simply can't let you go back to the school."

She plunged her heels fiercely into Parson's ribs and tried to leap away into the wilderness of manzanita stumps. He reared and would have launched out into them if the boys had not closed in to make a knot of plunging, wheeling, bewildered horses. They held their tools high, like lances, above the scrimmage, but the hazardous flourishes of ax and pick were too much for her. She pulled up her horse. Even in open country it was doubtful whether she could have got away from them. Up here, it was hopeless. She patted Parson's neck to settle him down, and wished she could quiet the boys as easily. Van and his red horse executed one more carelessly graceful curvet, and came to earth inches away from her. Van leaned over to look earnestly into her face.

"Promise, Miss Blossom. Please promise."

It was such a childlike petitioning that her answer was as to a child. "I can't make a promise like that because it wouldn't be honest. When we got to a phone I'd have to break it."

Fitz slipped her reins out of Miss Blossom's relaxed fingers, and flipped them over Parson's head, so that he had her helplessly on lead. "Ride on," he directed Van.

And thus they went on out of the manzanita wastes and into the dell where the Lime Kilns stood.

"This is about the most sheltered place," said Fitz, and got off his horse.

"Make up your mind, Miss Blossom," said Van. "Either swear not to tell a soul what you saw or spend the night here. Which do you choose?"

"She's already chosen," said Fitz curtly. "Didn't you hear what she said? Let's make it quick. We don't want to be after the bell getting in."

The other two boys climbed down. Miss Blossom remained seated. Now, while they were off, she would watch for a chance and make a bolt for it. But Neil—*Neil*—went to Parson's head and took a grip on the reins just below the bit. She had counted on him, if it came to a showdown, to restrain Fitz's recklessness and Van's fanaticism!

He spoke with determination. "Help her down."

Fitz reached up and took her arm. He smiled at her. "Sorry, Miss Blossom, but that's the way it is. Be a good sport. You may as well get down because if you don't, you know, I'll pull you off."

Miss Blossom decided on dignity to the last ditch. Her only chance now was to make it so easy for them that they'd feel too utterly like heels to go through with it. She descended in silence and watched Neil lead Parson down the trail and twist his rein around a bush. If Parson were only a dog! He simply didn't give a damn what happened

to her. Her chin quivered in self-pity. Neil came back to
his own horse and got his lasso. She had seen him secure
a struggling yearling with a couple of flips of a tie rope.

"Over here," said Fitz. He led her across the round
stones that had tumbled down from the crumbling masonry to the tree growing up through the center kiln. Van
walked at her other side. When they reached the tree, he
stooped to shift the stones at its base so that they were
more nearly level. He took off his windbreaker and spread
it over the improvised seat. Fitz slid out of his too and
held it out for her.

"Put this on," he said.

They were going to have the genius to carry this through
on a chivalrous plane. But surely not the rope! Surely when
it came to tying her up! She put her arms into the sleeves,
disguising her shudder.

"Sit down the way you'll be most comfortable," said
Fitz. "We may be able to come back for you this evening,
but we can't be sure."

She sank down on the stones, raised her knees, and
folded her arms.

"You'll have to be against the tree more," said Neil who
had now joined them.

She adjusted herself, still without speaking.

Neil took her hands and fashioned knots over her wrists
and ran the rope around her and the tree several times. She
found that her hands were well past each other and a small
experimental tug told her that the lines that held them in
that position were taut. Neil, his task completed, stood up
and looked at Van. They couldn't really go off and leave
her here! They were playing a game. It wasn't real to them.

"You are doing a very despicable thing." Miss Blossom
managed a disapproving schoolroom voice.

"Change your mind, Miss Blossom," exclaimed Van
impulsively.

"You still have time to change yours," said Miss Blossom, pressing her advantage. "But if you were to carry this through," she added severely, "the fact that you are under age would not help you with the police."

She could have bitten her tongue off, for this enabled Van to straighten his shoulders manfully. "We'll take what comes," he said.

Fitz was already back at his horse. "We've got to run for it," he told the others.

Neil lingered behind Van. "There won't be really anything to hurt you. You'll just be uncomfortable."

Miss Blossom raised her chin and looked the other way. Neil joined the others.

There was a scrambling of hooves, and she turned to see them run their horses heedlessly through the wash filled with mud and loose rocks and disappear from the hollow. Fitz was leading Parson. The commotion of their passage was quickly stilled, and Miss Blossom was alone with the mountain, her thoughts, and the quiet approach of the night-born fog.

12

Mr. Arbuthnot: Latin

Water that had been brought to the boil in the kitchen cooled on the unconnected electric grill in the Faculty Common Room. The sun withdrew its warmth from the windows and there was no glow from the hearth to take its place. At four thirty, pried from his couch by a habit so inveterate that it had won out over his disinclination to mingle, Mr. Dingle arrived. He inserted the plug, drew a stool almost into the fireplace, seated himself, and applied a match to the crumples of paper that stuck out from between the faggots. Cold air scurried over his shoulder blades while he waited for the fire to gather strength. He loathed this life. Such small adjustments were necessary to make it congenial. Separate quarters, say Stone Cottage wired for modern improvements, a servant to see that they were always ready for him, a working day confined within definite limits, and all rude scramblings with the non-academic hours of raw youth delegated to subordinates. Twice this long-dreamed-of arrangement had seemed to be within his grasp, and twice the cup had been dashed from his lips.

Nine years before, when circumstances, so distasteful that he had been able almost completely to forget them, had forced him to absent himself from a superficially tolerant but basically conventional Southern city, his

well-bred air and a chance encounter in a San Francisco
salon had resulted in the offer of a teaching position at
Drake's Anchorage. He had taken it then because he had
no choice. He had stayed on because he saw its possibili-
ties. Even at its lowest ebb, Drake's Anchorage had been a
sound financial institution. So Mr. Dingle had martyred
his fastidious tastes and maintained a splendid decorum
throughout the brief stays of a series of headmasters im-
ported from the East. Just as it had appeared that virtue
must inevitably be rewarded, two of the shilly-shallying
old founders had died and Alrik Lind, inheriting his grandfather's claim, had persuaded the other owners to appoint
him head of the school. Mr. Dingle had dissembled his
bitterness and succored his dreams by directing his charm
toward the conquest of Mrs. Cnut-Sorenson, who had
arrived in the vicinity a few months after Alrik Lind. Mrs.
Cnut-Sorenson's husband had survived his grandfather by
only six months, and his sudden demise had brought to
her the Sorenson share of Drake's Anchorage. Mr. Dingle
was quick to apprehend that Mrs. Cnut-Sorenson wished
also to express her personality through the school. It was
not long before he had fostered with her a gracious al-
liance composed in equal parts of admiration for their
own sophistication and tacit contempt for the crudities of
Alrik Lind.

Events had culminated more rapidly than he had dared
hope. If on certain aspects of them he preferred not to
dwell, he nevertheless had been prepared to profit by them
through the good offices of Mrs. Cnut-Sorenson in which
he had felt himself secure. He had thrown himself un-
conditionally into their course with the conviction that
success this time was certain. And then Mrs. Cnut-Sorenson, with no advance warning, had deserted him. She had
listlessly relinquished the school to the Señora de Herrera
and to her protégé, Monsieur Trougnac. To Monsieur

Trougnac whom Mr. Dingle, with what he had considered farsighted cunning, had been building up! Mr. Dingle was not emotionally equipped to attempt the domination of the Señora de Herrera. He knew his limitations, and so, unerringly, did she. Mr. Dingle was out. That purring lynx had the ownership of the school in her paws without ever having had to show her claws. Others had done that for her. The more he ruminated upon the past, the more he contemplated the future, the more sickly Mr. Dingle became.

The water boiled again, and he set a pot of tea to draw. Mr. Arbuthnot entered.

"Oh," said Mr. Arbuthnot.

"Will you do the honors?" said Mr. Dingle. "Apparently we are to be unsupported."

Mr. Arbuthnot proffered a tentative equality. "Those of us who remain must stick together," he suggested in what he hoped was a jocose voice. It didn't come out very well, but it was a beginning.

Mr. Dingle accepted his tea and moved to a more comfortable chair without comment.

"I wonder what Mr. MacDowell will do with himself now." Mr. Arbuthnot was anxious to share. "I understood from him last night that he had no resources except his car and that it was not entirely paid for. He had no idea where he was going. I offered him what cash I had but he didn't accept it. Did you talk to him before he left?"

Mr. Dingle, as well as Mr. Arbuthnot, had endured much from Mr. MacDowell, but he was too disinclined to acknowledge a kinship with Mr. Arbuthnot to join him in gloating over Mr. MacDowell's downfall.

"No," replied Mr. Dingle. "I merely inferred that he had departed this life when I found both the ninth and tenth grades in my classroom for the first period this morning."

"You should have seen him slamming things into his car. He didn't attempt to pack—just dumped everything in together, and was off in half an hour. I also offered him what I thought was a rather good suggestion, but I fear he was too angry to take notice of what I was saying." Mr. Arbuthnot waited.

Though purpose had died in him, Mr. Dingle had trained himself too assiduously to be able to ignore a conversational ball when it was tossed directly at him. So, "What was the suggestion?" he asked.

"I reminded him of the old ranch house on the headmaster's land over toward Inverness. It was opened up and stocked, you know, for the December All Day Ride. I suggested that he make it his headquarters while he considered what to do next." Mr. Arbuthnot shot Mr. Dingle a sly glance. "And then too, I reminded him, there is the possibility that he might be recalled. Our situation—is not stabilized?" He made it sound like a question. Mr. Arbuthnot longed to know what had put an end to the chumminess between Mr. Dingle and Monsieur Trougnac. "Do you expect Monsieur to remain in charge of the school throughout the entire term?" Was Mr. Dingle now excluded from participation in policy-forming conferences as completely as it had always been Mr. Arbuthnot's fate to be? His nose quivered appreciatively, and Mr. Dingle saw it.

"Before you rejoice too indecently at the plight of others," he said acidly, "you might pause to consider your own! The school is disintegrating at so rapid a rate that the question of who is in charge of it will soon be immaterial."

It was sweet to see that he had been able to get under Mr. Dingle's skin, but he desired more the intimacy of mutual commiseration which it still seemed to him he might attain. Mr. Arbuthnot replied, "I'm far from rejoicing. I was just going to remark the same thing. I expect Mr. Weber to fall out next. This is his free weekend, you know."

"Is he taking it?"

"Went off without even waiting for lunch. The way he's been conducting himself lately, I'll be surprised if he gets back Monday."

"I have a headache," said Mr. Dingle. "I think I'll go and get something for it from the nurse."

Mr. Arbuthnot gazed at the coals of the fire till long after the room was dark. No one else came in for tea. These long Friday afternoons, with so few duties, had always proved duller than the other ones. Today, in spite of all that had happened, was no exception. He became aware that he was going to miss Mr. MacDowell. Even his ragging had been some sort of companionship. He got up to wander aimlessly toward his room.

As he went down one side of the courtyard, Van, Neil, and Fitz came up the other side, as unobtrusively as their boots permitted. They stopped in front of Nat's door, knocked, and disappeared inside. Nat had not gone back to the infirmary, but he was still confined to his bed except for meals and classes. Mr. Arbuthnot told himself that too much excitement was not good for Nat. Those big healthy boys would tire him out. And what could they want with him? Mr. Weber was not here to intervene. Mr. Arbuthnot took himself across the court. In a shadow thrown by a column that stood between him and the corner light, he paused with his hand on the knob of the door.

Miss Blossom's ears caught the steady clop-clop of trotting horses. Although the period since she had ceased to struggle with her bonds and had given herself over to a trance of misery stretched eternally behind her, her watch indicated that it was only a few minutes past six. She roused sufficiently to recognize that the boys would have had to turn around immediately they reached the corrals to be returning so soon.

There were two horses. They were passing her by. One was on lead. Astride the other there was a small hunched figure. As it came up against the sky on the other side of the hollow, Miss Blossom recognized its back.

"Mr. Bjornstrom," she called.

He pulled up and turned his horse. "Miss Blossom! Where are you?" He got a flashlight switched on and with it searched her out.

"Over here."

He dismounted and came to her. Miss Blossom was beyond surprise, beyond making explanations, almost beyond fear. He clucked under his breath when he saw the rope, and immediately set about untying it.

"There you are," he said a few minutes later, and began to recoil the rope.

Miss Blossom rubbed her chilled hands together and stumbled mutely to her feet. Mr. Bjornstrom took her arm. "Make it all right to the horse? I can bring him nearer."

Her knees sagged and her feet were stumps in which pins and needles were awakening, but with his assistance she got to the horse. "Why, it's Parson," she said wonderingly. She leaned her forehead against his mane and shed her first tears. Mr. Bjornstrom must have been coming for her and not for Miss Breckenridge.

"Here, here," said Mr. Bjornstrom. "None of that. Now, up with you!"

He got her shoved up into the saddle. He remounted, flicked his reins across Parson's rump, and they started at a jog trot on the trail back to the school. Miss Blossom bumped along, clinging to the saddle horn. Finally feeling came back into her hands and feet and she could manage the stirrups and reins and find her seat and the rhythm of the trot. They had covered almost half the distance to the school before she spoke.

"Who sent you after me?"

Mr. Bjornstrom was so close behind her that he must have heard her question, but he did not answer until after she had repeated it. "Nobody," he said.

"But then, how did you know I was out here?"

"I got eyes," he said, "and those boys don't lie well. I saw 'em sneaking in with a spare horse. When I asked 'em where you was, all they could think of was that you'd hitched a ride into San Rafael."

"How did you know where they'd been?"

"I seen their tools," said Mr. Bjornstrom. His words dropped definitely into the night air.

They quickened Miss Blossom's reviving consciousness to encompass a new field of suspicion. Was Mr. Bjornstrom also aware of what lay near where the trail builders had been? Without some additional reason, how could he possibly have suspected that the school's most trustworthy boys had mistreated Miss Blossom? And now, having discovered her outrageous predicament, why did he prefer that the incomprehensible remain unexplained? He had not been surprised.

"You know then!" She spoke her conclusion before she thought.

Mr. Bjornstrom neither affirmed nor denied. His silence could only mean that he was involved in some way with the death of Miss Breckenridge.

Somewhere not too far from the school there must be policemen. How solidly satisfying now, if she could speed her roadster down the highway and come upon the black and white frown of a prowling patrol car! The thing to do was to get to her car. How could she know what Mr. Bjornstrom planned to do with her? The boys, too, had been kind at first. She was free now. She was ahead of Mr. Bjornstrom on the trail, and the corrals were not more than a half mile

away. She kicked Parson into a run that rapidly widened
the space between her and Mr. Bjornstrom.

"Hey!" he called.

She did not answer, but leaning forward slashed her
reins back and forth on either side of Parson's outstretched
neck. She came up out of the fields and down the dirt road
without checking his speed and the astonished horse had
to choose between either sliding on his tail or taking the
corral gate. He had played a lot of polo. He sat, and Miss
Blossom tumbled off him.

"What do you think you're doing?" bellowed Walter
from the door of the barn.

Miss Blossom did not reply. She opened the gate, shooed
Parson in, slammed the gate, crossed over the road, and
ran down the trail. As she passed Stone Cottage, it seemed
so tranquilly unchanged that it challenged the reality of
the last two hours. She almost looked in to see whether the
Paisley shawl could be still on the bed where she had so
often seen it. Actually, however, she didn't pause, for she
knew that her glimpse of that rigid foot and the icy feel of
it against her hand had been no nightmare.

She ran straight for her car, fumbling in an inside
pocket for her keys. Her stall was the last but one before
the door that led into the passage between the infirmary
and the Common Room. She noticed that the last one,
which had always been reserved for Miss Breckenridge,
was empty. She wondered whether she could think back to
the last time she had seen Miss Breckenridge's old Chevrolet standing there. That would be for the police, not for
her. Once she had been able to reach them—

"Miss Blossom! You shall not leave now! Where have
you been? What do you do there?"

Miss Blossom hung on the door she had just opened
and swung forward to look over the hood of her car toward
the voice that had shot icicles of terror into her heart. The

Señora de Herrera had come out of the school and at her elbow stood Monsieur Trougnac. The light from the passageway behind picked out half of the accusing face that was turned toward her. The other half was lost behind the long shadow of his nose.

"Just—getting something—out of the—pocket—of the—"

The lighted half of the face began to twist down under the nose, and the walls of the school, the very door on which she was leaning, slid with it. Only the nose remained vertical, reaching toward her, growing longer. Paisley ripples spreading from it, humming, singing a harp-like melody in her ears. With a tired sigh, Miss Blossom dropped on the ground behind her car.

Miss Blossom was trying to rise up, but there was a weight on her chest and she couldn't move her arms, "Wicked, wicked," she murmured. "That's what she said. All wicked." They had tied her up again. They were smothering her. She tore her eyes open, to find herself gazing up into the intent eyes of the nurse. Miss Burtt's hands were on Miss Blossom's shoulders. She was beginning to smile. Miss Blossom made another attempt to rise. "I've got to get away," she pleaded. "Miss Breckenridge said I had to get away, and now she's dead." Miss Burtt's hands were inexorable, and her smile went on developing. Miss Blossom moaned, and waited helplessly for the teeth to be bared, for the howl to spew forth.

The nurse said soothingly, *"Not* dead, just gone away."

"Poor little one. The week has been too much for her." Soft fingers brushed her forehead. There was an odor of kid gloves. She turned her head and saw that it came from a fold of fine dark fur. She followed the line of the fold upwards into the dusk and saw the face of the Señora de Herrera bending down toward her.

"Oh," said Miss Blossom. "I must have fainted."

"What happened to you?"

Through the gap between Miss Burtt and the Señora, Miss Blossom could now discern the head and shoulders of Mr. Arbuthnot, and behind him a white blur that was the face of Mr. Dingle. It was Mr. Arbuthnot who had asked the question. He was animated with what seemed to Miss Blossom ghoulish interest.

"Don't question her," said Miss Burtt. She pressed her fingers on Miss Blossom's wrist. "She must rest a while."

The Señora moved away from her toward the door, and Miss Blossom realized that she was lying on the couch in the Faculty Common Room. She caught sight of Monsieur Trougnac standing on the hearth and involuntarily shuddered.

"Someone build up the fire," said Miss Burtt. "I'll get a blanket."

"I'll do that," said Mr. Arbuthnot.

Miss Blossom watched Monsieur escort the Señora out of the room. She left with a kindly word of encouragement for Miss Blossom, with a gentle regret that an appointment in the city called her. Miss Blossom replied with a haunted smile. Miss Burtt returned with the blanket.

"We'll just take off that coat first," she said, and helped Miss Blossom to a sitting position so that she could remove it. "Why, you're wearing two!" She looked at the neckband of the windbreaker in her hand. "Fitzsimmons Eubank," she read. Monsieur Trougnac stood in the doorway again.

"What is that?" he asked.

"He lent it to me," said Miss Blossom in a small voice. She couldn't think of any plausible reason why, so she added nothing more.

"Let me take it to him," said Mr. Arbuthnot, reaching eagerly out for the jacket. "My corridor, you know."

Miss Burtt removed Miss Blossom's own windbreaker, seemed to note her chafed wrists without commenting on them, and settled Miss Blossom down under the blanket she had brought.

"Now," said Miss Burtt, "she'll be all right in a little while if you people go away and let her be quiet. You just lie still, Miss Blossom. I'll see that you are sent in something to eat. Would you like some soup? Anything else?"

"Thank you," said Miss Blossom. "Just soup."

"I do not see—" began Monsieur Trougnac.

"Later," said Miss Burtt.

From their curiosity, sharpened by needs Miss Blossom could not know but only fear, Miss Burtt was for the time protecting her. Mr. Dingle, Mr. Arbuthnot, and Monsieur Trougnac filed unwillingly from the room ahead of the nurse. She closed the door behind her and Miss Blossom was alone.

The springy mattress, the enfolding blanket, the crackle and smell of the fire were grateful to her, but she could not forget that her refuge was temporary. Beyond that door, the world was hostile, and she felt that she must get up and force herself out into it again. Until she had made contact with the police, she must not rest. There was the telephone, just across the hall in the dispensary. What did one say? She imagined herself hissing into the ears of the operator, "Murder! Police! Quick!"

She imagined Miss Burtt listening from her adjoining living room. Much better if she could get away and give the alarm in some less melodramatic fashion. She remembered that the man who had looked for the Stinson Beach robber had come from the sheriff's office in San Rafael. He was the one to get. She could drive down to Olema and call San Rafael from a public telephone in the filling station on the corner.

The door she was watching swung open softly, and
her heart leapt into her throat. Mrs. Bjornstrom pushed
through it slowly, balancing a bowl of soup and a plate of
crackers on a large aluminum tray. She set the tray on the
tea-table and looked enigmatically down on Miss Blossom.
Miss Blossom's relief at the demonstrated innocence of
Mrs. Bjornstrom's approach dwindled when she reflected
that Mrs. Bjornstrom might have come from a conference
with her husband.

"Don't you want to sit up?" said Mrs. Bjornstrom.

"I guess I'd better." Miss Blossom brought her aching
arms out from under the blanket and hunched herself to
a sitting position. Mrs. Bjornstrom placed the tray on her
knees. "Thanks," said Miss Blossom.

She found she was so hungry that she wished she had
ordered a full meal. As she sipped the soup and nibbled the
crackers, Mrs. Bjornstrom watched her with arms akimbo.
Miss Blossom avoided her eyes.

"What kept you out so late?" asked Mrs. Bjornstrom.

"I got stuck in a canyon."

"You should keep to the trails."

"Um," said Miss Blossom, and forgetting her spoon,
lifted the bowl and drained what remained of the soup.
She had to put her head back so very far, and she was so
very tired that her eyes ached, and so she closed them. She
could scarcely wait to snuggle down under the blanket.
Dimly inaccurate, she dropped the bowl toward the tray,
and was not even aware that Mrs. Bjornstrom caught them
as they slid from her knees. Mrs. Bjornstrom frowned
down on the freckled nose, the parted lips, the dark lashes
dropped so conclusively on the flushed cheeks. Miss Blossom's head hung back over the pillow; her hand and one
foot trailed on the floor. Mrs. Bjornstrom flattened her
out and pulled the blanket up to her chin. Miss Blossom's
muscles were limply yielding.

13

Miss Blossom: Instructress of Small Boys

Pool and backgammon went forward in the Games Room. Till after eight o'clock, boys lingered around the piano in the Great Hall, waiting for Miss Blossom to appear for the Friday Evening Sing. Clyde La Montt's mother phoned from Florida, and Willard Capon's father from New York. The boys were well. Clyde had got 100 per cent in algebra and Willard wanted a trumpet. For each call, Monsieur Trougnac unlocked the Office door and hovered over the child who talked. In the Doghole, Mrs. Bjornstrom read aloud about the boyhood of Will James. Mr. Dingle conversed in the Great Hall, and Mr. Arbuthnot kept the pool score. Mr. Pyke listened to the Fanny Brice program in his own room, and Monsieur Trougnac patrolled the courtyards. Van made several surreptitious and fruitless trips to the barn, during the third of which Walter told him he was getting too big for his pants. At nine-thirty, Miss Burtt administered poison-oak lotion for ten minutes, and afterwards looked in on Miss Blossom and spread another blanket over her. At ten o'clock the last bell rang. In the rooms of the boys, the lights went down. Fog, drawn inland by the warmth the sun had left in the valleys, climbed up and over the black ridge. Behind it, the stars shone down on Drake's Anchorage and the incoming tide. One by one the masters' lights blinked off.

Through the redwood logs on the hearth in the Common Room, hidden fire crept cell by cell, so that the structure became a great cherry-colored crystal imprisoned in white ash. The spring tide approached its full flood and thundered through the caves in the cove. Miss Blossom moaned and turned, pushing against the blanket, till her face was toward the fireplace, and the glow from the logs struck a gleam under her lashes where her eyes had opened a little way. But she did not struggle through to consciousness, and lay quiet for another hour. Then the sudden small moment of change mysteriously arrived. With leaping light and a purling tinkle, the outlines of the logs broke down into a lavalike flow of embers. Miss Blossom's eyes opened wide upon it.

It was a moment or two before she roused above a purely sensuous reception of the phenomenon. Then she was perplexed by the inconsistency of an open fire in her bedroom. She felt the rough blanket under her hands, became aware that she was still in her clothes, and finally, when she caught the shimmer of reflected light on the brass tea-table, memory of all that had happened flooded over her. She jerked to a sitting position, looked at her watch, and held her throbbing head in her hands while the realization that it was now three-thirty in the morning deepened her dismay. How could she have gone to sleep and remained dead to the world for—something over eight hours? And she was still so tired that every muscle in her body shouted to be allowed to rest again in the warm hollow out of which she had arisen. The room was not really cold, but the air felt chilly against her back. She brought her feet and most of the blanket to the floor and stumbled over it to reach her coat which she saw lying on the arm of a chair by the fireplace. She put on the coat, sat down in the chair, and pulled the blanket up over her knees. This headache made it so hard to think.

Could there have been something in that soup that Mrs. Bjornstrom had brought her? Had a knowledge of that been in Mrs. Bjornstrom's face as she had watched her drink it? Who else might have drugged her? The nurse? The cook? Or was everyone in league to keep the body of Miss Breckenridge from being discovered? They had all retired smugly outside and mixed their potion and said, "There! That'll hold her. You take it in, Mrs. Bjornstrom. She'll never suspect you." She pictured a guard watching on the other side of the Common Room door, but she couldn't put a face to it. If in moments of terror she suspected everybody, when she reflected reasonably she could suspect nobody. People whose habit it was automatically to put the well-being of children ahead of their own convenience simply could not be moved to anything so violently unconventional as murder. There was the body, but there must be some other explanation for it.

She would put an end to this by telephoning. She pushed the blanket away and went to the door. In the corridor outside, she tried to retain her confidence. It was not quite so dark as it had been that other night, and that experience should help her now. The entryway into the infirmary yawned. She chose to go down the passageway toward the Office under the starlight. As she came opposite each courtyard, she surveyed it carefully. No lights were burning anywhere. She found the Office door locked. She told herself she had known that it might be, and retraced her steps. That meant she must use the extension in the dispensary. How did Miss Burtt sleep this night? She disregarded unpleasant associations and made for the phone.

She stuck one finger under the instrument to hold down the bracket on which it rested before she lifted it quietly with her other hand. What was she going to say? She must speak very softly and yet make herself quickly understood.

She assembled her sentence and raised her finger. So long, it took them. She waited, concentrating on the words that she had ready so that they would not slip away. All the world except the waves was sleeping. Even the phone! She realized that no hum vibrated from the piece against her ear. It was a dead thing! She laid down the instrument, pulled up the wire, and slipped her fingers along it till she came to a prickly end. Here was a fact—more definite than her suspicion that her heavy sleep had been unnatural. Someone in the school was determined that she should not reach the police with her story.

There was still the car. She hurried from the dispensary to the outer gate. It made a scuffing noise when she opened it, and so great were her newly stimulated fears that she made no attempt to close it again before she tiptoed away across the gravel. She felt in the usual pocket for her car keys. They were not there. She tried her other pockets. She remembered running down here. It was a foggy memory of terror and ended in obscurity. That must have been just before she had fainted. She had no knowledge of what she had done with the keys. When she came to her car, she found that the door was standing open. Maybe inside? She felt the plate over the ignition switch. No, the keyhole was empty. She searched the floor of the car and the ground by the running board as thoroughly as she could without turning on a light. She could remember, now, how she had hung on the swinging door when the ground had seemed to be coming up to meet her. If she had dropped them when she had fainted, they must be somewhere around here. But perhaps she hadn't dropped them. What more logical than that the person who had cut the phone connection had also taken her keys while she slept?

Three, and five, or six—or seven? Say something under ten miles to Olema. She could do it in an hour on Parson. She would *not* go back in that school again. She picked her

way up the trail past Stone Cottage. When she crossed the
road to the corral gate, she wondered whether she could
get the horse out without waking Walter. Why not wake
Walter? It did not seem possible that he could be in on
this conspiracy. She crossed the saddling corral to the gate
of the one where the horses would be. Maybe Walter would
take her out in his truck, she was thinking, as she went
through that gate. The corral was empty. She didn't believe it at first. She went up to the lean-to against the barn
where the mangers were. Not a horse in the corral. Walter!
Walter too? A soft stomp from within the barn reminded
her that there were horses—of a sort—in the stalls. The
stallion, Roy Mungeson's lamed Eloise, and Walter's white
Arabian. She chose the Arabian. It was a skittish beast,
either a little loco or suffering the consequences of an outrageous past. She wished she knew its name—her name.
She was a mare. Walter had been ridiculed for buying her
for the school a month or so ago, so he was riding her
himself to gentle her, which he insisted could be done, so
that she would become a mount they could risk offering
to one of the boys.

The Arab was awake and trembling when Miss Blossom approached her stall. That was it. Walter called her
the Arab. Miss Blossom whispered to her soothingly as
she moved in beside her to untie her and bring her out
where she could be saddled. She was not supposed to be
vicious, just easily frightened. Miss Blossom managed her
with the little croons and pats that had never failed her,
but the Arab continued to tremble while she was being
saddled. She tried to rear at the approach of the bit, and
Miss Blossom held her breath for fear the thump of her
feet would bring Walter. She waited, and then tried again.
The horse would not take the bit. Miss Blossom patted her
neck. With the third attempt, she was able to slide the bit
between the teeth, and the bridle over the twitching ears.

She moved the Arab out on the road, a dainty, terrified ghost in the starlight. Maybe the stallion would have been less difficult to manage, but it was too late to change now. Any minute, Walter's head might appear at the window of his cottage. Miss Blossom put distance between herself and the corral buildings by walking and leading the horse. She trusted that the sounds the Arab made in this manner would appear to Walter, if they roused him, to be merely those of a grazing horse that had wandered back to the corral. Where the road curved, she risked getting on. It was well that she had waited. Arab shied and plunged so recklessly that they were off into the fields before Miss Blossom had found her other stirrup. Miss Blossom managed to bring her around in a circle and back on the road at a place some distance up, and here, when Miss Blossom tried to head up the road, Arab came to a dead stop. They skirmished. Whenever Miss Blossom got her pointed away from the barn, the Arab would only back.

"Even the damned horse," Miss Blossom muttered.

At the end of her patience, she smacked Arab smartly across the rump with her long reins. Arab bolted, but in the right direction. Miss Blossom was able to keep her on the road, and the angle of ascent gradually slowed the horse. When she could get her breath, Miss Blossom talked and patted, and pulled ever so gently on the reins. On the top of the ridge, Arab went from a stiff-legged lope to a shivering halt. This ride was going to be as fraught with frustration as everything else that Miss Blossom had gone through. She had to content herself with a mincing crablike walk downhill. At every shadow, at every leaf that rustled, Arab shied. Arab trusted neither the night nor Miss Blossom. "Walter will murder me," said Miss Blossom, and was so upset by her choice of words that Arab shied in sympathy.

The farther they progressed down the slope, the deeper the forest and the heavier the shadow under the trees. The road twisted back and forth for the accommodation of automobiles, and the night became too black for Miss Blossom to see the turns. She had to trust to Arab, and Arab seemed to prefer running into a tree trunk to being helpful. She would walk off a curve and stop chest-deep in brush as if, so far as she could make out, that spot was Miss Blossom's intended destination. By hit and miss, they reached the coast road, and here, where it was lighter, Arab discovered fresh terrors. There were culverts, fence posts, and occasionally old newspapers and cartons. The twinkle of a star, caught in an abandoned tin can, was enough to send her up in the air and down in a ditch on the other side of the road. Miss Blossom gave up an abortive intention to trot. There were too many interruptions to make it worthwhile. She was so impatient she could not pity the horse, and so pulled her up so sharply when she shied that Arab lost rather than gained confidence. When Miss Blossom thought she must be nearly to Olema, she found that she was just passing the end of the logging road. She tried futilely to keep her imagination from following it up to its head.

How cruelly solitary was the body that lay there! How powerless to shed light on its misfortune! How finally separated from sympathy! She reminded herself that sentience had mercifully departed from it. Death had placed a period to a focus of relationships that reached far back into the past and that even in life had been secret. She must stop feeling one thing or another about Miss Breckenridge.

Yes, it was wasteful to pity Miss Breckenridge, but there was more to it than that. Death hadn't separated the past from the future of those whose existence had been related to hers. Else why had Miss Blossom battled windmill after windmill to arrive on this road at this hour upon this mission? What were others, even more nearly concerned, about under the cloak of night? What purposes, hidden from Miss Blossom, might not have drawn them back to this very neighborhood? She looked over her shoulder, half expecting to see the nodding beams of a car's headlights coming down through the trees.

Arab stopped in her tracks, turned her head, and whinnied. Another horse answered, and Miss Blossom heard the easy beat of its hooves as it came closer through the darkness. At first it was a dull sound. Then it acquired a clickety-click accompaniment. That would be gravel thrown up from the hard margin of asphalt. The conviction took root in Miss Blossom that when she had first heard the hoofbeats they had been upon the soft dirt of the logging road. She felt an urge to race away into the darkness ahead, to keep ahead of that unknown rider until she should reach the security of Olema. But Arab was tensely awaiting the arrival of a friend. She had turned clear around now, and was pawing the ground. Unless she whipped the horse into an ungovernable frenzy, Miss Blossom doubted that she could move her from that spot. The first signs of the approach of the other horse that Miss Blossom could make out with her eyes were four white socks moving in the rhythm of the sounds. Then a massive black horse materialized above the feet. Twinkletoes.

"Walter?" inquired a voice that she recognized. Twinkletoes was reined in beside her, and Arab leaned against him for comfort.

Miss Blossom reeled under the implications of the headmaster's presence. He had not accepted his banishment, but was here, fighting back with all his power, and God knew what tools, for possession of his kingdom. He had probably been here all the time, moving about at will under cover of darkness. From the conflicts engendered by his determination must have arisen the sickness of spirit, the series of unexplained accidents that had afflicted the school all week. Even to the death of Miss Breckenridge, his most staunch advocate?

"Who is it? That's not Walter." The headmaster leaned over and put his hand on her arm. "Why, Miss Blossom!"

"You!" croaked Miss Blossom.

"Yes." He removed his hand from her arm.

A sudden surge of pain swept over Miss Blossom. It was not pity, for he so definitely did not invite that. It was more a flashing perception of beauty in jeopardy, if not already destroyed, a suspicion that it is evil and not divinity that shapes our ends. Her pain became purely a fear of the unknown, and her flight was not so much from a man as from a view of life that she did not want to accept.

She lashed both the neck and hindquarters of the Arab and, as the frantic horse reared, yanked her head so that she came down facing up the highway. Miss Blossom slashed again, but it was unnecessary. Arab was flying down the center of the macadam road in blind terror.

For the while, Miss Blossom was obliviously one with the maddened horse, but as she came opposite the first of the cluster of cottages that made up Olema, she regained sufficient presence of mind to begin trying to slow down the Arab. It was hopeless. They shot through the quiet town with undiminished speed. On north of Olema the Arab flew, seemingly tireless, heedless of rein or bit or Miss Blossom's hand and voice. Here there was rising ground, and that might help some, but with the rise came curves, and the Arab slithered drunkely on the high crown of the road as she rounded the turns. As her pace slackened a little, Miss Blossom attempted to rein her to the graveled edge of the road. The pull of the reins was a distraction but not a deterrent to the blowing horse. With her head pulled side-wise, she ran now on the side of the slick hump. At the next curve, she went into a skid from which in her exhausted state she could not recover. She went down on her knees and her rider went over her head. The hard pavement came up toward Miss Blossom too quick for thought.

14

Mrs. Gordon Maxwell II: a Mother

The alarm clock sounded in Walter's quarters next to the barn at six o clock. He reached over with a groan to push down the button, and rubbed a stiff shoulder. Walter found it difficult to pull out in the morning. The rodeos of his youth left him with joints that protested. In most respects, this job was a sinecure for his old age—he was in his early forties—but this morning there were two things he had to get done before Saturday morning study hall freed the boys at ten o'clock. He boiled himself some coffee while he got into his clothes. His real breakfast would come later, down at the school, after he'd got up the horses. He swore softly as he remembered the unnecessary labor he had let himself in for. When Mr. Bjornstrom had become curious about the absence of Twinkletoes, Walter had conceived what to him appeared to be a good plan. To forestall similar questions from anyone else who might chance to see the empty stall, he had put all the stock out to pasture last night. Although it was too short for them yet, the horses were eager to smell at the new grass. He had planned to put it up to the boys themselves to get in what horses they wanted today. Be good experience for them, he would tell them. They wouldn't find them all, and Twinkletoes would be one of those they didn't find. Then late last night the

Head had wakened him and ordered him, without explanation, to see that the horses were back in the corrals by the time the boys would be using them.

Grumbling to himself, Walter entered the barn to discover the absence of the Arab. Twinkletoes, too, was out again. What the hell did the Head think he was doing? Glumly he brought out Eloise and slung his saddle on her. It would probably lay her up for another week but he sure as hell wasn't going to walk! The sky was beginning to redden when he rode Eloise down toward the sheltered hollow where he was most likely to find a dozen or so of the horses. He was in luck. Over half of them were there, and he was able to change mounts before he had done Eloise much damage. Another hour saw them all back in the corral, just in time for him to get up to breakfast at his usual hour. Walter had so far softened as to have a strong preference for regular meals.

When he had washed up, he came out to see the Arab standing with hanging head at the corral gate. When he found her raw knees and Miss Blossom's saddle on her, Walter seethed with anger, surprise, and concern. Arab had been badly skinned up and soaking wet. She was probably ruined for good. Walter was surprised that she had returned. Must have run a good many miles down the pavement. He led her inside and rubbed her down and gave her some oats. She submitted to everything without a quiver. She was either ruined or cured! But what had happened to Miss Blossom? While he worked over Eloise, he tried to remember more of the noises he had ignored last night because they had occurred after the Head had been in to see him. Whatever craziness Miss Blossom had been up to, the fact that the horse had come back without her obligated Walter to locate her. What had she got her little nose into?

When he arrived at the kitchen, it was almost eight o'clock. Breakfast would be well along in the dining room.

He settled himself at a table in the corner and fell upon a goodly pile of hot cakes that the cook supplied. Walter had made it definite when he had taken his job that his duties should never extend beyond the corrals. He often marveled at Mr. Bjornstrom that he was willing to preside at a table and roil his stomach by diverting his attention from his own needs to see that little Willie finished his grape nuts. That was the sort of thing marriage got you into. Not until Walter had downed a half dozen hot cakes and finished his first cup of coffee did he take up his investigations.

"Miss Blossom at breakfast?" he asked one of the waiters.

No, was the reply, she hadn't showed up.

Walter polished off another plate of cakes and finished his coffee. Then he made his way toward the Office. He didn't want to tangle with Monsieur, but he'd have to find out what had become of the little fool. Fortunately, Miss Parelli was alone in the Office.

"Howdy," said Walter.

"Howdy, yourself," replied Miss Parelli. She had several drawers open and looked a little befuddled, but she answered cheerfully.

"How're they treating you?"

"If they don't get that new secretary soon, I'm going nuts! Monsieur—" She caught back the words that had come to her lips, and indicated the litter of papers and manila folders that were spread over her desk with a despairing gesture. "Oh, I'll live through it, I guess. You want something?"

"I was kind of anxious to see Miss Blossom. Do you think you could take time off to look in her room for me, quiet like?" When she hesitated, he added, "I'll stay here and take the blame with Monsieur if he comes in."

"Sure," said Miss Parelli. "It won't take but a minute." Miss Parelli was longer than she had promised. When she returned, Miss Burtt came with her.

"Miss Parelli tells me you are looking for Miss Blossom," she said curtly. "May I ask why?"

Walter repressed the rejoinder, "None of your gol-darn business."

Miss Parelli caught his eye guiltily. "She wasn't in her room, and her bed was made. Naturally, I was surprised, so when Miss Burtt came in, I asked her whether she knew anything about Miss Blossom. She didn't and she was looking for her too."

"Miss Parelli tells me you are looking for Miss Blossom. May I ask why?" said Walter to Miss Burtt.

Miss Burtt was stiff. "I see no occasion to joke. My reason is that Miss Blossom was not well and spent the night on the Common Room couch. When I went to see whether she was ready for breakfast, she wasn't there. Now, what is your reason?"

"Well," said Walter slowly, "looks like she's ridden out on a crazy horse and got herself throwed. Now don't go making a to-do about it. I'll find her and bring her in. Chances are she's just shook up a little."

The lines about Miss Burtt's mouth were hard. "Let us hope that that is all. I shall want to see her as soon as she comes in. Be sure and bring her straight to me."

"Yes, ma'am," said Walter, and got himself out of her neighborhood without more palaver.

Why Miss Blossom had got up out of a sick bed to ride off on horseback in the middle of the night he couldn't savvy, unless she was for some reason trailing the headmaster. The idea was crazy, and he wasn't going to discuss it with Miss Burtt—with anybody, for that matter.

The other thing he had to do before ten o'clock he could combine with his search for Miss Blossom. Arab had almost certainly been on the highway, and Walter had business on the highway, down near Stinson Beach.

He would search that direction first. He backed out the pickup and rumbled up the road. On the floor of the truck jounced the left front wheel of Miss Breckenridge's Chevrolet, newly sheathed in a repaired tire. Miss Breckenridge had been waiting for three weeks for a new seventeen-inch tire. She had no spare.

On the coast road he slowed down so that he could search the ditches and neighboring fields for Miss Blossom. At the infrequent ranch houses that were anywhere near the road, he stopped and inquired, but no one had seen either a girl or a white horse. Miss Breckenridge's car was parked two miles north of Stinson Beach, on the narrow road that had the cliff on one side and the lagoon on the other, in one of the few places that it was possible to get off the highway. Walter replaced the wheel and commandeered the driver of a truck whose way he was blocking to help him shift the car around so that he could raise the rear end with the hoist in his pickup. Funny she'd been going toward the school when she'd had her puncture; he'd supposed she'd been leaving it.

On the way back he again saw no sign of Miss Blossom and concluded uneasily that she must indeed have gone north—toward Inverness. He took the school road in his lowest gear and babied the Chevy around the turns. Even so, it was in the ditch most of the time. A shiny new car caught up with him and had roaring fits every time he slowed to negotiate a turn. He reflected that that wouldn't be the doctor; it could only be a mother. He pulled out his watch. Ten minutes to ten. Mr. Pyke would have to spell him at the corrals so that he could search the road to the north for Miss Blossom. With some difficulty, he wangled the Chevy into the shed where he kept the pickup. When he had finished, he saw that the car which had followed him had stopped too and that Mrs. Maxwell had gotten out of it and was watching him.

She was pretty as a picture. She had on a short red coat and the sort of shoes that indicated that she had come to spend a day in the country. She looked a lot like Gordie. Now she looked like Gordie when he was about to ask whether he could put the bars up another hole on the jumps.

"Good morning, Walter! It's an awfully nice morning, isn't it?"

"Sun's out again," allowed Walter.

"Walter," she approached her subject without further generalities. "Walter, you and the headmaster, you're really very good friends, aren't you?"

"You could put it that way," admitted Walter.

"You—you'd want to do anything you could for him, wouldn't you?" she pressed him.

"I reckon so," he replied.

He reached toward his plug of tobacco and then switched to his cigarette papers out of deference to her presence. He didn't like the direction the conversation was taking. For all her innocent looks, he had a feeling she'd have a way of digging what she wanted to know out of a man.

"Walter, the headmaster never did go to Chicago." He felt her eyes upon him as he flicked a nice amount of tobacco into a gingerly held paper, licked the edge of it, and rolled a cigarette. "Where do you suppose he is?"

"Your guess is as good as mine, ma'am."

"You don't seem very surprised at my news."

He gave her a straight look over the top of his lighted match. "I am, though. Where did you get it?"

She hesitated, searching his expression for a clue, and then with a decisive movement opened her bag and took out a folded square of yellow paper.

"There. Read that. You'll see why I want you to help me find him."

The telegram was addressed to her, dated the previous evening in Chicago, and signed by Lars Aakrog. It read:

> MUCH DISTURBED BY SITUATION DRAKE'S ANCHORAGE STOP NEWS INADEQUATE STOP YOUR LETTER MOST WELCOME STOP ALRIK HAS NOT CONTACTED US STOP TROUGNAC REPLIES WHEREABOUTS UNKNOWN STOP HAVE OFFER FOR SCHOOL STOP LUELLA ADVISES SELL STOP DESIRE CONSULT ALRIK STOP IF YOU REACH HIM PLEASE REQUEST PHONE WITHOUT DELAY.

Walter stared for a long time at the paper, hindered in his memorizing by the plethora of "stops."

"Well," said Mrs. Maxwell finally, "do *you* know anything about him? Can you tell me how to find him?" When he still did not look up, she added, "Walter, I just don't feel that Monsieur Trougnac *wants* Lars Aakrog to talk to the Head. Why did he send Miss Breckenridge away? He hasn't said anything to the parents who stirred up the trouble. So far as I know, nobody's tried to do *anything*. What's *happening*, Walter?"

Walter pushed back his hat and scratched his head. "I don't rightly know. I keep out of the mess down yonder." He hated to disappoint her but his orders were strict. "I'm right sorry I can't help you."

Mrs. Maxwell replaced the telegram in her bag. "I'm not giving up. I believe I can get to him through *someone* here. I've come prepared to stay for the weekend."

He liked her spunk and her loyalty. "Monsieur will probably jump down your throat," he warned her, "but it looks to me like your figuring's pretty good."

"I used to stay over, you know, when Gordie first came. He won't be able to stop me now." She was suddenly smiling with tears in her eyes. "And thank you, Walter. Thank you so much!"

"Well, I don't know what for," said Walter uncomfortably.

"You make me feel better—really!"

There was a flash of red as she hopped back in her car, and a grinding of gears as the car got under way. Walter felt a rising resentment against the Head. The damned fool. Why must he play such a lone hand? Well, no use fretting over what he couldn't fathom. And now the boys were coming up the trail. Walter sent Garnett Haydon back down with an S O S for Mr. Pyke.

Mrs. Maxwell drove her car into Miss Breckenridge's parking space with the air of one who has come to stay. She deposited her overnight bag in one of the guest rooms behind the dining room and went to look up Gordie. She caught him just as he was leaving his room. He was booted for the trail, but looked genuinely pleased to see her.

"I say, Mom, the new bridle's swell. You want to come up and see me put it on Horace?"

As there was no one around before whom he would feel embarrassed, she gave him a real hug with her kiss.

"I'd love to, darling, but not right away." She wondered whether it would be a mistake to hold him up now. But there would never, she realized, be a perfect time for what she intended to do. She plunged. "Before you go up to Horace, will you let me have about five minutes? I want a little help from you."

He followed her readily back into his room. She shut the door and sat down on the bed. He came of his own accord to lean beside her.

"What about?"

"Gordie, I need to talk about something that you don't want to talk about."

When he moved away to sit on the edge of the chair on the other side of the narrow room, she didn't try to hold him. She didn't even look at him for fear her eyes would plead unfairly and thus justify his withdrawal. She gazed down at her lap, fingering the clasp on her bag. It came to her that a noncommittal equality would be the best approach. She took out the telegram and offered it to him. Gordie stood up to receive it.

She allowed herself to watch his face as he read it. She longed to know what had been said among the boys during the four days since she had last seen him, what concepts had been presented to him for the first time, and in what way! She had expected him to learn from Alrik, but not like this. Was Alrik in contact with the boys? If the headmaster was putting the relationship he had built up with them to the test of treating them like men, what a hard decision it must have been for him to make. If he lost, he had done them a frightful injury; but if he won out, they might have acquired wisdom that would stand them in better stead than all their English and mathematics and other academic lessons put together.

If she herself had not loved Alrik, she would not have had the purpose or the understanding to appeal to Gordie as she was doing now. Was that good or bad? She thought it was good. If she managed to carry it off, she would have treated Gordie as an adult and not as a child, and that she felt would be a gain. What value was innocence that had to be preserved through avoidance and built up as ignorance? She realized that she was probably doing some growing up herself. If Alrik won! If Alrik came through all right! Where was he? What was he feeling?

"That's in confidence, Gordie," she said after she had allowed him time to struggle through the unfamiliar terminology of the telegram. "I don't expect you to tell anyone else about it, and I don't expect you to tell me anything that you have learned in confidence from anyone else.

"But this is what I think. It seems to me that if the headmaster did not go where he said he was going to go, it was because he thought he could stay here and clear up this trouble. He wouldn't just disappear. I think there is at least one person in this school who is helping him find out the things he needs to know. Now I don't know whether it's one of the faculty or one of the boys, but I want the news in this telegram to reach him.

"Gordie, if you have heard anything that leads you to believe that there is such a boy, I want you to go to him and say that I have an important message for the headmaster. I'm going to stay at the school over the weekend. Tell the boy I am hoping that he will come and talk to me. Will you think that over, son?"

Gordie gave her back the telegram and met her eyes without self-consciousness.

"I'll see what I can do, Mom," he said.

They smiled at each other.

"And now," she said, rising briskly, "you want to get up to the corrals, and I had better go to the Office and get myself accepted as a weekend guest.

"I brought along a pair of jodhpurs. If Walter has a horse he'll let me use, perhaps this afternoon or tomorrow you'll show me Horace and his bridle in action."

15

James Quigley: Sheriff

Sheriff Jim Quigley had hardly got through the door of his office when a deputy thrust a phone at him. "Point Reyes Station calling the sheriff," he was told. He sat down in the chair pushed out for him.

"Sheriff Quigley speaking."

The man calling identified himself as Paul Silveira, a rancher between Olema and Point Reyes Station. He said he had a girl there who was asking for the deputy who had been looking for the Stinson Beach robber. In response to the sheriff's questions, he said that he could get nothing else out of her. Not her name, nor where she lived, nor why she wanted the deputy, nor how she had been hurt. Yes, she did look mauled about, but she'd come up to him, where he was picking up his empty milk cans, under her own steam. That had been about seven-thirty. He would guess she was from over Inverness way by the look of her, and that she had been thrown from a horse, but she wouldn't talk. He lowered his voice to add that he thought she wasn't quite right in the head, and that he'd be relieved when that deputy—or *any* deputy—took her off his hands.

"Ask her if it's Frank Zanetti she wants," said the sheriff.

After a pause, Silveira replied that that name seemed to suit her.

The sheriff promised speedy action and hung up.

The sheriff of Marin County had strength of character and brains but no spectacular window dressing. His control over his department had been established by a solid continuity of good sense rather than by either bluster or brilliance. He was a middle-aged man with grayish tones in his skin and hair who, were it not for the assurance implicit in his speech and carriage, might have been summed up as fatherly.

Since Thursday evening, his men had unearthed no evidence that the large, blond stranger who had slugged the proprietor of the Shrimp Shop had appeared on any of the county roads. Zanetti, usually a competent man, was convinced that he had traced the man to Drake's Anchorage, and he had wanted to override the hostility that he had met there and go back Friday with a search warrant and a force large enough to comb every inch of the school and the surrounding hills. The sheriff had restrained him, pending the report on the fingerprints, that had been teletyped to Washington, from the cup Zanetti had picked up in the barn. When word had come back, Friday evening, that the prints were indeed those of a veteran, but that the veteran was Alrik Lind, the headmaster of the school at which they had been found, Zanetti had been downcast. Now the sheriff was quietly pleased that Zanetti was going to have an opportunity to pick up the trail that he felt he had muffed.

"Well," he said to Zanetti who had been watching him since he had heard his name mentioned, "this call may lead you to the guy who pulled the Bartello holdup. There's a girl who wants to talk about it out at the Silveira ranch. You know it?—Good. She wants you, and according to Silveira she's badly shaken up. Phone back for what help you need when you get the facts. The girl may need an ambulance."

Zanetti made the twenty-one miles in something under thirty minutes. At the ranch house, Mrs. Silveira told him her husband was back at the barn if he was wanted, and ushered him into the parlor where the girl was lying on the couch.

"Here she is," said Mrs. Silveira. "I'll be getting back to the kitchen." They were not a curious couple. She even closed the door.

"You're the very one!" said the girl on the couch with relief. "I saw you from the window."

The skin was raw on her left temple, cheekbone, and jaw. To these patches, evidently, the Silveiras had applied mercurochrome. Her left sleeve and the left leg of her jeans were rolled up, and her arm and knee had been similarly treated.

"Looks as if you'd put a neat print on the highway," Zanetti told her. "Did you roll off a horse?"

"Yes," said the girl, "but I'm all right. I guess I hit equally all over."

"I guess you did. And now what window did you see me out of and what's your name? Just so I can keep things straight as we go along."

"My name's Meredith Blossom, and I saw you at Drake's Anchorage. I teach there."

"That so?" exclaimed Zanetti, his interest quickening. "You've seen the fellow I was looking for?"

She held up her hand, "No, no! Not that at all. This is something else."

She took a deep breath and looked at him solemnly. Zanetti swallowed his disappointment.

"Well then, what *is* the trouble?" he encouraged her.

"I want to report," she said formally, as if it were a lesson she had learned, "that I found a dead body in the woods yesterday afternoon about four thirty. It's at the top of the logging road that leads west off the coast road, halfway between Olema and the road into Drake's Anchorage."

As she recited her piece, Zanetti regarded her with heightened perceptivity. She was under a strain that he judged was the result of something more than her bodily misfortunes, spectacular though they appeared. She was completely rational, and she had what he would classify as an honest, law-abiding face. He got out his notebook and jotted down the information she had given him.

"Four thirty—yesterday?" he repeated suggestively.

"Yes," she replied. When he continued to wait expectantly, she colored. "You're wondering why I didn't report it sooner."

"That's right."

"I tried to—but first I got lost, and then my horse threw me." He wrote that down too, and she watched him uneasily.

"Do you know what caused death?"

"No."

"Any signs of violence?"

Faintly, "I didn't notice any. I—went away quickly."

"Would you say the body had been there some time?"

"I don't think so."

"You're sure it was dead?"

"Oh *yes!*"

"What did it look like?"

"It was covered up."

"How? With brush?" She shook her head. "A blanket?" She nodded.

"Could you identify the body?"

"I— No."

He felt that she was holding things back, but that her story so far as it went was genuine. He went out to the two-way radio in his car and communicated with his chief.

Sheriff Quigley told him to take her to the foot of the logging road and to wait for him there. Zanetti sought out Silveira, took his statement of how and where he had met up with Miss Blossom, and returned to the girl. She got up readily from the couch but staggered when she tried to walk. She was so pale that her freckles stood out. Yes, she answered, as he took her arm and led her to the car, she had lost consciousness when she fell and she now had a headache. As soon as she was in the car, she leaned back and closed her eyes. He put off further questions.

He didn't try to get her attention again until he had stopped at the end of a road that seemed to tally with her description a few miles south of Olema. Yes, she told him, this was the logging road.

"We'll wait for the sheriff, here. Now tell me, how did you happen to fall off your horse away up on the other side of Olema? Where were you going?"

"I wanted to telephone for you from Olema, but I couldn't get the horse stopped. She bolted. She started from here and I couldn't get her stopped in Olema. She finally fell on a curve, and I don't remember anything more till I heard that man banging his cans. I was down on my back in a ditch."

"What made her bolt?"

"I guess I did," said Miss Blossom. "She was a crazy horse. I was in such a hurry. I whipped her—" Miss Blossom dropped her head against the back of the seat. Zanetti let her alone.

When the sheriff arrived, he was not unaccompanied. With him in his car were three more deputies. Behind traveled an ambulance, and seated beside its driver was the coroner, old Dr. Peacock. Assistant District Attorney Bliss Truax brought up the rear in his roadster. Zanetti got out and went over to the window the sheriff had rolled down.

"How's the girl?" asked the sheriff.

"Pretty groggy," replied Zanetti. "She's had a knock on the head. I haven't questioned her much." He reported his small store of additional information.

"What's the road like?" asked the sheriff next. Zanetti had not looked. Together they went over and inspected it. It was unsurfaced and ungraded. They walked up it a little way but found no distinctive tire marks. The wide ruts had no doubt been packed down by the logging truck for which the road had been cut. Between them were fresh-looking hoof prints.

"Who owns this land?" asked the sheriff.

"Drake's Anchorage property," replied Zanetti.

The sheriff nodded. "Well, let's go on up. I'll get in with you. Be a good thing if you'd do the same thing, Truax," he said to the assistant district attorney who had joined them. "No use messing the place up any more than necessary."

"That's a good deal," agreed Truax. He was a small thin young man in a navy-blue business suit. He hadn't been in office long. If it turned out to be a murder that they were investigating, it would probably be his first experience with a case of that sort.

The sheriff and Truax climbed into the back seat behind Miss Blossom. Zanetti, after telling the deputies in the sheriff's car to wait and signaling the ambulance to follow, took the wheel. "Room for two cars to turn, up there?" the sheriff had asked Miss Blossom, and she had replied that she thought there was.

"How did you happen to find the body, Miss Blossom?" the assistant district attorney asked.

"I was out riding," said Miss Blossom.

"You were alone? No one else knows about it?"

"I was riding alone," replied Miss Blossom.

"And then you got lost, Zanetti says, and your horse ran away and you were knocked out. Is that all that's happened since then?" Truax pressed her.

Miss Blossom raised her hand to her forehead. "It's all so mixed up," she murmured. Her hand dropped down, palm up, between her and Zanetti.

With all that mercurochrome and those mussed-up braids, she looked to be hardly more than a child. Her cheek lay against the seat and her eyes were closed. "Better hold up a while," Zanetti advised. Then he saw her lashes lift and close again quickly. The suspicion re-awoke in him that she was taking refuge in weakness to avoid awkward questions. Ten to one this had something to do with that school. He remembered his reception there on Thursday afternoon. Could the fellow who had disappeared have got mixed up with someone at the school and been fatally injured? Was that what she was afraid of? Had she found his body out in the forest? He had to return his attention to the road and another steep turn. He found himself nosing into a small clearing where a ring of ruts encircled a woodpile. "This looks like the end of the road," he said.

"Keep off there for now," said the sheriff. Zanetti had already signaled the ambulance and come to a stop.

The sheriff and Zanetti made a quick survey of the ground around the pile of logs while Truax helped Miss Blossom out of the car. Dr. Peacock came up to take her other arm.

"Up here," said Miss Blossom. They went with her up the draw. She stopped on the far side of a log with a hollow behind it and raised apologetic eyes to Zanetti. "The body's gone," she said.

Truax broke the small silence that followed her statement. "What the hell do you think you're doing? Bringing us all out here on a wild-goose chase!"

"Really and truly," Miss Blossom was still appealing to Zanetti. "It was just as I told you."

"Could you have mistaken the place?" asked the sheriff. "Zanetti, take a look around."

Miss Blossom was definite. This was the log.

"Describe what you saw," commanded the sheriff.

"I stood just here," said Miss Blossom, "and right below me, in the hollow, sort of half under the log—" Her face stiffened in revulsion as she gazed at the spot. "—there was a red Paisley shawl spread over something."

"How did you know what was under the shawl? What made you so sure it was a body?" the sheriff asked her.

"I picked up a corner of the shawl. I saw a bare foot. I touched it."

"This is some nightmare she had after she fell off that horse,'" said Truax. "She's imagined the whole thing."

"Oh no!" exclaimed Miss Blossom. "She was here!"

The sheriff nudged Truax with his elbow before the latter could speak.

"And then what did you do?" the sheriff asked sympathetically, "Well—I sat down. I thought I was going to faint, you see."

"But you didn't?"

Miss Blossom had covered her face with her hands. "No."

"So then, what did you do?" The sheriff's voice was still gentle.

"I—went to my horse. I knew I had to get to the police."

"You didn't look at the corpse again?"

"No."

The sheriff spoke abruptly. "Then how did you know it was the body of a woman?"

Miss Blossom's head jerked up.

"You know something—or you recognized something—that gave you the identity of the corpse! Quickly! Who was it?"

Miss Blossom twisted her hands. "I don't know! Oh I *don't* know!"

"Careful," said Dr. Peacock. "Remember that possible concussion. I think you ought to postpone questioning her."

"My opinion is that we can call the whole thing off," said Truax.

Zanetti was waiting to receive the sheriff's attention. To answer Truax, he held out a couple of inches of red yarn. "This was on that bush that sticks out down there," he said. "And I don't believe she's as pooped as she makes out. This has something to do with that school and she's trying to avoid having to say so."

When she found all eyes centered on her, Miss Blossom said pleadingly, "I don't really know anything."

"Maybe not," said Zanetti exasperated, "but you have suspicions!"

"Could I just sit down somewhere?" petitioned Miss Blossom. She looked reproachfully at Zanetti. "I don't know what to think, and I certainly don't want to say what isn't true."

"Let us be the judge of what's true," said Truax, a shade pompous.

The sheriff led her back to the running board of the car. As he walked, he rolled the bright piece of yam meditatively between his fingers. "Now this red Paisley shawl," he said when he had seated her. "Do you know who it belongs to—or rather, do you know of someone who has one like it?"

Miss Blossom sighed. "There was such a shawl," she admitted, "on the bed in Stone cottage."

"And it isn't there now?"

"I don't know."

Zanetti asked, "This Stone Cottage—would that be the one halfway up from the main building to the corrals?"

"Yes."

"The bed was covered with an army blanket on Thursday afternoon," said Zanetti positively.

"But that doesn't necessarily mean anything," said Miss Blossom, "because she'd probably gone by that time."

The sheriff raised an eyebrow. "Who slept in that bed in Stone Cottage who was probably gone by Thursday, Miss Blossom?"

"Miss Breckenridge, the school secretary."

"Her clothes weren't gone," said Zanetti.

"Ah," said Truax. "When did you last see the secretary?"

"I can't remember her after Tuesday."

"And why did Miss Breckenridge leave?" inquired the sheriff.

"I wasn't informed." Miss Blossom met his gaze stubbornly.

"But you were so upset when you saw the shawl," he said, still speaking easily, "that you ran back and jumped on your horse without actually stopping to see whether it was the body of Miss Breckenridge that lay underneath it. Is that the way it was?"

"Yes, that's what I did."

The sheriff allowed his gaze to wander up the canyon and take in the matted undergrowth and fallen timbers. "You had brought your horse down through that?" he questioned admiringly.

"Oh no," Miss Blossom explained quickly. "I left him at the top and walked down."

The sheriff looked at her sternly. "Then by what route did you get down to the bottom of this road to start your runaway?"

She blushed. "All right!" she said, after she had locked glances with the sheriff. "I *did* go back to the school. While I was there I was—delayed, by several circumstances. But I do not believe that anyone at Drake's Anchorage was responsible for Miss Breckenridge's death—if she is dead—I don't even know that! Therefore my delays were accidents, and I don't intend to talk about them."

Truax bristled, but the sheriff held him in check.

"Then I take it," he said smoothly, "that these signs were not left by your horse?" He helped her to her feet to look around the back of the car at the clear-cut prints of a horse and some dung that could not be more than a few hours old. "On your way to Olema, last night, you were startled by someone coming down this road? And that is when your horse ran away? Did there seem to be—two riders?"

"Oh no!" she gasped. "Oh no!"

"But there was one." His grip tightened on her arm. "You recognized that one. Who was it?"

"But it— Oh but he couldn't possibly—"

"Tell me who it was."

"The headmaster," she breathed.

The sheriff and Zanetti exchanged glances. "If I remember your report correctly, Zanetti, you were told that the headmaster was in Chicago?"

"That's right, but they were cagey about that too." He remembered Mary Parelli's duplicity with some bitterness. She'd let him believe also that there was no other secretary than herself.

"And the headmaster," the sheriff continued in a thoughtful voice, "is a big, light-haired Scandinavian? Didn't he come into some other land too, over by Inverness?"

"By God!" said Zanetti. "The old Lind place! Of course. And that cup they razzed me about! There's only one man, and he's that man!"

"Well, we want a talk with him, anyway," said the sheriff. "Zanetti, you take Prentice with you and see if you can locate him at the Lind ranch. I'll take Miss Blossom up to Drake's Anchorage and begin there. Doc, it looks as if there'll be some delay before we have a job for you. You and the ambulance may as well go back to San Rafael. You want to come with me, Truax, or will you wait until we have a body to go on?"

16

Michael Sterne: School Doctor

Sheriff Jim Quigley slowed down when he entered upon the flat stretch of road that ran along the ridge above the school. He was taking in as much as he could of the general layout of the place which he knew only through Zanetti's report. "Plenty money," was his initial reaction.

"Find the head of that trail along here?" he asked Miss Blossom who was sitting in the seat beside him.

"Right across from the corrals," said Miss Blossom.

He pulled up at the spot she indicated. Boys and horses peered curiously at him from the other side of the fence.

"All right, men," said the sheriff to the two deputies in the back seat. "Both of you out here. Milton, you stay where you can check on whoever goes in or out of the school by the road. Keep an eye on the trails, too. Let anyone you talk to believe we are still looking for the man Zanetti was after before. Don't arouse antagonism, and don't talk to the boys. They're sensitive about that.

"That last goes for you too, Bullard. I want you to follow this trail down to the school. Cover the whole length of it carefully and give Stone Cottage the works. You'll find me down at the school."

In his rear-view mirror, while he was issuing his directives, he saw Walter Huggins climb out of a pickup that was parked in front of a shed a short distance back up the road. Huggins reached them as Bullard started down the trail. He nodded to the sheriff and looked across him at Miss Blossom.

"The both of you sure are a mess," he said.

"I'm sorry about the Arab, Walter," Miss Blossom apologized immediately. "Is she— Did she get back all right?"

"She's here, thinking over her sins. But how come you took out the Arab, and run her on the highway? I been down as far as Stinson Beach looking for you. I was just starting up the other way. Where'd you find her, sheriff?"

"Couple of miles north of Olema," said the sheriff.

"Why weren't the horses in the corrals last night, Walter?" asked Miss Blossom as if she was almost afraid to hear his answer. The sheriff pricked up his ears.

"They was hankering after the new grass. I let 'em out. You'll have a pack of explaining to do when you get down to the school. The nurse is looking for you right smart. She said you was to go straight to her."

"I've already had first aid," said Miss Blossom. "Now all I want is a bath." She sounded relieved, and the sheriff grinned to himself. Miss Blossom had checked Huggins off her list of suspects.

"I see you have," said Walter.

"A crack on the head is nothing to play around with," said the sheriff as he let in the clutch. "You'd better let a doctor look you over. Still got that headache?"

"It's not too good," admitted Miss Blossom.

"Well, you're for the nurse," said the sheriff. "Let her put you to bed and you keep mum about what's happened. I'll do the investigating, and if you'll promise not to talk to anyone else, I'll let you alone till you've had a few hours' rest. Is that agreed?"

"I should say so!" replied Miss Blossom.

On the terrace in front of the school, a man and a woman were standing. Miss Blossom introduced them to the sheriff as Monsieur Trougnac and Mrs. Maxwell. The sheriff cut short their exclamations.

"Get her to where she can lie down," he said, "and don't confuse her with questions. She's had a bad fall from a horse." Monsieur Trougnac was as Zanetti had reported him. He thanked the sheriff stiffly for his assistance and said he would take Miss Blossom immediately to the infirmary.

"I'd like to have a talk with you when you are free," the sheriff told him.

Monsieur Trougnac looked disapproving. "Is that necessary?"

"Yes, I think it is."

"Would you like me to show him where the Office is, Monsieur Trougnac?" Mrs. Maxwell asked.

"If you would be so kind," said Monsieur Trougnac.

"I'm sorry—to be such a bother," said Miss Blossom. Now that she was standing, she seemed to be dizzy again. Certainly ever since she had stepped from the car to receive the support of Monsieur Trougnac's arm, she had been very pale. She leaned away from rather than toward him as he led her down the terrace. The sheriff watched them until they had disappeared around the corner at the far end.

"I do hope she isn't badly hurt," said Mrs. Maxwell. "What happened?"

"I didn't see her until it was over," replied the sheriff. "Are you one of the teachers?"

"No. I'm just here visiting my son. The Office is in through here."

"A very pleasant place to visit," said the sheriff tactfully as she took him through the Great Hall. "They can put you up right here?"

"There are two guest rooms, but they're not used much. I came out this morning for the weekend. The boys, you know, get on better if the parents don't stay around."

"Very sound."

"Miss Parelli," said Mrs. Maxwell as she opened another door, "here is Sheriff Quigley. He's just brought poor Miss Blossom back from a fall off a horse. He'll wait in here till Monsieur Trougnac comes back."

"Thank you, Mrs. Maxwell," said the sheriff.

"Not at all," she said pleasantly, and departed.

"But how did *you* happen to find her?" asked Miss Parelli.

Noting the way the question was phrased, the sheriff decided that he would begin with the bookkeeper.

"Miss Parelli, I am here to ask questions as well as to return Miss Blossom. I hope you will answer them as accurately as possible"

Miss Parelli eyed the notebook he had taken out. She assumed an air that sat oddly upon her pert face and skittish attire. "I must refer you to Monsieur," she replied, "on all matters pertaining to the school."

"These matters go beyond the school. I am questioning you as a resident of Marin County. As a citizen you are obligated to help the officials of your county uphold its laws."

"Gosh gee," said Miss Parelli. "What's happened now?"

"That's what I'm trying to find out. So tell me, first, when you last saw the school secretary, Miss Breckenridge."

The sheriff maneuvered Miss Parelli through her perturbations of conscience and curiosity with a light firm hand. His written notes followed a rambling thread, but before Monsieur Trougnac returned he had got this sequence in his head: During the rest period on Wednesday afternoon, Señora de Herrera had brought her children into the Office, returning them a couple of days late for their second term. Miss Parelli had been sent to take the two boys to their housemother. She had returned to find Monsieur Trougnac alone in the Office. He had informed her that Miss Breckenridge was to be replaced. She had not seen the secretary again. She had seen Miss Breckenridge's car, however, on her way to and from the school ever since Thursday morning. It was parked beside the road just north of Stinson Beach.

Upon Monsieur Trougnac the sheriff had to make a more direct attack before he could pry any information out of him.

"You admit that Miss Breckenridge has been for at least twenty years a resident of this county and an employee of this school, Monsieur Trougnac, of which you say you are the acting head. Under those circumstances you must see that since you can't tell me where she is you will have to answer the questions which my search for her make necessary."

"About Miss Breckenridge, I have answered. Your other questions I do not answer. They do not concern Miss Breckenridge."

"Let me determine that."

"I determine! This is a private school. The police have no business here—"

"Would you say—" The sheriff let him have it, "Would you say that the police had no business here if I were to tell you that on your property Miss Breckenridge had been murdered?"

Monsieur collapsed on the nearest chair with a little gurgle. His face was a haunted sheet of terror. Miss Parelli had more wits about her. Her eyes were like saucers but she was not long without the power of speech.

"Do you know that, or do you just think that?"

"I just think that," admitted the sheriff with rueful respect.

"Why? If you want us to help, I think you ought to tell us what's happened."

"Yes, yes," whispered Monsieur Trougnac, almost visibly leaning on Miss Parelli for support.

Sheriff Quigley considered the punctured martinet. The conclusion that he came to decided him to change his method of approach. He told the two of them in as few words as possible what he had learned from Miss Blossom. Miss Parelli was excited to fierce indignation and a hunger for vengeance. But for Monsieur Trougnac, the mere realization that an investigation of this nature was to take place at Drake's Anchorage was a catastrophe so colossal that he had capacity for no other emotion than despair. He was no longer hostile but simply desolate.

Monsieur Trougnac had last seen Miss Breckenridge at about eight o'clock on Wednesday evening in the door of the Faculty Common Room. Others present had been Mr. Dingle, one of the teachers, and Mrs. Cnut-Sorenson, one of the school's owners. The subject of their discussion had been a projected sale of the school to a Señora de Herrera. Monsieur Trougnac had apprehended the secretary eavesdropping and had discharged her. He had not seen her again, had not been surprised that she had left no forwarding address, had not thought to look in at Stone Cottage.

When asked how he had been able to inform Miss Parelli six hours before he discharged Miss Breckenridge that she was to be replaced, he replied that Miss Breckenridge's conduct had shown him that it would be necessary. This led to a halting delineation of the circumstances surrounding the departure of the headmaster.

Monsieur Trougnac answered listlessly, but shock might have provided him with this mask of innocence. So the sheriff recorded all his replies in his little black book. However, the trail here, so far as rediscovering the body was concerned, was cold. Time later to delve into the complex of motives and animosities that was unfolding before him, which might or might not relate to the death of Miss Breckenridge. Small wonder, though, that the staff had been disinclined to be communicative. He was glad his children went to public schools.

The morning was getting well along and he wanted to tackle Miss Blossom on the "accidents" that had kept her from contacting the police while the body was being moved. He obtained a list of the school personnel which included their years of service, secured a promise from Monsieur Trougnac that he would call them together in the Faculty Common Room during the rest period that would follow the lunch hour, and left the Office.

He walked along the terrace in the direction that he had seen Monsieur Trougnac take Miss Blossom. When he got to the north side of the school, he saw Bullard coming down the last stretch of trail. He went to meet him.

"How'd you make out?"

"The old woman's things are still in the cottage. Closets and drawers undisturbed. She didn't start packing, and I don't think the motive was robbery. There was a bunch of jewelry on the bureau and a pocketbook in the top drawer. Had money and whatnots in it, a checkbook, and this piece of paper. I brought it along because aside from the checkbook it was the only piece of writing in the whole place. No bills, letters, or anything like that. This is in shorthand."

The sheriff looked at the crumpled sheet he held out. "Did you bring the checkbook?"

"No, I didn't. Had a balance of between three and four hundred dollars. The stubs all just said 'Cash.' There was a key that looked as if it was for a safe-deposit box. I brought that."

"I was thinking about the handwriting, but we can get that in the Office. She worked there twenty years. That's probably where her papers are." He studied the shorthand note a moment longer. "Whoever wrote that was angry."

He handed it back to Bullard. "Get Bernardi to work it out. What about prints?"

"Well, I don't know about the door. The only smooth places were the surfaces of a big iron latch. The ones I got there were so superimposed that I couldn't make much out of them. They could be all hers, or even some of Zanetti's. I found a swell set on one of the windows that didn't correspond to any of the others in the room." He took a canvas bag from his pocket and shook its contents gently into a handkerchief. "But here's the real McCoy."

The sheriff saw pieces of clear glass that seemed to be the remains of a square bottle. The stopper, which had not broken, was of clouded glass, had a round knob on it, and was an inch in diameter.

"No label?" asked the sheriff. "I see traces of glue."

"I know. I looked for it, but I couldn't find it anywhere in the bushes. The bottle wasn't in the cottage. A piece of it caught my eye about twenty paces to the left of the trail not far above where you first saw me, I think it was thrown, probably in the dark, caught first in the bushes, and then dropped on through them on the rock. The pieces are quite large."

"Prints?"

"Yes, but blurred. I just picked it up. I was going to take it where I could get at it better—"

"O. K. I don't suppose you saw a Paisley shawl."

"Nary a Paisley shawl. But when I looked for it under the army blanket, I saw that the other covers were all messed around. That was the only place in the room that wasn't in order."

"And the foot was bare," said the sheriff.

"That's what I was thinking," said the deputy. "There was a lot of funny-looking underclothes on a hook on the closet door."

"How far down from the road is the cottage?"

"About a quarter of a mile, and steep."

"Horse get down it?"

"Could, I guess. I saw no sign that one had, but it's practically all rocks." He reached in his pocket to pull out another bundle. "Here's one more thing that sort of clinches it. Finding these was what made me look sharp for a bottle."

The sheriff found the wad of cloth to be made up of three towels. Stamped across the end of each one was the imprint, *Drake's Anchorage.* "Where'd you find these?"

"Hanging to the back side of a bush a dozen feet from the door. Looked as if they'd been thrown, too. Just like I felt about the bottle. Whoever got rid of the things was either in a hurry or didn't care if they were found."

The sheriff held them to his nose and then returned them to Bullard. "Have them tested. Take my car and go back by way of Stinson Beach. See what you can find in a Chevrolet parked a mile or so this side of it." The sheriff gave him the details of what he had got from Miss Parelli. "I'll be busy here some time," he concluded as he dismissed the deputy. "If you're not ready to come back by the middle of the afternoon, and Zanetti hasn't reported in that he's over here, send someone else back with the car."

The sheriff entered the door immediately behind him and came suddenly upon a sallow, embarrassed man who was obviously standing rather than walking.

"Good morning, good morning!" said the man with a nervous smile. "To what do we owe this visit? Nothing serious, I hope?"

The sheriff looked him over. "We brought in one of the teachers who'd been abandoned by a runaway horse," he told the man. "Can you show me the way to the infirmary? I want to see how she is."

"Dear me! That must be Miss Blossom! Of course. Just follow me up this way. When did it happen?"

"Quite early this morning, I believe."

"Extraordinary! She's said to have a very good seat. Miss Burtt, oh Miss Burtt."

They had come to an entryway and through a door on his left the sheriff saw many bottles on shelves. He drifted in there when the man had gone on up a narrow corridor. There were, of course, a variety of bottles bearing druggists' labels, but the uniform rows with plain red-bordered labels and glass stoppers were all round in shape.

A hefty, severe woman in the uniform of a nurse approached him through another door. "Mr. Arbuthnot says you are asking about Miss Blossom. She is resting comfortably, thank you."

"I'm glad to hear that. I'd like to talk to her for a few minutes."

"I'm sorry," was the answer. "That is impossible."

"Oh, I won't bother her long," said the sheriff. "I have to make a report. Some routine questions. You know how that is."

"Quite impossible," repeated the nurse firmly.

"I'm afraid I must insist," said the sheriff, just as firmly.

The nurse went back into the room from which she had just come. "Dr. Sterne, will you talk to this officer, please?"

Dr. Sterne came into view in the doorway. "Why, good morning, Sheriff," he said, walking forward. "What brings you here?"

"Good morning," said the sheriff shortly. "I want to see the girl we brought in here."

"You may look in on her, if you wish," the doctor replied, "but I've administered an opiate. Probably I can supply the information you want for your report—"

"What did you do that for?" interrupted the sheriff, chagrined to the point of rudeness. He shouldn't have let the girl get out of his hands.

Dr. Sterne's expression of solicitude cooled, but he answered smoothly, "Her condition required it. She was hysterical and I was uncertain of the extent of the head injury."

"She wasn't hysterical the last time I saw her, and I need to talk to her. How long will she be out?"

The doctor looked closely at him. "Was there more to this runaway than I understood?" he questioned. "What did happen that upset her so? I expect Miss Blossom to sleep most of the rest of the day."

The sheriff regarded him morosely. "Miss Blossom was upset because when she led us to where she had found the body of the school secretary it was no longer there."

"Good heavens! What are you talking about? Do you mean Miss Breckenridge is dead?"

"It looks as if she's been murdered, but were short the body. That's why I want to talk to Miss Blossom. Can't you bring her out of it some way?"

"Sorry." The doctor shook his head slowly. He sat on the edge of the desk and traced a pattern in the linoleum with one well-polished toe. "What a thing to have happen—now," he said thoughtfully. "I don't like it." He shook his head and repeated almost to himself, "I don't like it." He looked up at the sheriff. "You have only Miss Blossom's story, or something more to go on?"

"A good deal more," said the sheriff.

The doctor sighed and picked up his bag. "A sorry business. But I'll have to be on my way, unless, of course, there's anything I can do to help you."

"I'd like to hear anything you've picked up about the people around here—their relations with Miss Breckenridge, for instance. You must have been in and out a good deal."

"Yes, that's true, but—you say you think she was murdered! I know nothing about anyone that could conceivably have led to murder."

"What is it that's occurred to you, though?"

The doctor spoke reluctantly. "Well, I suppose I'd better come out with it at once or you'll think it's more important than it is. You're bound to hear it sooner or later. It's one of the school's cherished traditions—perhaps I should say legends."

"Let's have it. I don't go off at half cock."

"I'm sure you don't. So—the thing that I thought of immediately was the long-standing feud between Miss Breckenridge and Mrs. Bjornstrom. Nobody knows why—I don't know that it's even true—but they are reputed to have lived side by side for a quarter of a century without speaking to each other. That's all I can tell you."

"Thanks," said the sheriff. "I'll check into it. Anything you can think of about any of the others?"

"Nothing, except the typical antagonisms that a woman like Miss Breckenridge would be bound to stir up in a place like this. But this is nonsense! Why these people— You know, you'll really have to look elsewhere for a murderer. And now I'll have to get on with my rounds. I've a heavy schedule."

The sheriff accompanied the doctor to his car which was parked just outside the infirmary. "I'll have to ask you a few more questions, Doctor. They're what I'll be putting to everyone connected with the school after lunch. If you'll give me a few minutes now, I won't ask you to come back."

The doctor stood with his hand on the door of his car. "Ah yes. That's what I feared. This thing's going to get damned unpleasant before you're through, isn't it?"

"It's quite possible."

"The publicity," sighed the doctor. "Well, let's have them. Perhaps you'd like to get in and have a smoke while you're putting me through the jumps."

"I'll do that," said the sheriff, and went around to enter the luxurious postwar car by the other door. "I'd like to know where you were last Wednesday night from eight o'clock on."

The doctor had played chess with a Reverend Carstairs of the Seminary until midnight. He surprised the sheriff by offering Miss Blossom as his voucher for the later hours of the night. The sheriff sighed moodily as he made a note of another chapter of pertinent events that was locked up in the sleeping Miss Blossom.

"And Friday? Last night?"

The doctor had dined with the Blodgetts of Inverness, He thought he had gone home about one o'clock. He admitted that he had been called from the dinner table to attend a case and that he had been gone about an hour. He would not divulge the name without having first secured the patient's permission, and he refused even to ask for that permission unless the sheriff could show greater reason for requiring him to supply an alibi.

The sheriff eased himself out of the seat and gently closed the door. "Been on some tough roads already, haven't you?"

"What do you mean?"

"These scratches." The sheriff ran his finger meditatively along the side of the door. "A narrow road and a good deal of brush. Both sides of the car. Know where you got them?"

"Could have been in a dozen places. We doctors have to take our scratches in our stride, scars incurred in the line of duty."

"Be seeing you," said the sheriff with a short nod.

17

Mr. MacDowell: Science

"We found the body and we found Lind, Sheriff—both of them on the Lind ranch!"

As he leaned out the opened door of his car to communicate his good news, Deputy Zanetti's shoulders bulged with content under his black leather jacket, and his rather round red cheeks and deep-brown eyes all somewhat ludicrously twinkled at the amazing expedition with which he had accomplished his mission.

"Well, I declare," said his chief, and put his pipe back in his mouth.

The deputy grinned sheepishly. The sheriff watched the doctor's car as it was shifted into high gear and gathered speed for the ascent behind the school. A clatter of cutlery and conversation was issuing from the dining-room windows and there was no one on the terrace.

"Oh hell! Was I talking out of turn?" asked Zanetti.

The sheriff relented. The deputy was so obviously bursting with his story. "No, that's all right," said the sheriff. "I'll get in with you and you can drive down the road a piece and tell me about it. I'll want to be back here at one o' clock."

Zanetti drove to the sweep of road that went farthest out on the cliffs, and parked where they could see the surf on the rocks below.

"This all right? I brought you a couple of hamburgers. Want to chew on them while I shoot?" He was still humble.

"Good enough," the sheriff said. "We've got half an hour, so give me everything."

Zanetti needed no second invitation. "Prentice and I drove straight for the ranch. After we got on the Inverness road, we went by several places where trees had been felled and new roads started into the hills on the left—clearings left ready for building next summer. They looked like good bets for anybody who would be wanting to get rid of a body in a hurry. We were going to take 'em in coming back."

The sheriff nodded, and Zanetti continued. "The lane into the Lind place had wide ruts full for about a quarter of a mile. We stopped where the deep ruts turned left into a sort of creek bottom. It was lousy with cobblestones but there was no water in it and it had evidently at one time been the route of a logging road. The other lane went on straight but looked less traveled. I waited at the fork and sent Prentice to follow the creek up a way to see if a road led out of it again on higher ground. Before he'd even got out of sight, he turned back suddenly to look at something. He waved an arm at me and disappeared up a bank of scrub oak and manzanita. I hopped it up to where he'd left the creek bottom and saw what had stopped him. Enough water had seeped up from somewhere to form a skim of ice over a puddle of silt against a rock. The sun hadn't reached the ice yet but it had been stepped on.

"We didn't know how near we were to the ranch house so we weren't making any more disturbance than we could help, but I risked calling loud enough for Prentice to hear to ask how he was doing. He said he was going slow trying to follow broken twigs. The ground was too firm there for prints. He got to the body at ten-twenty. I made a note of the time. That was only forty minutes after we'd left you!"

"Good work! Could you identify the body from Miss Blossom's description of Miss Breckenridge?"

"I didn't go up then, but Prentice was pretty sure, and we had Lind do that definitely—later."

"That was well done, too."

Zanetti glowed. But as he went on with the rest of his story, his elation became less exuberant.

"There was something about the fellow," he said, "like— well, like a lion that's been caged up to ship to a zoo."

"What did he have to say? Where did you find him?"

"I left Prentice in there and drove the car on up the road. A couple more turns and I could see the old ranch house. It lay about a hundred yards away in the middle of a meadow. There was smoke coming out of the chimney at the back. I drove around there and knocked. I figured that if he didn't come to the door, I could circle the house and catch him before he'd got across the meadow in any direction. I didn't have to go after him though. He opened the door at once.

"He fits Bartello's description all right, but the more I saw of him, the less he seemed like the kind of a dope that would knock out Bartello from behind because he didn't have the price of a cup of coffee."

"He has another reason for hiding out," said the sheriff, "that smells even worse."

"He's a hard man to read. I said I wanted him to identify a body we'd found on his property. He came right along without asking any questions.

"I sent him ahead of me up the bank toward where Prentice called to me that he was. Prentice had pulled back that Paisley shawl that Miss Blossom kept talking about so that we could see the head and shoulders of the stiff.

Except for the pallor, she just looked as if she was asleep. It was an old lady in a pink flannel nightgown with her hair done up in toilet-paper curlers.

"I watched his face, but I couldn't get a line on him. He touched her cheek. Then he stood up and looked at me. 'Eliza Breckenridge,' he said, 'my secretary at Drake's Anchorage.' Just like that. 'Any idea how she got here?' I asked him. He said, 'No,' looked down at the body again, and asked me, 'How did she die?' I felt kind of silly and looked at Prentice. He said he hadn't touched the body except to uncover the face.

"I said we were leaving that for the coroner, and Lind turned around and went back down to the creek bottom and toward the road, studying the way as he went along as if he was completely on his own. Prentice stayed with the body and I followed. The fellow was treating me like the tail of the kite so I guess I threw a little weight around and said, 'Get in the bus.' There was a little flicker in his eyes and then they sort of went dead and he got in. That was when I began feeling I was on the wrong side of a shady operation."

"It's not all pleasant," agreed the sheriff.

"After I'd buzzed Bernardi and told him to send the coroner back out and notify the district attorney's office, I tried to get a statement out of him. He admitted that he'd been up to the top of the logging road when he met Miss Blossom but said there was no body there. When I asked him whether he'd been looking for it, since he was so sure it wasn't there, he shut up like a clam. He also admitted that he'd been in the barn when I first went up to the school, Thursday afternoon. He'd gone over to the Lind ranch on horseback while I was down below. I tried to find out why he was in hiding but it was no soap. You say you got the dope on that?"

"The teacher that's in his shoes says he's gone for good on uncontested charges of perversion."

Zanetti digested that in silence. Then he said, "Hell, I don't know what he *is,* but one thing he isn't—well, he's like no Peeping Tom that I ever ran in. If he's still here—after that— Could he be after the person who brought the charge against him? Was that Miss Breckenridge?"

The sheriff shook his head. "Seems to have been made by a group of parents. There's only one of them at the school now. I don't know how she fits in— Then there's another parent about to buy the school. Miss Breckenridge's trail ends at the door of a conference about that—eavesdropping. Looks as if she was against the sale—"

The sheriff balled up the papers in which his lunch had come and got out of the car to toss them over the cliff. They blew back over his head. His eyes traveled along the definite blue edge of the Pacific to the bump of the Farallons.

"Well, if she was playing Lind's game," Zanetti's voice brought him back to the car, "why wasn't he more cooperative when I was questioning him about who could have killed her?"

The sheriff got in and lit his pipe before he replied. "I don't know—yet. But from what I learned from Monsieur Trougnac, and from the impression that he's made on you—I'm wondering if he could have been in the clear. The thing could have taken him by surprise. He evidently learned Monday night that he had to get out or see the school publicized Tuesday morning by a story that would ruin it. If someone—and he wasn't sure who—had taken that underhanded way of getting the school away from him, he'd make it appear that he'd gone, and then try to determine who that person was, so that he could move against him. Maybe Miss Breckenridge found out for him."

"The Frenchman?" said Zanetti.

"Not necessarily. There's probably a lot more to this than we know yet. I'll see what I can find out from the teachers after lunch before I tackle Lind. Where is he now, by the way?"

"Truax is trying to see what he can get out of him. He came out with the coroner again. I told Lind we'd want him for further questioning and he agreed to stay on the ranch. I left Prentice there."

"Have you heard anything from Bullard?"

"Bernardi gave me a message for you. Bullard didn't find that Chevrolet. And I was going to tell you— When I slowed down to give Milton the high sign on the way in here, I noticed what looked like an old Chevy in one of the sheds up there. I didn't stop. Do you want me to go back now and see?"

The sheriff glanced at his watch. "Ten minutes to one. I'll go with you and see what Huggins has to say if it *is* Miss Breckenridge's car. The bookkeeper seems to be sure that it was still out on the road when she came to school this morning."

On the way up the road, Zanetti said, "What Bernardi told me about the setup at Stone Cottage reminded me that Thursday, when I was in there, I thought the old woman had been using a cleaning fluid."

The sheriff nodded. "That would tie in. A woman that age would succumb to ether—if enough of it was used. You said the windows were open. If it was ether, I wonder how long the odor would cling.

"The secretary was discharged on Wednesday evening. You were there on Thursday. She must have been put under some time Wednesday night—early enough to enable the body to be removed and the place cleaned up before daylight. And it wasn't premeditated or they'd have done a better job of making her disappearance look normal. Whatever it was she found out was dangerous enough to stampede somebody into getting her out of the way immediately.

"Now that looks—a sane person wouldn't commit murder to avoid being shown to have made libelous charges, nor yet, I wouldn't think, to secure control of the school, however rich it is. No. I think—we're going to have to look beyond the school for the motive."

In the shed, the sheriff read "Eliza Breckenridge" on the registration card in the Chevrolet. "Seen Huggins lately?" he asked the other deputy who had followed them into the shed.

"Gone down to eat," said Milton. "When do I eat?"

"Patience, Big Boy," grinned Zanetti.

"You can take the car and run out now while Zanetti stays here. I'll walk down the trail and meet Huggins," the sheriff said. But as Milton was getting in, Walter's head appeared above the level of the road. "Hold it, Milton. I may want to contact headquarters."

Walter altered his course when the sheriff hailed him and came toward them without quickening his pace, chewing on a toothpick.

"I'd like to ask you some questions, Huggins."

Walter took the toothpick out of his mouth and thoughtfully broke it up. "I don't aim for to be curious," he said, "but you fellows have been pussyfooting it back and forth here all morning. Before I answer any questions, I want to know what you're about."

"Didn't Monsieur Trougnac tell you I'd be expecting to have a talk with you after lunch?"

"Monsieur and I don't see much of each other."

"You don't have a very high opinion of Monsieur Trougnac?"

"I said, what's this all about?"

"Were investigating the death of Miss Eliza Brecken-ridge."

The remnants of the toothpick dropped from Walter's large fingers. "God a'mighty!"

"How does her car happen to be parked in this shed?"

Walter twisted a finger in one ear and looked perplexed-ly at the car. "Why, I pulled it up here this morning after I'd mended a tire for her. She ain't got—didn't have—no spare."

"Did she ask you to do that?"

"Yeh."

"When?"

"Well, in a manner of speaking, she did. She told Mr. MacDowell to ask me." He turned apprehensively to the sheriff. "How come you're wanting to know? When did she die? How did it happen?"

"We don't know. That's why we're asking. Her body was found this morning."

"You trying to tell me she was murdered?"

"That's right. When did Mr. MacDowell tell you to move the car?"

"Night before last when he left the tire." Walter's face had become cautious. "I mended it yesterday."

"Did he say when she'd given it to him?"

"He picked her and it both up the night before that. He forgot he had it in his car till he come to load up his duds."

"What do you mean, 'load up'?" asked Zanetti.

"Your man hunt lost him his job. Didn't you know that?"

"You mean this MacDowell left the school for good on Thursday evening?" the sheriff asked.

"Yep."

"Where did he go?"

"He didn't know where he was going. Right at first he thought he would get drunk, and then he'd see."

"Where's his home?"

"Some place in Georgia. I don't think he was aiming for there though."

"She must have been with them when they came in Wednesday evening—with MacDowell and that other fellow," exclaimed Zanetti. "That makes her still alive at midnight."

"If MacDowell told a straight story," said Milton from his seat in Zanetti's car.

"Well, this other fellow—"

"Who is also missing," Milton interpolated helpfully.

The sheriff said, "Milton, stop joshing and call the office. Have them put out an all-points bulletin for Mac-Dowell. Tell Bernardi he can get the information he needs about MacDowell from Zanetti's report on the Bartello case. You had his license number in there, didn't you, Zanetti?"

"Yes, it's in there."

"If you think MacDowell had anything to do with killing off Miss Breckenridge," said Walter, "you're barking up the wrong tree."

"Well, he was probably the last person to see her alive," said Zanetti.

Milton leaned away from his microphone to question Walter. "What time did MacDowell leave here, Thursday?"

Walter looked at Zanetti. "When did you go by? He came up right after."

Zanetti spoke to Milton. "I'd say he left about six-thirty."

"And this is Saturday," said the sheriff. "He could be halfway across the country."

"Not unless he got a job first," supplied Walter.

"You mean he was low in funds?" asked the sheriff.

"I loaned him five dollars. He said he didn't want to get any drunker than that."

"Give them that too, Milton," said the sheriff.

"Bernardi wants to talk to you, Sheriff," said Milton.

The sheriff got in beside him and rolled up the window. Bernardi's voice came metallically out of the receiver. "About those prints, Sheriff. They're none of them Lind's, and the ones on the window and the ones on the bottle aren't the same. We've sent both sets to Washington."

"Get hold of MacDowell's prints. Didn't he have a California driver's license? Try Sacramento on that. What was in that note?"

"Part of a conversation between two people—about which of them was to move into the headmaster's rooms. One's Dingle, or Dinkle, I think, but the other's beyond me—something like T R U N A C K. Do you want Bullard back out there?"

"Yes, and I can use a couple more men besides him. They can bring out that note. Heard anything from the coroner?"

"Not yet, Sheriff, but he said he'd rush it."

"Have three men ready to come out here at six, and alert the rest of the force."

"O. K., Sheriff."

18

Mrs. Bjornstrom: Housemother of Small Boys

Five persons were waiting with Monsieur Trougnac when the sheriff passed through the sabbath quiet of the school in its rest hour to enter the Faculty Common Room. From their demeanor, it was obvious that Monsieur had announced the reason for their having been called together. The sheriff nodded to Miss Burtt and to the man she had spoken of as Mr. Arbuthnot. He asked to be introduced to the three men whom he had not yet met.

"This is Mr. Dingle," said Monsieur, "and over here are Mr. Bjornstrom and Mr. Pyke."

None of the three moved forward to shake his hand. The sheriff had dipped sufficiently into the affairs of Drake's Anchorage to know that among them existed antagonisms, but the attitudes of all six people made it evident that toward him they intended to preserve a united front.

"Thank you," said the sheriff. He selected an easy chair with its back to the west windows and moved it so that from his seat he could face the couch that was centered in the room and the other chairs that were grouped around the fireplace. "I suggest that you make yourselves comfortable."

"It is not possible that we remain long," said Monsieur Trougnac.

"I'll cut it as short as your cooperation makes possible. Please sit down."

"Well, let's get on with it," said Mr. Pyke. He seated himself, and the others moved to follow his example.

"That's better," said the sheriff. "An investigator is always resented by the people into whose lives he forces an entrance. And in this situation, where you feel responsible for the children in your care, and where you are already handicapped by the attack that has been made upon the good name of the school, I realize that I am doubly unwelcome. I have several men working with me. I assure you that nothing that we learn which is not necessary for the conviction of the murderer of Miss Breckenridge will go beyond us."

"It is our opinion," said Monsieur Trougnac, "that the criminal who hid here Wednesday night was discovered by Miss Breckenridge, and that he killed her."

"Were not forgetting him," the sheriff said. He consulted the list he had taken from his pocket. "Where is Mr. Weber?"

"This is his free weekend. He will return tomorrow evening," answered Monsieur Trougnac.

The sheriff got from them that Mr. Weber had left in his car at noon on Friday, that he had also been absent from the school all of Wednesday night. On where he might have spent that night or where he might be now they professed to no opinion. They knew of no animosity between him and Miss Breckenridge.

"And Mrs. Bjornstrom?" He looked at her husband.

Monsieur Trougnac answered. "She is with the small boys. After the rest hour she will be free."

"I want to see every adult at least briefly this afternoon. That includes your domestic staff, Monsieur. I've instructed my men that no one is to be permitted to leave the school property without a pass from me."

"That's an extreme measure," said Mr. Dingle. "You're not even certain that Miss Breckenridge is dead."

"Since my talk with Monsieur, the situation has changed. The body of Miss Breckenridge has been found and identified, and in a short time I shall have a report of the coroner's autopsy." The sheriff spoke mildly but he was alert to the attitudes of his listeners. "Our knowledge of the circumstances of her death is not yet complete, but we are rounding it out hourly. I am expecting help from you in putting together the information we are collecting.

"My tentative picture is this: Miss Breckenridge was discharged and told to leave Drake's Anchorage at eight o'clock Wednesday evening. She died in her bed, probably from a lethal dose of ether, some time after midnight that night—or, I should say, Thursday morning. Her body was then removed, either by car or by horseback, to the place on the ridge from which the school obtains its firewood. It was seen there by Miss Blossom at four-thirty Friday—late yesterday afternoon. By a series of events which it is not plausible to consider were all accidents, Miss Blossom was prevented from notifying my office of her discovery until this morning. Shortly after nine o'clock, when we arrived with her at the spot where she had seen the body, it was no longer there. An hour later, my men discovered it, hidden under some brush up a dry creek on the Lind ranch. Some time between Friday afternoon at four-thirty and Saturday morning at nine, the body had been moved again, and again either by car or by horseback."

The sheriff paused to consider the effect of his words. The only sound was the boom and sough of the waves. The faces before him were evasive.

"I see that you recognize that all this could not have been accomplished by someone unfamiliar with the school. While I have been talking, you have been remembering occurrences of the past week that you don't want to admit are suspicious, even to yourselves. The more you hold out on me, the longer you'll have to live with them. The franker you are with me, the sooner we'll get at the truth, which I am supposing is what most of you want."

His audience was still unresponsive. "Well," he said, "as Mr. Pyke suggests, let's get on with it."

The sheriff moved into his inquiry gently, shifting away without demur from subjects which concentrated the tension in any of his adversaries—for so he had to regard them. He asked each of them to tell what he had been doing on the nights of Wednesday and Friday. Appearing to be concerned with the details of their comings and goings, he was listening for indications of motive. He was coursing his field, probing for weaknesses in their common defense that he could return to later, for cracks into which he could insinuate wedges of dissension.

When the bell rang indicating the end of the rest period, both Monsieur Trougnac and Mr. Pyke rose to go.

"I'll have to ask you to remain," said the sheriff.

"But look here," said Mr. Pyke, "I've got a game on, and I've told you I don't know a damned thing that'll help you."

"It is necessary that someone be with the boys," said Monsieur Trougnac.

"Sorry," said the sheriff. "For your own protection— for the protection of Miss Blossom—I can not allow anyone to leave this room until my men arrive. It won't be long now."

"I'll be damned if I can see that," said Mr. Pyke.

"Well frankly, I made a mistake about Miss Blossom," said the sheriff. "Really two. I've told you that I let her be given an opiate before I'd got her complete story of last night."

Mr. Pyke slowly turned a brick red. "You mean you think that *I*—" Words failed him.

"I mean I'm taking no chances," the sheriff replied. "So far, none of you has given me the complete cooperation I requested. It follows that I must hold all of you suspect."

"Well, I'll be damned," said Mr. Pyke, and sat down again. Monsieur Trougnac walked the length of the room twice, and then subsided on the window seat with his head in his hands. The shouts of young voices echoed down from the trail up past Stone Cottage. The sheriff ran his eye over the restless group. Their solidarity, which had been weakening under his questions, had been further confused by his last words. He went back to the sick headache which Mr. Dingle said had kept him awake until midnight of Wednesday.

"Did you have to leave your room, Mr. Dingle, to obtain the sedative which you say caused you to sleep soundly through the late hours of Wednesday night?"

"No. I had something of my own."

"But Friday afternoon when you complained of a headache, you told Mr. Arbuthnot you were going to the nurse for a remedy."

"I wanted something stronger."

"I see. You've had a bad headache all week. You told Miss Parelli your anger at Miss Breckenridge was making you ill. Is that what caused your headache?"

"It was rather the general situation," said Mr. Dingle.

"You alone knew that if Miss Breckenridge did not appear the following morning, Monsieur Trougnac would simply conclude that she had accepted her dismissal."

"You can say the same thing of Monsieur. And if you're making a point of that, you'd better inquire why a light sleeper like Monsieur Trougnac, who leaps out into the corridors every time a boy snores, didn't hear Miss Blossom and Mr. MacDowell and Mr. Arbuthnot running around."

Monsieur Trougnac raised his head. "I heard them. I was in the Office. I did not wish to be disturbed." Monsieur Trougnac encountered the sheriff's gaze and parried

the question he saw forming there by offering the assurance that others had known that the secretary was leaving.
He was sure that he had told Miss Burtt.

"Did you pass on that information, Miss Burtt?"

"I did not," said Miss Burtt. "It was not a matter that
concerned me—beyond the fact that the quarrel between
Miss Breckenridge and Monsieur and Mr. Dingle was so
violent that it was upsetting a boy who was ill in the infirmary and I had to go out and ask them to be more quiet."

Mr. Dingle looked at her venomously, "It seems to me
unwise, Miss Burtt, for a person who has ether in her possession and understands its use to be so free with imputa-
tive statements. What were you doing with bottles Friday
evening when I came into the dispensary and *smelled* ether?"

Miss Burtt allowed a contemptuous glance to rake her
attacker and then said to the sheriff, "It isn't necessary for
me to reply to such an irresponsible question."

"It's true, Miss Burtt," agreed the sheriff, "that smells
and bottles are not out of place in a dispensary, and that
we have plenty of evidence that you were incapacitated
Wednesday night, but I'm curious about one aspect of
that: It's strange that the only insulin reaction you have
suffered since you came to the school should have occurred
on the night Miss Breckenridge met her death. Have you
an explanation that would make that coincidence a little
less glaring?"

"It doesn't seem strange to me," said Miss Burtt. "I'm
more a housekeeper here than I am a nurse. My duties
were multiplied by the beginning of the term and the unexpected absence of the headmaster. On top of that, there
was the nervous strain of being held accountable by the
doctor and the parents for not having seen what was happening to the boys. The doctor will tell you of the talk we
had that afternoon. I went to bed so depressed that I failed

to note the signs of developing insulin shock that would ordinarily have warned me."

"That seems reasonable," said the sheriff, "Now Mr. Arbuthnot—" He was stopped by the sound of heavy feet coming up the passageway. "That will be the men." He met them in the corridor, closing the door behind him. Bullard and Zanetti had arrived with the two additional deputies he had requested.

"Couldn't get anything out of Huggins," said Zanetti, "If he saw or heard anything either night, he's not saying."

"That's to be expected. He's covering for Lind. Did you see the girl in the Office?"

"Yes, she's in there. Says she has to work overtime. I only stopped long enough to find out where you were. She's a kid that's grown up around here, and she hasn't known any of these people long enough to be involved."

"Keep your shirt on," said the sheriff. "I only want you to find out whether she has any idea what Monsieur Trougnac does in there nights. While you're in there, go through the secretary's desk, but don't spend too much time on it now. Have Miss Parelli take you to the science laboratory and give that a once over. See what kind of containers the chemicals are kept in. Check on the ether supply.

"And, Bullard," he turned to the other deputy, "let me have Bernardi's version of that note and then close up Stone Cottage. Your main job is to get the prints of everyone here."

"Kids, too?" inquired Bullard.

The sheriff frowned. "Not until you've found out whether any of the adults' prints mate up with those you've got. Not today, anyway. Here's a list of them to go by. Better add a Mrs. Maxwell. She's a visiting parent around somewhere. You may as well get Miss Blossom's while you're here, and those of the faculty I've got rounded up."

The sheriff left Albertson, one of the newly arrived deputies, at the door of the Common Room, and took the other one, Roma, with him and Bullard down the infirmary corridor. They found Miss Blossom behind the third door down. Bullard recorded the prints of her right thumb and fingers without disturbing her deep sleep.

"Roma," said the sheriff, "your job is to see that no one—not even the nurse—gets close to this girl. Check the windows, and whether there's another entrance to the infirmary. Then stay in the hall with her door open. I want to talk to her as soon as she's awake enough to make sense."

When the sheriff and Bullard returned to the Common Room door, Albertson said, "A dark thin guy with a nose wanted to leave, but I told him he'd have to wait for you."

"That's right. You come in, now, and take notes. I've been making a poor job of that."

Monsieur Trougnac ceased speaking abruptly as the sheriff re-entered the room. He left the phrase "—under no circumstances—" hanging in the air. Mr. Arbuthnot was looking scared and a shade rebellious. "Sorry to keep you waiting," said the sheriff. "This is Deputy Bullard. I'm going to ask you to let him make a record of your fingerprints."

To his rapid glance around the room, the face of the man whom the sheriff considered most capable of concealing his emotions betrayed the greatest shock. It was the face of Mr. Dingle. No one said anything. Bullard did his job quickly and departed.

After he had dismissed Mr. Pyke, the sheriff returned to his prey. "Mr. Arbuthnot, by your own account you did a good deal of traveling around both in and outside the school on Wednesday evening. I'm aware that you have left things out of your story. I'd like to have them now please."

Mr. Arbuthnot did not reply at once. He cracked his knuckles. Finally he said, "I have nothing to add." He had not looked at Monsieur Trougnac but the sheriff felt a general tension relax at his words.

"That's it!" he exclaimed. "You're holding back information because it involves students."

"The boys know nothing," said Monsieur Trougnac. "They must not be brought into this."

"I certainly don't want to unnecessarily," the sheriff told him. "But we may have to come to that. Mr. Arbuthnot, if you are shielding one or two, you may be doing so at the price of forcing me to interrogate the whole kit and caboodle of them."

"Mr. Arbuthnot has no information," said Monsieur Trougnac.

Mr. Arbuthnot squirmed under the sheriff's stare. "Why don't you ask Mr. Bjornstrom how he happened to go out looking for Miss Blossom during dinner on Friday," he blurted out.

"Why, you blasted little snooper!" said Mr. Bjornstrom whose contributions so far had been monosyllabic.

"I was about to return to Mr. Bjornstrom." The sheriff looked expectantly at the old man. "Did you go out to look for Miss Blossom?" The man's beady eyes fell before those of the sheriff. "You've got quite a bit of explaining ahead of you, Mr. Bjornstrom, so you may as well begin."

"I haven't done anything," mumbled Mr. Bjornstrom.

The sheriff walked over to stand immediately in front of him. "You're right, there's one thing you didn't do," he told him. "When my deputy talked to you on Thursday afternoon, you'd already seen the body. Why didn't you report it?"

Mr. Bjornstrom's shoulders hunched over until the sheriff could see the scraggly locks on the back of his neck.

"Nothing to do with me," he said.

"He hated Miss Breckenridge," said Mr. Arbuthnot.

Mr. Bjornstrom jerked his head up. "I did not!" he shouted. There was sincerity in his voice.

"Well, anyway, his wife did," Mr. Arbuthnot insisted.

"You don't know what you're talking about. Shut up!" Mr. Bjornstrom returned fiercely.

"I believe it's time for me to talk to Mrs. Bjornstrom," said the sheriff. "Albertson, will you go after her? The rest of you can go."

Miss Burtt was the first to get to her feet. "I hope you will be successful, Sheriff," she said before she departed. "The school will be a healthier place when these old in-grown grudges are rooted out of it."

Her heels clicked away. Monsieur Trougnac and Mr. Dingle followed her wordlessly. Mr. Arbuthnot hesitated beside Mr. Bjornstrom's bent shoulders. He looked uncertainly from them to the sheriff, and then he too went out.

"You suspected your wife?" the sheriff asked Mr. Bjornstrom. "You know, I wouldn't, if I were you. But don't tell anybody I said so."

Mr. Bjornstrom stood up and became as straight as his years and his limp permitted. "I never did! Only people wouldn't believe now what it was my wife had against her." His expression of relief was thrown slightly askew by a wink. "They didn't none of 'em see Eliza when she was young." Mr. Bjornstrom started off as if he intended to be well away from there before his wife arrived. In the door he turned to look once more at the sheriff. "You sure enough got it right, my wife didn't kill Eliza—not now. She wouldn't have waited forty years. So I'll give you something else to chew on. She's dead, Eliza is. All you can see— To you she was just an old woman. But I'm telling you, Sheriff, no man that was a *man* would kill Eliza, no matter how old she was!"

The sheriff was left in an empty room to ruminate upon masculinity and the youth of Miss Breckenridge. He was a family man, but in response to something in the old man's voice his pulse had stirred. Escaping the intrusion of a dream forsworn, he went out to his car and buzzed headquarters.

"Any reports?" he asked Bernardi crisply.

"Yes. At two o'clock, MacDowell phoned in from a public campground down in the Big Sur, reversing the charges. He said he'd just heard we wanted him, and that if we'd see that he got some gasoline he'd be right up. I fixed it with the highway patrol. He's long about San Jose now, and should be in by six. Sounds like a gay bird. His print wasn't on his license."

"Well, don't lose track of him. Anything come in from Washington?"

"Not yet."

The sheriff went to look in on Miss Blossom. She was still asleep. Miss Burtt watched him resentfully, but made no comment. As Albertson still hadn't arrived with Mrs. Bjornstrom, he asked a tall, light-haired boy who was sauntering in the corridor to lead him to the science room.

"Keep you working pretty hard here?" the sheriff asked the boy as they walked along together.

"Hard enough, sir," replied the boy. "Did you bring Miss Blossom in? Is she going to be all right?"

"I think so. What do you know about Miss Blossom?"

"Why, Mr. Arbuthnot said she'd had a fall from a horse."

"Did that surprise you?"

The boy who was nearly as tall as the sheriff, opened a door that they had come opposite. "Here's the lab," he said. The sheriff saw him take in the presence of Zanetti there before he backed away to allow the sheriff to enter, "There you are, sir."

The sheriff questioned once more as the boy was turning away. "About Miss Blossom?"

"Oh—why yes. She rides quite well as a rule."

This he threw airily over his shoulder as he went back and turned into the doorway of a room they had passed on the way down. The sheriff noted its location and joined Zanetti.

"There's no ether here," said Zanetti, "but he's got about everything else. And the uniform bottles are square."

"If the room wasn't locked up, it would have been an easy matter for anybody take it."

"It wasn't locked," said Zanetti, "but I've found that the prints that predominate in this room correspond with the ones on Bullard's bottle. They're blurred on the bottle, but there's enough of them to cinch it. Of course the bottle might have been picked up with a cloth and handled carefully. Somehow I don't think that fellow—"

"He's on his way up from below Carmel now," the sheriff told him. "Bringing himself in."

"That's a good sign," said Zanetti. "What do you want me to do now?"

"Go give the hired help a once-over. I'd like to get back to town before six. I've got Mrs. Bjornstrom to see, and then if Miss Blossom isn't awake, I'm going to pour a bucket of cold water over her. If you run into Bullard, tell him to try to wind his end up by five o'clock. Both of you meet me at the cars then."

Albertson was waiting with Mrs. Bjornstrom in the Faculty Common Room when he returned there.

"Mrs. Bjornstrom," said the sheriff, "there is an apparently widespread belief that you and Miss Breckenridge were enemies. Now that she's dead, I think it would be a good idea if you'd tell me how much truth there is in that."

"Not enemies," said Mrs. Bjornstrom positively. "I just didn't want to have anything to do with the likes of her and she knew it."

"I see" said the sheriff gravely. "What made you feel that way?"

Mrs. Bjornstrom pursed her lips. "I never was one to tell tales, and now she's dead."

"But the way she died puts a different face on things. You must help the law find out who killed her. Do you think there was anyone in her past who might have come back wanting to do that?"

Mrs. Bjornstrom looked scornful. "Not them. That wouldn't be what they come back for!"

"They do come back though?"

"Such disgraceful carryings-on," said Mrs. Bjornstrom. "I wouldn't dirty my mouth talking about them."

"When was the last time they came back?"

"The last time was when one of them died here. That was enough for the other that was with him. Till then they'd been back every summer."

"Died? How do you mean, died?"

Mrs. Bjornstrom said primly, "The headmaster told me not to talk about it. He said if we was to stay on, we must let the past bury the past. Not that he ever knew the half of it, but I wasn't the one to tell him."

"I'll have to have the facts, Mrs. Bjornstrom. If you are to clear yourself from suspicion, you must hold nothing back. Now who was it that died?"

Mrs. Bjornstrom folded her hands and looked into the past. "Him that's the grandfather of the headmaster, Alrik Lind the elder. Dropped right down there on the floor of Stone Cottage and never said another word. Rog Torvaldson came hurrying down and sent Gudmund off for the doctor. They put him in her bed, and for two days and nights she and I took turns nursing him, but there was nothing a body could do. Rog was all the time saying it was his fault Alrik had got so excited. He kept asking Eliza to forgive him, but she paid him no mind, tagging along behind her like a puppy, and him an old man!

"When Alrik died—it was well after midnight, and my turn to nurse him, but Eliza had come and pushed me away—Rog sat on one of the rocks in the trail and cried like a baby. Eliza went out and I heard him calling after her but she wouldn't talk to him. She went off toward the cove, foggy as it was. The doctor went out and brought him in and gave him a drink of whiskey. It was then they fixed it up about Rog's selling the doctor his share of the school."

"Was that the school doctor? Dr. Sterne?"

"Yes, the same one. Rog wanted to go back to Chicago and stay there. He said he was old, and tired, and sick of the sound of the sea, and that the school was a foolish dream he wanted to forget. I always did think it was just an excuse they had to come and see Eliza. The doctor had to promise that the others wouldn't know—Lars Aakrog and Oscar Liljeborg. They had a pact among them. But they ain't none of 'em been around since Alrik died."

"What about the grandson? He must know."

"If he does, he hasn't said. He's not one for telling what he knows, either. And anyway, he wasn't there then. He didn't come till the next day. And he wasn't interested in the school then. He was busy getting his grandfather buried. They cremated him, and put his ashes down in one of the caves in the cove. There was all sorts of difficulties, but Eliza would have it that way, and he humored her. She said Alrik had said that was what he wanted, but I don't believe it, because he never talked after he keeled over. Eliza just never would do anything the way other people would do it. Even dying."

Mrs. Bjornstrom had finished her tale. "There now. You see, I had no cause to bother with Eliza. It was never

Gudmund she was after. It was them as had money she took."

The sheriff felt the dovelike eyes of Albertson upon his neck and had an unnerving suspicion that he was beginning to blush. He stood up.

"Thank you, Mrs. Bjornstrom. That will be all now."

Without waiting for her to go he beat a retreat into the infirmary. "Miss Blossom!" he bellowed. "I can't wait all day. I've got to have a talk with Miss Blossom!"

"Here I am," a faint voice answered him.

19

Mrs. Cnut-Sorenson: an Owner

"Any activity up here, Milton?" the sheriff asked when he had stopped his car beside the deputy who was stationed on the road above the school.

"Nothing in or out but a grocery truck. I knew the driver so I let him make his delivery. At two o'clock, sixteen boys came up and got horses and went down to the polo field. You'd said go easy on the kids, so I didn't talk to them. About an hour later, a teacher named Pyke came up and got a horse and went down there too. They're just back now and putting up their horses. They still add up to sixteen. That's all there is— Oh yes, Huggins wanted to take a horse trailer and a blond kid into San Rafael, but I told him he'd have to clear through you. I guess he gave up the idea. The kid hung around for a while and then went back down the trail."

"Tall, tan, brown eyes?"

"Yeh, nice-looking kid."

Lights were winking on in the buildings that lay below them and, as Milton answered, a faint jangling alarm drifted up. The boys who had been meandering in and out of the corrals responded as if to a fire. They streamed across the road and disappeared toward the school. Zanetti, who had turned his car over to Bullard and Albertson so that he and the sheriff could compare notes on the way into town, laughed.

"The only people who react normally around here are the kids and those six waiters."

"Let's have that list of the waiters," said the sheriff. "Here, Milton, they live out. Let them go home when they're through work and come back again in the morning. The old cook, Olsen, can do the same. And there's one teacher on the loose, name of Weber. He's not expected back until tomorrow, but if he turns up, let him go down. Otherwise, no one in or out without my O. K." Milton accepted the list but looked melancholy until the sheriff added, "Turn that information over to the man sent out to relieve you." They left Milton on the dark hilltop and drove rapidly toward San Rafael.

"That bunch of boys may act normally, but they're not all innocent," said the sheriff. "I hate to drag the whole lot into this, but none of the adults will give me a line on which ones to question. Three times when I got to a dead end I had a feeling it was because there was a boy or two at the other end of it. That blond kid that was up here is interested in Miss Blossom, and there was a gap in her story."

"Oh, you talked to her again after all?"

"Some, but I didn't finish with her. She was so set on getting out of the infirmary that I had to see her transferred to her own room before I could get anything out of her at all. I put Roma where he can keep an eye on her door, and I'll give her another whirl in the morning." The sheriff buzzed his office. "Bernardi? MacDowell showed up yet?"

"He's in the bag," came the answer. "The San Francisco police have shunted him on the bridge and I've got a patrol car waiting for him on this side. The coroner's report's come in too. Cause of death, suffocation."

"Good enough. Put MacDowell into my office. And send men out to replace Roma and Milton at Drake's Anchorage, and Prentice at the Lind ranch."

The sheriff replaced the microphone on its hook and frowned at the road ahead. "We're getting the dope faster than we can put it together. Things are breaking almost too well. Got any ideas, Zanetti?"

"Well, the thing that interests Monsieur Trougnac after lights out is finances."

"Uh-huh," responded the sheriff. "We don't know enough yet about the people that own the place. I'll call the Chicago police on the three old men back there. One of them, Torvaldson, sold his share, *sub rosa,* to Dr. Sterne, a year and a half ago. Then there's this Mrs. Cnut-Sorenson in Ross, and the Señora de Herrera in San Francisco. Lind, too. You didn't tackle him from that angle. Wonder what Truax got out of him."

"I'll wager not much," said Zanetti. "Do you want me to take on some of these people tonight?"

The sheriff considered as he entered the outskirts of San Rafael. "Well, suppose you drop around and see Mrs. Cnut-Sorenson. Six o'clock's as good a time as any to find her at home. I'll go over to San Francisco to see the Señora and look up a couple of other things. That nurse interests me."

"That's a good deal," said Zanetti. "It's a cinch we aren't going to find out anything from what the secretary left around. Nothing in the safe-deposit box but a few thousand dollars in bonds and a will leaving everything to the school. Bullard found nothing in her cottage. And when I went through her office desk there wasn't a bill or a scrap of private correspondence in it. Looks like her murder *must* have something to do with the school because she had no personal life at all."

"Don't you fool yourself!" said the sheriff.

As Zanetti turned an inquiring face toward him, they were interrupted by a voice from headquarters, "Calling all cars. Calling all cars—"

Over the radio came the description of Nils Berg, World War II veteran, born Columbus, Ohio, aged twenty-four, blond, blue-eyed, six feet two, weight 210, arthritis in right knee probably causing limp, wanted for questioning in Drake's Anchorage murder, suspected of assault and robbery at Stinson Beach, disappeared in vicinity of Drake's Anchorage early Thursday morning, probably wearing—

"Washington identified the prints, and they put Berg inside that cottage!" said the sheriff. "Where the hell *is* that fellow? I'll find him if I have to put the whole damned force on it!"

They had drawn up at the courthouse as the broadcast was being concluded. He dismissed Zanetti with a gesture and strode down the steps into the honeycomb of offices that made up his headquarters. He barked orders right and left, but got himself under control before he entered the room where MacDowell was waiting.

"Glad you turned up," he told him. The sheriff settled himself into the familiar lines of his own chair and prepared his pipe as a further solace while he summed up MacDowell. "Smoke?"

MacDowell grinned self-derisively.

"Lundberg," the sheriff spoke into his inter-office phone, "get me a couple of cups of coffee and a package of cigarettes—" He looked at MacDowell.

"Camels," said MacDowell.

"Camels—and some ham sandwiches," finished up the sheriff. While they waited for the coffee, the sheriff found out that MacDowell had first heard that Miss Breckenridge had been killed and that he himself was wanted for questioning from a regular news broadcast over the radio of a man who was camped next to him.

"Camping?" asked the sheriff.

"He was," said MacDowell. "I was just there."

He wolfed down his sandwich, and then seemed ready to talk over his coffee and cigarette.

Said the sheriff, "Tell me everything you remember about Wednesday night."

"I take it I may begin with when I picked up Miss Breckenridge on the coast road?"

"What were you doing before that?"

"Having dinner with a nice girl."

"Well, start with Miss Breckenridge for now."

"I've been trying to collect my memory of that night on the way up here. This is as near as I can recall it." MacDowell inhaled meditatively. "About eleven-thirty I bowled through Stinson Beach, and just north of it recognized Miss Breckenridge's Chevy. I slowed down enough to see that she was sitting in it, so I pulled up and walked back. I asked her if she was intending to spend the night there. She had a flat, but she wasn't doing anything about it. She'd have let me drive right on past. I've been thinking it's too bad I didn't."

"How did she seem? Worried? Angry?"

"No. That's what I was trying to bring out. You'd have thought she'd just stopped there to look at the moon in the lagoon, only there was no moon and the tide was out and she was surrounded by the stench of the mud flats.

"She snapped out of it, though, and took charge of me in her usual form. I had to jack up her car and take the wheel off and put it in my luggage compartment. While I was doing it, she told me to turn the wheel over to Walter before classes the next morning and to tell him to mend the tire and bring the car back to school before noon. When we started on, I asked her why noon—was she going to take the afternoon off? As she practically never left the place—even on weekends—I'd only asked her that to get a rise out of her, but she answered seriously. She said, 'If it comes to that, I will.' Naturally I asked, 'If what comes to what?'"

MacDowell paused dramatically, and shook his head impishly at the eager sheriff. "She never told me. Just then my headlights picked up a fellow walking along the road ahead of us. She said, 'There's that poor young man again. Stop beside him.' She took charge of him, too. She opened the door and said, 'Get in, young man.'

"From what I learned the next day, I can see that I didn't just imagine that he hesitated, but he didn't have a chance against her. From there up to where I dropped her at the head of her trail, she was arranging his life for him. He acted like a lost dog that's found a new home, but leery at the same time. He wouldn't tell her anything except that he was sick and broke and out of a job. She was going to fix that all up the next day, and he was to spend the rest of the night with me.

"Well, as I say, she took my flashlight and got out at the top of her trail—that was probably about twelve fifteen. She stood there and reminded both of us of the things she'd told us to do first thing in the morning, dismissed us from the presence with a satisfied nod—and disappeared—"

There was a suspicion of a break in MacDowell's voice. He lit another cigarette and avoided looking at the sheriff.

"Did she tell you where she'd been? How it happened— if it was her habit not to leave the school—that she was on that road in the middle of the night?

"She said she'd taken a walk and missed dinner at school, and driven down to Stinson Beach for something to eat."

"Where'd she eat?"

"I didn't ask her."

"Think back again. Was there nothing else she said? Did she tell you she'd been discharged?"

"No. I got that from Monsieur the next day. She acted as if she held the world in the hollow of her hand and was pleased with it. But first there was her tire, and then there was this man. I'm sure she didn't talk about anything else. I've tried to give you an impression of how she acted."

"Who do you think killed her? Have you any theory about why?"

MacDowell brought his hand down over his face and pulled at his chin. "I suppose you've heard about all that business of the Head?" The sheriff nodded. "Well, she was wearing his colors. I'd say, without anything to base it on, that she'd hit on some way to clear his name. She could have said to—" MacDowell thoroughly snubbed out a half-consumed cigarette. "Well, I hate like hell to say this, when I don't know where it leads, but the only thing I've been able to think of is that she must have found a boy who admitted having started the stories about the Head. She'd said, 'Confess, or else—I'll give you till noon tomorrow.' Something like that." He gestured impatiently. "But that's crazy! The boy would have had to be crazy to—" He had completely lost his earlier insouciance.

"About the rest of the night," the sheriff brought him back to his story. "Have you anything to add to what you told my deputy last Thursday concerning the man you picked up? What do you think happened to him?"

"I suppose he made off as soon as I went to sleep. I'd picked him up too near the place where he'd made the stick-up."

"We have evidence that's almost conclusive that he was inside Stone Cottage."

"The devil, you say! How do you know? Have you got hold of him?"

The sheriff told him of the identity of the prints on the window. "Yes, that's the same guy, all right," said Mac-Dowell wonderingly, "but if he went in there for anything, it was to get a pat on the head and be told he was a nice doggie."

"I suppose you give the boys a sort of general science course? Your room is very well stocked with chemicals."

"Oh, I tried to give them a taste of this and that. What are you up to with that question?"

"You keep ether there?"

"Naturally. Why?"

"Miss Breckenridge died from an overdose of ether. There is none now in your laboratory. In fact, a broken bottle from your laboratory, bearing only your finger-prints, was found in the bushes between the school and the cottage. Have you any idea how it got there?"

MacDowell gripped the edge of the sheriff's desk with fingers that whitened. "Very pretty," he said. "You feed a starving man, kill him with kindness, while you get his story—and all the time you have that up your sleeve."

When the sheriff made no immediate rejoinder, Mac-Dowell lit another cigarette with hands that trembled slightly, slid down in his chair, crossed his knees, and folded his arms. On his palish, high-strung face was the expression, "So what?"

The sheriff relented. "Well, don't go off the deep end. It could have been a plant, you know."

MacDowell regarded him suspiciously. "You were wait-ing for me to say that."

"So I was," agreed the sheriff. "Well, that'll be all for tonight, MacDowell. Don't go out of this county, but go somewhere and get some sleep. We'll talk some more to-morrow. Leave your address."

MacDowell's resentment evaporated as quickly as it had arisen, but he smiled ruefully as he stood up. "Address? Well—make it the Lind ranch on the Inverness road." He turned to go.

"Hold on a minute," said the sheriff. MacDowell waited with his hand on the doorknob. "What takes you way out there?"

"Food and a bed. Did you forget I'm broke?"

The sheriff looked hard at him for a moment longer. "O. K. Go ahead."

Zanetti nosed his patrol car through the long vista of moss-covered elms whose leaves made a sea-green tunnel of the avenue in summer. He had delivered papers along this beat. The boy of fifteen years before threatened to determine the psychological approach of the sheriff's deputy to a woman who dwelt within one of the rococo frame mansions which were set far back from the avenue behind grilled gates, stone pillars, and the shrubs of fifty years.

He was left standing in a broad dark hall by a noncommittal servant. After a five-minute interval, the servant returned to usher him into an equally broad and dark library. Mrs. Cnut-Sorenson was at home and would see him. The servant pulled heavy curtains across recessed windows, put a match to a fire already laid, flipped a switch that shed pools of reds and golds and peacock blues under half a dozen ornate standing lamps. Another five minutes passed.

Her evening dress was peacock blue, too. It rustled, and opalescent lights fountained from her ear lobes, wrist, and waistline, as she walked toward him past the lamps. When she sat down, the light revealed her face. Her eyes were not quite blue enough and her skin was not quite young enough for the peacock dress. She was a tense blonde.

"I have an engagement, but I have been expecting you to call." Her accent was what Zanetti called Bostonian. "Although I know nothing that can help you in your investigation of the death of the secretary at Drake's Anchorage, I shall be glad to give you the few minutes necessary for you to find that out for yourself."

"That is very good of you," said Zanetti. "Will you tell me the nature of your relation with the school? I understand you became connected with it through an inheritance. I'd like to have your description of that."

"That's very easily answered. My late husband's grandfather was one of its founders. He died early in 1945, and the fifth interest passed to my husband. When my husband was killed, it came to me."

"And you have been closely associated with the school since that time?"

"Not immediately. I was prostrated by my husband's death. Friends suggested that in the little children of Drake's Anchorage I might find an interest that would make life bearable. I have none of my own. I came here with that hope in— I think it was November of that year."

Mrs. Cnut-Sorenson folded her hands and lifted her head and on her lips appeared a tremulous smile. From the dexterity with which she fell into the stained-glass-window pose, Zanetti gathered that it was an attitude that she had frequently used with great effect.

"You must have been amply repaid," he said in a voice of veneration.

"Indeed yes," she breathed.

"And yet you have decided to sell the school."

His words shattered her trance. Her glance jerked to meet his, and there was a second before the fear that he read in it was transmuted to pain.

"You are unkind to remind me of that," she accused him.

"I'm sorry," he said humbly. "I suppose it is on account of the death of Miss Breckenridge?"

"Oh, no—no! She had nothing to do with it!"

"Then what has decided you to give up what means so much to you? The disgrace of the headmaster?"

She hesitated, and then bowed her head. Her fingers, still folded, pressed hollows in the backs of her hands.

"Yes," she whispered. Over her face stole a mantle of shame. Zanetti's calculations were thrown off by this manifestation of extreme sensibility. "I am forced to separate myself from it all."

He began on another tack.

"On the night Miss Breckenridge was killed, you were out at Drake's Anchorage. We are asking everyone who was at the school that night for a full account of his movements. Will you let me have that now, please? How did you happen to go there that evening?"

She made no objection to answering.

"It was at Monsieur Trougnac's request. A message reached me at my hairdresser's in the city that he wanted to see me on urgent business."

"Do you know at what time he called you?"

She looked surprised. "Why, I believe it was about two thirty."

"And did you go out immediately?"

"No. I wasn't free till four. And then—I—" Again she was troubled, and seemed to be weighing her words. "I went to see the father of the boy who—had been—wronged—by the headmaster."

"Then you went out to Drake's Anchorage?"

"Yes. I stopped for something to eat, and went on out."

"At what time did you arrive there?"

"I'm not sure. I imagine—about seven o'clock."

"You are speaking of the period now, Mrs. Cnut-Sorenson, that we have been reconstructing very carefully. We have the testimony of the staff at Drake's Anchorage. I'm asking for yours as further corroboration. I believe you arrived at seven ten. What did you do then?"

She wet her lips. "I was extremely upset by what Mr. Pidgeon had told me. I went to see the nurse, Miss Burtt. I was anxious about the—welfare—of the other boys."

"You still took this interest, even though you had decided to sell out?"

"I was not aware that there was an opportunity to sell the school until my conference with Monsieur Trougnac."

"Will you tell me about that conference, please?"

When she came to the place in her story where Monsieur Trougnac flung the door open to reveal the secretary in the passageway, Zanetti asked her to be detailed in her description of Miss Breckenridge.

"She was malevolently—gleeful," said Mrs. Cnut-Sorenson. "I thought her eyes weren't quite sane. She hardly seemed to hear Monsieur shouting at her. You would have thought it was we and not she who had been discovered in a compromising position. As she went away, her laughter sent chills down my back. Outside we heard the engine of her car roaring. When she backed away from the wall I wouldn't have been surprised if she'd plunged right off the cliff.

"Indeed, I think you are most likely to find that she was not murdered at all, but that in some wild gesture of insanity she did mischief to herself."

"That's an interesting theory," said Zanetti. "So then you concluded your business and went straight away from the school?"

"Yes, I was sorry to desert those who were not to blame. But I was simply too shocked and too disillusioned to continue with it. I said I would advise the other owners of the school to accept Señora de Herrera's offer and left immediately. I haven't been back since."

"Who are the other owners?"

"Mr. Lind himself is one of them. It is his disappearance that has kept us from completing the transaction. The others are the three founders who are still alive, Mr. Aakrog, Mr. Torvaldson, and Mr. Liljeborg."

The servant returned to the door of the library.

"Dr. Sterne is here, madam."

20

Mr. Weber: Mathematics

After the long week of severe cold, the air was softening and there was a feel of rain in the gusts of wind. Again and again, the tall eucalyptus trees in the grove that bordered the meadow around the Lind ranch house dipped lithely almost to the ground. Curling branches, with long bruised aromatic leaves, and curling fronds of bark whipped from the trees and slithered through the air to brush against the sides of the house. The headmaster of Drake's Anchorage and Mr. MacDowell sat in darkness in the kitchen, with their old-fashioned wooden chairs tipped back and their feet on top of the still-warm range. They smoked, listened to the sighing eucalyptus, and were themselves silent. Sheriff's Deputy Sugs, who had relieved his fellow deputy, Prentice, some three hours earlier, had accepted the hospitality of a couch in an adjoining room, but they did not know that he slept. In any case, now that Mr. MacDowell had told the headmaster what he knew of Miss Breckenridge's death, there did not seem to be anything else to say.

Drops of rain mixed with the potent wind and kissed the cheek of the man who stood at the edge of the meadow and looked longingly at the dark house. Nils Berg, washed back into these lonely reaches by the guilt of his act at Stinson Beach and the fear of what he had seen in Stone

Cottage, had been without food for one day and with-out shelter for two. The woods, strange and pregnant with storm, frightened him more than the knowledge that there were now three people in the house that when empty had been his refuge. He dodged the bowing eucalyptus, which seemed with each sway as if they must uproot themselves, and moved farther and farther out into the meadow. An alien dart of lightning escaped from the mountains, un-familiar thunder rumbled, and down from the breathless hush that followed poured the rain. With bent head he plodded to the back door, stealthily lifted the latch, and entered. Perhaps they were all asleep.

The headmaster gripped Mr. MacDowell's elbow when he would have moved, and they waited for the intruder to disclose his purpose. Nils, who could not see them, tip-toed awkwardly toward the cupboard where he had found the canned goods stored. His movements, and the breath-ing of the other two men, were inaudible under the rain which now beat madly upon the roof. Nils selected a can at random, found a can opener in a drawer, and moved with outstretched hand across the middle of the kitchen in search of one of the chairs he knew to be there. He tripped over Mr. MacDowell's foot. He got to the door before Mr. MacDowell caught up with him. He lunged away from Mr. MacDowell and fell so heavily back into the arms of the headmaster that both of them were carried to the floor.

"Halt!" yelled a sleepy and desperate Sugs from the opposite doorway. He hadn't been able to put his hands on his flashlight. "Stay where you are or I'll shoot! What's goin' on?"

"There's a lamp on that shelf beside you above the pump," the headmaster told him. "If you'll light up, we'll try to find out. Matches in the can beside it."

Sugs fumbled with a match and the wick. A flame first flared and then smoked up the chimney. When he had

the lamp adjusted, it disclosed Nils Berg stretched out
on the floor. The headmaster was sitting on his chest and
Mr. MacDowell on his ankles. Nils was offering no resis-
tance. The headmaster looked down into his pleading face
and seemed to find it droll. He removed himself from the
man's chest, picked up the can of artichoke hearts and the
can opener, and held them out to Nils.

"With the compliments of the house," he said gravely,
"Mac, get off the poor guy and let him enjoy his supper."

"My God," said Mr. MacDowell, "it's Nils Berg, the
Stinson Beach fellow!"

"Huh!" said Sugs.

Nils sat up and accepted the can. He looked indecisive-
ly back and forth between Mr. MacDowell and the artichoke hearts.

Mr. MacDowell was allowing himself to become excited.
"You can support my story! Why, you may even have the
dope on what happened to Miss Breckenridge! You were
there! The police know you were there. What happened?"

Nils got to his feet and backed against the wall. "I
didn't do it! I tell you I didn't do it! But they'll say I
did—" He turned toward the wall and hid his face on his
arm and blubbered. The other three men looked at each
other, almost equally embarrassed.

"Oh, hell!" said Mr. MacDowell. "I know you didn't do it."

"He's all in," said the headmaster. "We'll get a meal
down him. Build up the fire, er—Sugs. Mac, go out and
get more wood. I'm going to mix up some biscuits."

"It's raining."

"In the shed."

Mr. MacDowell turned up his collar and braved the elements. Sugs stuffed the stove with the kindling at hand.
Nils turned around and dumbly watched. The headmaster
spoke to him from over his flour and baking powder.

"You there, Berg! Pump up some water for me. And you might give yourself a wash while you're at it. Better open that draft, Sugs."

As if angry at having been so long pent up, the rain increased in pulsing spurts, each incredibly heavier than the one before it. Hail thudded down with the rain and shouted on the roof. In half an hour, they all fell to on coffee, fried Spam, biscuits, and molasses. Over a third cup of coffee, Nils Berg began to talk of his own accord.

He wiped his mouth with the back of his hand. "That's the best coffee I ever had in my life."

"Boiled," volunteered Sugs.

"Cigarette?" said Mr. MacDowell. He offered a flattened package. "Camaraderie of the trenches."

"I don't know who done that to the old lady," said Nils. "I wasn't even sure she was dead."

"Did what?" asked the headmaster.

"Tied a towel all wet with chloroform over her face. I took it off her, and I opened the windows and the door. I was going to carry her outside, but then I got scared she was already dead." He looked unhappily at Mr. MacDowell. "She'd been good to me. She was the first person who didn't say everything was my fault before I'd even opened my mouth. But I couldn't stay there like she said, I had done something bad she didn't know about." He reached inside his shirt and pulled out what appeared to be a soiled packet of paper napkins and handed it to Sugs. "Here's what I stole. It's all there. I ain't opened it up since. Was the old man—? Did he—?" He looked prayerfully at Sugs who was busy opening up the package.

Sugs was counting. It was a task that took his complete attention. "Thirty-one, thirty-two, thirty-three—" And then he was down to the silver. The headmaster and Mr. MacDowell realized that this was a business which must be completed before the story could go on. "Forty-one dollars and eighty-five cents. Six bits extra." He wrapped the bills and the coins back up in the napkins and straightened out his legs to insert the package in his hip pocket.

"An honest cop," observed Mr. MacDowell regretfully. "I think we might have split the six bits."

"He probably forgot to ring up one meal," Sugs explained to him. "No," he said to Nils. "Pop wasn't hurt, but he was out cold for two hours."

"If you come forward on your own with what you know about how Miss Breckenridge was killed, maybe they'll let you off easy," suggested Mr. MacDowell.

"I should think we could fix up something like that," said the headmaster.

"Well, I don't see—" Sugs began.

"After all, he's our prisoner, not yours," Mr. MacDowell reminded him.

"That's so," Sugs admitted uncertainly.

"Nils Berg, I hereby give you your freedom," declaimed Mr. MacDowell. "Walk out that door and come in again." Nils got trustfully to his feet.

"Here, now, not so fast!" said Sugs.

"I think we can dispense with the formalities," said the headmaster. "Sit down, Berg, and begin at the beginning of your story. What time did you go up to Stone Cottage?"

Nils subsided in his chair and massaged his knee as he strove earnestly to recall the events of Thursday morning. "I don't know. I'd been asleep. I think it was near morning, but it wasn't light yet. I woke up and I knew that soon they'd be looking for me. I found the door we'd come in by and when I got outside it I could hear the breakers right underneath me. I was scared I'd fall over. I held on to the cars and the wall until I got to the back side of the building. There was a trail there that went up. I thought it must be the one she'd gone down, so when I got to that little house I thought she must be in there. I wanted to

tell her all about what I'd done. I didn't know where to go.
I thought maybe she'd tell me what to do. After a while I
knocked—just a little knock, but the door opened by itself
and that awful smell came out. I said something but she
didn't answer and I was afraid to yell loud. I went in and
felt around and I found her on the bed and did like I said.
When I couldn't find her heart beating I thought it was
already too late and I'd better get away from there. Nobody would believe me how it happened. I remember now,
it was beginning to get light then and that's why I couldn't
wait to think what to do. She was dead then. Sure she was
dead then! Wasn't she?"

"I think you did the best you could, Berg," said the
headmaster. "It was probably too late to help her."

"If I hadn't picked her up," said Mr. MacDowell. "If I
hadn't just happened to come from Stinson Beach that night!"

With his elbows resting on the table and his chin in
his hands, the headmaster had been leaning forward, intent on Nils' story. For a moment after Mr. MacDowell's
exclamation he continued to sit without moving. Then he
shifted to press his clenched fists against his forehead, and
let out his breath in a slow sigh.

Mr. MacDowell stared incredulously at the bowed
shoulders of the Head and choked with thick anger against
the Judas who had brought him to that pass. "By God,"
he said, "we've got to find out who's behind all this! Look
here! If it was already getting light when Berg left, then
whoever moved the body must have been practically on his
heels. They wouldn't have dared do that after the rising
bell. Now how did they do it? The sheriff seems to think
it was taken out on a horse."

The headmaster looked up. "I'd have heard anyone getting up a horse. I was right over the tack room. But a car,
now— Don't I remember hearing— Berg! Did a car pass
you?"

"I got off the road when I saw headlights coming."

"But there *was* a car— On the school road? Before you got out to the coast road?"

"I think there was two—maybe three."

"Good lord!" said Mr. MacDowell. "One of those would be old Weber—coming home with the dawn! And he said—" He got to his feet and his chair clattered to the floor behind him. "Let's get out of here! We've got to see Weber."

"You got to stay here," said Sugs. "That's orders. The sheriff's coming in the morning."

"Not for me, it isn't," said Mr. MacDowell. "You couldn't have orders about me. You didn't know I'd be here when you came on duty."

"You think Weber knows?" said the headmaster.

"Of course he knows—if he's sober enough to know anything! He saw them, and the murderer is a man because Miss Breckenridge is the woman. My God!" he added, as the memory of Mr. Weber's phrase painted a macabre picture in his imagination.

With the prospect of action, the headmaster was himself again. "We'll all go together in MacDowell's car," he told Sugs, "and you can call your headquarters from Olema. The sheriff didn't know you'd have Berg for him. Sugs, Sugs! This is your big moment! Don't muff it!"

All of them except Nils were now on their feet. He remained clinging to the arms of his chair. "You said you wouldn't turn me in."

"Man, you're turning yourself in!" Mr. MacDowell clapped him on the back. "You're the guy that's solved the murder. Come on! This is your big moment, too."

They piled on top of each other in the little convertible and bumped and clattered down the uneven road through the storm. Out on the paved highway, Mr. MacDowell skidded around the turns. Hail was no longer falling but it was a scattered hazard on the wet macadam. At Olema, Sugs was so distrustful of the dozen feet that separated him from his charges, while he was in the phone booth, that his report to headquarters was not too coherent. Relayed to Zanetti, at home in bed, the message was that the whole Breckenridge case was breaking wide open and that the sheriff couldn't be contacted. At the corrals, Deputy Gleysteen held up the car. They could not go down to the school that night. Orders! There was argument back and forth. Gleysteen made the point that since Sugs had notified headquarters of the reappearance of Berg there was undoubtedly at that moment at least one squad car on the way out to the school. The thing to do was to wait for it. They went into the barn to get out of the rain, and Walter joined them.

"Walter, do you know whether the sheriff talked to Mr. Weber?" Mr. MacDowell asked him. "He didn't drink himself right out of the picture, did he?"

Gleysteen interrupted. "Weber? That's the fellow who came in a couple of hours ago. What about him?"

"Weber back before midnight on Saturday night?" exclaimed Walter. "Why, it's the son-of-a-gun's free weekend!"

"Was he sober?" the headmaster asked the deputy. "We think he can identify the murderer."

Gleysteen said, "He was half-seas over—and he had a bee in his bonnet."

They stared at each other and arrived together at the same conclusion.

"Sugs!" said Gleysteen. "Get down there fast and take charge of the guy before something happens to him. I'll keep your men."

"Sugs needs help. We'll all go. Come on, Mac," said the headmaster.

There was a concerted movement toward the car.

"You've gotta wait here!" said Gleysteen.

"Don't be a damned fool!" said the headmaster without stopping. "Sugs doesn't know anything about the place. Come on, Walter! Berg, you keep the deputy company."

While Sugs and Gleysteen hesitated, the three Drake's Anchorage men threw themselves into the car and it began to pull off.

"Don't get left behind, you lug!" said Gleysteen.

Sugs lunged for a grip on the car door and hoisted himself on the running board. Fortunately, there was a lull between showers.

At the school, the headmaster ordered Mr. MacDowell to drift to a stop without headlights before the Great Hall. "No use being any more conspicuous than necessary till we see whether anything's afoot. Don't use your flashlight, Sugs. Just follow me."

"Deputy Redlick's on patrol here somewhere," whispered Sugs as they crossed the Great Hall and turned toward the north courtyard.

"He'll probably find us before long," said the headmaster. "First thing is to see whether Mr. Weber's in his own rooms."

Walter sniffed. "What's that stink? There's a fire smoldering somewhere."

They quickened to a run down the passageway to Mr. Weber's rooms. Sugs flashed his torch. Trickling languorously from all around the frame of the study door were telltale wisps of smoke. Sugs stopped the headmaster who already had his hand on the doorknob. "Wait! Once you open that it'll blaze up. Whatcha got to fight fire with?"

"Right you are, Sugs! Walter, get the fire extinguisher by the infirmary. Mac, the science lab." As he spoke, the headmaster pulled one down from the wall by the washroom and readied it for action. He looked at Sugs. "Try it now?"

"If there's a man in there, we'll have to work fast. Can we get some wet cloths quick?"

"In here."

As the headmaster and Sugs came back out of the washroom with drenched handkerchiefs, Walter returned from one direction. From the other, came Mr. MacDowell, with Deputy Redlick in resonant pursuit. The doors of the curious were opening along the corridors through which they had sped.

"Here we go!" said Sugs and threw wide the, door of Mr. Weber's study.

A tidal wave of smoke and heat surged out. The group that had collected in front of the door fell back coughing. The headmaster and Sugs donned their masks.

"He's probably in bed in the next room," said the headmaster, "Hang on to me, Sugs!"

They stumbled across the smoke-filled study toward where the bedroom door should be. For a long second their progress was through murky dark. Then as they reached the open door the first rosy flares burst to illumine the objects in their course. In the time it took the men to fling themselves across the room, elfin flames sprang wickedly from the mattress of the bed, raced up a curtain beside it, tripped across a bureau scarf, dropped into a wastebasket, warmed and longing for their embraces. Sugs snatched a Navajo rug from the floor, and together they bundled it about the man who lay like a log on the bed that had become a pyre, and carried him out into the courtyard. Walter and Mr. MacDowell advanced into the room to fight the now-rioting flames.

Mr. Weber was unconscious but his pajamas had not caught fire, and the burning bedclothes they had dragged out with him had been smothered under the rug. "Stick by him, Sugs," said the headmaster. "Let the onlookers think a cigarette was the start of this—and maybe it was. But don't take any chances."

The pungent smoke was being dissipated in the court-yard by the now-gentle rain, but its odor, and the shouts of the rescuers and their audience, had aroused a good two-thirds of the school. Monsieur Trougnac and Mr. Arbuthnot, who were among the earlier bath-robed figures to arrive, stood gaping. When Mr. Pyke came, he assisted Sugs, under Miss Burtt's direction, to carry Mr. Weber into the infirmary. Mr. Dingle, having taken time even at this hour to comb his hair, was the last to appear. Monsieur Trougnac collected himself sufficiently to give him, with Mr. Arbuthnot, the task of corralling the excited boys back into their rooms. Deputy Redlick, torn fifty ways a minute, was just making for the patrol car that he had parked outside the infirmary to beseech headquarters for assistance when Zanetti rolled up, with another deputy, as if in answer to his yet unspoken prayers. Redlick thankfully turned over to Zanetti the authority that he had not had time to assume.

As the fire was now extinguished, Zanetti ordered everyone out of Mr. Weber's rooms and posted Deputy Shinn at the door.

"Where's Miss Blossom?" he asked Redlick next.

Redlick looked worried. "She must still be in bed."

"Well, get over there quick and find out. Bring her to the Common Room. I want to see all the adults in the Common Room. Get one of the faculty— Get Mr. Pyke to help you round the rest of them up. Find that parent and get her up, too."

Zanetti went to see how Mr. Weber fared.

21

Peter Van Tassel: Golden Boy

Zanetti's brief inspection of Mr. Weber and his more prolonged one of Mr. Weber's ravished bedroom left him morose. He'd kept them waiting fifteen minutes in the Common Room and he still hadn't found anything suggestive in the debris that he could question them about. Redlick, in the south courtyard near Miss Blossom's door, had seen and heard nothing until Mr. MacDowell had come charging into the science room. From then on, both he and Sugs had been too much the actors in the drama to observe. Mr. Weber had undoubtedly been drinking. He was a smoker. But Gleysteen had said that Lind and MacDowell believed that he could identify the murderer. If they had not come to look for him, before morning Weber must inevitably have succumbed to the fire gathering force beneath him.

When Zanetti entered the Common Room he was still undecided what course to follow. If one among them was so desperate as to have set that trap for Mr. Weber, could he risk sending them all back to bed to wait for the morning, the sheriff, and Mr. Weber's testimony? A pall of silence constrained the group, shepherded by Deputy Redlick. To Zanetti they all appeared rather wearied than fearful. He vented his dissatisfaction upon Monsieur Trougnac.

"I thought you said Mr. Weber wouldn't be back until tomorrow night."

"That is when I expected him," said Monsieur Trougnac.

The headmaster spoke. "How *is* Mr. Weber?"

During this interchange, Zanetti realized that his first impression had been wrong. There was tension in the room, but its source was not so much concern for the fate of Mr. Weber as awareness of the presence of the headmaster. There was a knock on the door. Redlick opened it and went out to confer in the passageway. In a moment he stuck his head around the door to say doubtfully, "There's a boy here says his names Van and that it's very important for him to talk to the headmaster."

Monsieur Trougnac spoke. "Let him return at once to his room!"

Zanetti remembered the sheriff's hunch. "Bring him in!" His pulse leapt when he saw the boy. He was immediately certain that this was the one who had caught the attention of both Milton and the sheriff.

The headmaster came forward. "What is it, Van?"

Monsieur moved as if to intervene. "You have not the right—" he floundered.

The boy disregarded Monsieur and addressed the headmaster with Spartan directness. "After I told you about Miss Breckenridge, last night, you didn't stay for my report, sir."

The headmaster said neutrally to Zanetti, "Van's investigations cover the period in which you are interested."

"I'd like to hear his report," said Zanetti.

"Let's have it, Van."

"Everything? In front of everybody?"

"I prefer it that way. And I think you haven't anything to say that would make you feel ashamed."

"No, sir."

"Begin at the beginning. Let the chips fall where they will."

"Yes, sir." The boy seemed able to forget the others in the dimly lit room. "Last Tuesday I began asking first one and then another of the fellows whether he had any bad sex habits. If a fellow looked uneasy, I'd ask him if—he'd had anything to do with you!" Van got the odious implication out with a rush. "That's what you *said,* sir!"

"Yes, I know, Van," the headmaster reassured him.

"This is abomination," said Monsieur Trougnac. "Van, I command you to stop!"

"Don't interrupt," said Zanetti.

Van ignored both of them and continued. As he progressed with his story, he spoke more and more naturally, and without faltering.

"Well, half of them, that is, half of those I asked—I left out the kids the way you said—half of them looked as if they thought I was out of my head, but thirteen of them had heard that there was a story about you and some other fellow. Only one of them wouldn't talk at all. That was Nathaniel Vaughan. I didn't handle him right, sir. He had hysterics, and Neil got the nurse, and she shut him up in the infirmary and wouldn't let me see him.

"But I went on with the other fellows till I found out that they'd all either got the story from Wyman Gould or Clarence Pidgeon or from some fellow who turned out to have heard it from one of those two. Pudge wasn't here, so I concentrated on Wyman. That is, Neil was already concentrating on him after something he'd said. I hung around till Neil had him down. While Neil—er—twisted his arm, I got his confession. It was the only way, sir!"

"Um. You think that under those circumstances Wyman would tell the truth?"

"Oh yes, sir! He'd given up, you know. He'd have to tell the truth after that."

"Um. *I* know, but— Well, we'll take that point up another time. Go ahead with your story."

"Wyman said he'd got the idea from the nurse and given it to Pudge and that so far as he knew that was the whole start of it. He said the way she hated you scared him, and he wished he'd never helped her spread anything about you."

"Miss Burtt!" exclaimed the headmaster. "Weber—" He started for the door.

"Sugs is with him," said Zanetti. "He's got his orders."

"Good old Sugs," said the headmaster. "But the nurse! Good God, what—" The headmaster looked as if he were having to revise a great many ideas. He sat down on the floor with his back to the fire, hung his elbows over his raised knees, and looked up at Van. "All right. What next?"

"Wyman promised that if we'd let him up, he'd tell me the whole thing after lights out. Mr. Arbuthnot was trying to get into the washroom, so we thought we'd better.

"That night, Wyman told me how it all started.

"Last fall he was in dutch a lot. One afternoon you told him to stay at the woodpile until he'd filled a box with kindling. He sat there till after dark and after it had begun to rain and you didn't miss him until dinner. You were mad, and you brought him in and had the nurse dope him up and put him to bed. Wyman was mad too, and that's when she began to talk to him—some then and more later. She told him he'd won a moral victory. She said that you were a tyrant and liked to get boys in your power, and that because he was strong he must stand up against you. I found out Friday she'd said the same things to Fitz after you gave him—after he got that black eye. And Wyman told Pudge, and Pudge talked to her, too. Pudge told Wyman he'd asked the nurse what made Nat different from the other fellows and that the nurse had said that it was because you got him off alone and scared him.

"Wyman said that was how Pudge got an idea what to tell his father so he wouldn't have to come back. Wyman said he was afraid of the nurse and he bet she'd scared Nat more than you ever had. He wanted to help get you back. I told him to keep mum until you'd said what to do, and as soon as he'd left I went up to the barn—but you weren't there. Walter wouldn't say anything except to wait till the next day. That was Thursday night, and Friday—we found Miss Breckenridge.

"I thought for sure you'd be at the barn when we got back, and you'd said not to do anything, so when Miss Blossom wouldn't promise to wait we had to tie her up. But you *weren't* there, and Miss Blossom got back anyway— and still you hadn't come—so we—put one of Nat's pills in her soup." Van paused, and for the first time dropped his eyes. "Maybe that wasn't a good idea."

"No, that wasn't very sound. I had told you not to try to do anything when you found out who was responsible for the story about me. What made you think that Miss Breckenridge's death had anything to do with that?"

Van looked up. "Oh, but I'm sure it *did,* sir! I haven't told you yet what Nat said when he got out of the infirmary Wednesday night."

"Wednesday night!" said Zanetti. "Tell us everything you know about Wednesday night."

Van glanced at him and then turned back to the headmaster. "Well, it was very late when he came and waked me up. His teeth were chattering. He told me the nurse was going crazy. He said she was afraid. He said that when people got very afraid they went crazy. I asked him what Miss Burtt had to be scared of, but before he'd talk about that he said he wanted to answer the question I'd asked him." Van hesitated, and doubt colored his voice. "This is personal, sir."

"It all is," the headmaster agreed with him. "But sometimes we have to talk about personal things in order to clear the atmosphere. Just be straightforward about it."

"Yes, sir. He said he had a habit he was ashamed of."

"Miséricorde!" moaned Monsieur Trougnac. No one else in the room stirred. The boy and the headmaster had eyes only for each other.

"—and that he knew it was wrong, and that he couldn't help it. He'd been told he would go crazy. I told him that was crazy, that I'd been in the same trouble myself, and you had told me not to worry myself sick about it, that after a while it would pass, and that you were right because it had."

"Insensé!" The whisper was despairing.

"That calmed him down. He said that was just what you'd said to him. That kid had been so frightened that he had hysterics when he had only that to conceal!" Van's voice was angry. "It was the nurse who did that to him! After you'd had him in your study talking to him, you'd taken him to the nurse for some pills to take when he couldn't sleep. And after that she would never let him alone!

"I still thought then that he was imagining part of it, for he said that she'd made him a prisoner in the infirmary. I asked him why he hadn't just walked out. He said that at first he'd been too sick and too scared, but that he'd made up his mind he couldn't keep still and let people think what wasn't true about the Head, and that during study hour he'd begun to try.

"The nurse was in the dispensary. He waited in the hall for her to go into her living room so that he could go by the dispensary door. But, he said, Mrs. Cnut-Sorenson came into the hall, and he had to duck into the living room himself. And this is where it ties in, sir. While Mrs. Cnut-Sorenson was talking, Nat looked out into the hall. Miss Breckenridge was out there, listening too. After Mrs. Cnut-Sorenson went away, Miss Breckenridge went in. It was what Miss Breckenridge said that scared Miss Burtt.

That he had overheard it scared Nat so much that he went back and got in bed and pretended to be asleep. And Miss Burtt even came back and looked to see if he was!"

"Let's have this Nat in here, next," said Zanetti, "I want this as straight as I can get it." In his eagerness, he was already opening the door.

"Oh, don't do that to him!" Mr. Arbuthnot's voice broke impulsively from the shadows in the back of the room.

"No," said the headmaster. "We won't do that. He's not ready for it. You'll have to take what you can get from Van."

As Zanetti turned back to look at the speakers, a car swung around the driveway outside the Common Room. Its headlights threw into brief relief the tense faces of Mr. Dingle, Mr. Arbuthnot and Monsieur Trougnac at the front window, and then the more stolid ones of Mr. Pyke and Walter, who were leaning against the wall by the side window. Mrs. Maxwell was at one end of the couch and Miss Blossom at the other. Mr. MacDowell was reclining in the exact center of it. The car drew up in the parking area, and Zanetti went down the passageway to the outer door.

"Dr. Sterne," those left in the room heard him say, "who is that sitting in your car?"

"A friend of mine," came the doctor's voice. "We were just starting home from an evening in Inverness when I got this call. I understand old Mr. Weber went to sleep and set his bed on fire. You haven't had any other trouble, have you?"

"That's Mrs. Cnut-Sorenson," said Zanetti peremptorily. "I want both of you to come into the Common Room."

If Dr. Sterne took exception to Zanetti's manner, he made it known only by remaining silent. There was the crunch of footsteps on gravel, and a moment later Zanetti led the two of them in. Mr. MacDowell gave Mrs. Cnut-Sorenson his place on the couch. The doctor did not accept his invitation to share the chimney seat, but remained standing near the door.

"I want to cooperate, of course, Deputy," the doctor said, "but I'd be easier if you'd allow me to look at my patient first."

"He's all right," said Zanetti callously. "Just smoked, not fried."

"But I'm afraid I don't understand," said Mrs. Cnut-Sorenson. "Wasn't the fire simply a case of drunken carelessness? Do you think it has anything to do with the death of Miss Breckenridge?" She caught sight of Van, who had retreated to the seat on the other side of the chimney. "Merciful heavens! What's that child doing in here? Monsieur!" She searched the dark side of the room. It was the headmaster, not Monsieur Trougnac, who came forward to answer her. Her displeasure subsided in a gasp of consternation. "Alrik! You here?"

"Yes, I'm here." The headmaster spoke with repressed anger. "And this—child—has been telling us of a talk that you had with the nurse that you have evidently withheld from the police."

A deep blush first stained Mrs. Cnut-Sorenson's face and she lowered her head. "I'm—sorry. I couldn't—I—" Then she raised her eyes to meet those of the doctor. "Oh, no!" Fear and revulsion came to dominate her expression, and the color drained from her cheeks until the rouge stood out on them when she turned back to the headmaster. "You mean—you *can't* mean—"

"Hold it," said Zanetti. "I'll take over now." He spoke to the deputy at the door. "Redlick! Bring the nurse in here, too."

The doctor wet his lips. "The patient—"

"Will do all right without her," Zanetti brusquely finished his sentence for him.

While they waited, Monsieur ventured, "I think Van shall go away now."

"Please, sir," said Van to the headmaster.

The headmaster and Zanetti looked at each other. "Stay," said Zanetti.

Redlick returned with Miss Burtt.

"Can not this inquiry be put off until tomorrow?" said Miss Burtt as she entered. Then the wave of concentrated hostility that her arrival aroused hit her like a physical force, even though three-quarters of the faces turned toward her were in shadow. She started to raise a hand to her throat, controlled it, and dropped it again at her side. But she was not quick enough to restrain the one startled glance that she threw at the doctor's averted face.

"Sit here, Miss Burtt," said Zanetti. He put her in the straight chair that Miss Breckenridge had always used at the tea-table. "And Doctor, here." He brought another chair forward so that when the doctor sat the light from the lamp beside the couch would fall also on his face. "Redlick, call headquarters."

Zanetti took a stand on the hearth with his hands hanging easily at his sides. He did not speak again till Redlick reappeared in the doorway. They exchanged a glance which seemed to make things clear to both of them, and then Zanetti addressed Mrs. Cnut-Sorenson.

"When I asked you a few hours ago about your movements on Friday evening, you told me that you had seen the nurse before you met your appointment with Monsieur Trougnac. Your statement was that the business between you 'concerned the welfare of the boys.' There were two witnesses to your talk. Miss Breckenridge listened not only to your conversation with Monsieur Trougnac but also to what passed between you and Miss Burtt. The other listener—" He allowed his glance to indicate Van. "The other—was one of the boys."

"Mrs. Cnut-Sorenson, we're waiting to be told by you what it was that Miss Breckenridge overheard. We have also the boy's testimony, but I'm giving you this opportunity to complete yours."

Mrs. Cnut-Sorenson gazed forlornly at Dr. Sterne's profile. He sat unmoving, arms folded, looking up at Zanetti with what appeared to be a receptive air. A small muscle in his temple pulsed as he alternately clenched and relaxed his jaw.

22

Alrik Lind: Headmaster

"I shall have to go back a little," said Mrs. Cnut-Sorenson. Zanetti nodded.

"In the afternoon, I saw not only Mr. Pidgeon but also his son. Mr. Pidgeon told me how the committee of parents who demanded Mr. Lind's immediate removal had been formed. He said that when he first arrived and questioned his son the boy was very upset. Clarence told him that he was not the only one with whom the headmaster had had improper relations, but he would not divulge any names except to say that another boy, Wyman Gould, would back up his story. Several of the parents were in the city that afternoon, bringing their boys back from the vacation. Among them were the Goulds. Mr. Pidgeon got in touch with Mr. Gould. Mr. Gould's son did not deny the story, although he said that he was not one of the boys who had been involved. His attitude seemed to them to confirm it. Mr. Gould called together the other parents. Mr. Pidgeon consented to the use of his son's name in the accusation that they decided to make, but only on the condition that he was not to be further interrogated.

"Since that time, Clarence had been confined to his room in the hotel, and during the two days that had elapsed his parents had been unable to get him to say more even to them. Mr. and Mrs. Pidgeon had quarreled.

Mr. Pidgeon was worried. I persuaded him to let me see his son—alone."

Mrs. Cnut-Sorenson's coolly factual attitude deserted her. Her bleak face revealed that what she must say next would be more difficult. Zanetti encouraged her.

"And he found you more sympathetic? He could talk to you?"

She took his cue gratefully. "He threw himself on my mercy," said Mrs. Cnut-Sorenson. "He poured it all out to me. He was afraid to tell his father his real reasons for not wanting to go back to school, and he was afraid not to.

"They all stemmed from the fact that he was overweight. He had been denied bread and potatoes and dessert and made to dig trail every day. That was all that he had against the school and against the headmaster.

"When I asked him what had induced him to say this other thing about himself if it wasn't true, he said it had just popped into his head after he had put in his long-distance call to his father. It was the most drastic reason he could think of; he hadn't realized it would have such disastrous consequences. He said—that the school nurse—had given him the impression that such relationships between the headmaster and his pupils were quite common."

"The little liar!" hissed Miss Burtt. "I'll sue! I'll sue for libel! I don't *believe* he said that." She turned arrogantly to the doctor. "Dr. Sterne, you know my character. Are you going to allow this woman to assail my professional integrity? You know better!"

Dr. Sterne spoke authoritatively to Zanetti. "It is extremely unwise for laymen to discuss matters of this kind. I suggest that you abandon this line of inquiry and send a competent alienist to attend the boy." He stood up and walked over to the couch. "With your permission, I shall take Mrs. Cnut-Sorenson home. In fact, as her physician, I insist on doing so."

"No, no!" said Mrs. Cnut-Sorenson. "Don't let him— Don't *touch* me!"

The doctor rested his hand on the back of the couch instead of on her shoulder but he continued to bend over her and his voice for her was tender.

"Luella, my dear, you are not yourself. And you don't understand what you're getting yourself into. Trust me. Come now, let me take you home."

Her palms were flattened on the seat on either side of her and she shrank stiffly away from his arm. "Don't— don't. Go away! Oh God, I tried not to see—not to believe!"

"Take your seat, Doctor," said Zanetti. "What was it you tried not to believe, Mrs. Cnut-Sorenson?"

Dr. Sterne looked toward the door, met Redlick's blank stare, thought better of it, and went back to his chair. "I remain under protest," he said, "and I shall make sure that your superior officer hears of your rash indiscretion."

Mrs. Cnut-Sorenson had relaxed and closed her eyes as soon as the doctor moved away from her. Now she raised her head to continue with a determination that lifted her above concern for how she might appear to others.

"In order to explain— In order to make comprehensible—Dr. Sterne and I were planning to be married," she concluded flatly.

"I went to the nurse intending to force her to clear the headmaster by threatening to insist, if she did not, that Dr. Sterne reveal what he knew about her. He had told me, I suppose for his own protection, that her name had been removed from the San Francisco Nurses' Registry and that a serious charge against her had been suppressed upon her agreement that she would quit the practice of nursing. He had said that he believed her to be thoroughly competent for the position at Drake's Anchorage and led me to agree with him that it would be a kindness to hire her.

"When I accused the nurse of maliciously misleading the boys, she did not deny it, but she laughed at the suggestion that Dr. Sterne would take any action against her. She said that he would never do that because he had more reason to conceal whatever it was that had happened than she had."

Miss Burtt broke in again. "She's twisting my words. I never said that. I couldn't help that other accident, and I had nothing to do with what happened here. Once more I am being persecuted for being ill. I have tried to rise above my handicap, to continue to be self-supporting in the work for which I am trained. But the odds are too great. I feel myself breaking!" Her movements became jerky and her eyes wide and staring. "I look strong, but I am not strong. I think—" She got dizzily to her feet. "I think I had better— Look at me! Look at me, all of you who are hounding me! This is what Mrs. Cnut-Sorenson did to me on Wednesday night, and you know what happened after that." She laughed wildly. "How could I have had anything to do with the death of Miss Breckenridge while I lay prostrated by an almost fatal insulin reaction?"

"By god!" Mr. MacDowell sat up and thumped the seat beside him. "You've overreached yourself! You should never have brought that up!"

Miss Burtt staggered toward the door, and a low animal moan rose in her throat. Redlick reached out an arm to support her.

"Don't let her pull that again," said Mr. MacDowell relentlessly. "She's acting. She was acting the other night!"

Dr. Sterne had reached Miss Burtt's side and was starting to open the door. "Young man," he said, "you don't know anything about this. Haste is imperative. Let us pass quickly." Miss Burtt sagged against him.

"But it happens that I do. I had enough medical training before the war to know when a normal person is

shamming a faint." Mr. MacDowell got to his feet and ges-
ticulated. "Why, the whole damned thing is as simple as
the nose on your face! She'd stopped Mrs. Cnut-Sorenson
from talking, but Miss Breckenridge had overheard—and
nothing was going to stop her. Van, what was it she said
that scared Miss Burtt?"

"That if the nurse hadn't told the parents she'd lied
by noon of the next day Miss Breckenridge would tell the
police she thought Miss Burtt and Dr. Sterne had killed
somebody!"

"So," continued Mr. MacDowell, "Miss Burtt fixed herself an alibi and killed Miss Breckenridge! Then she remembered that Miss Breckenridge had been told to get
out. When Dr. Sterne came, she told him that if he could
get rid of the body there was a chance that no one would
ever know what had happened to her. *Don't let them out
that door!*"

Redlick pulled Miss Burtt back and slammed the door.
She sank to the floor and Dr. Sterne bent over her, his
hand on her pulse. He pushed up one of her eyelids with
his finger. "You incompetent young pup!" he exclaimed
furiously. "This whole place is psychopathic. You are
endangering a life while you fabricate your wild hypothe-
ses. If you won't let me out, Deputy, you must go and get
some sugar and a cup of water!"

Miss Blossom moved impulsively. "You'd better let me.
But—" She sat again on the arm of the couch and spoke
challengingly to the doctor's back. "I don't know what
makes you so frantic. You certainly weren't when I called
you up the other night. And you said you'd come out early.
You wanted me to tell her that. Remember? What time *did*
you come? I waited around, but after eight o'clock I never
saw you!"

"That's my girl," Mr. MacDowell commended her. "You
didn't see him because he came before we were up. He

knew that insulin shock was a phony! But Mr. Weber saw him! Mr. Weber saw him with the body of Miss Breckenridge leaning against him in his car. Running into Mr. Weber unnerved him so much that he dumped the body up the first side road he came to. Tonight, Miss Burtt was making sure that Mr. Weber would never again be sober enough to remember!"

The doctor spoke savagely to Zanetti. "If you prevent me from attending this desperately ill woman on the strength of these libelously unsupported accusations, I swear it will cost you your job."

The headlights of another car rounding the corner of the school threw the tableau into brief chiaroscuro. Zanetti delayed his reply while the car parked and its occupants approached. The sheriff and two more deputies pushed the door open as far as it would go and stepped over the body of Miss Burtt.

"What's the matter with *her?*" asked the sheriff.

"I'm not sure there's anything the matter," said Zanetti.

Mr. MacDowell walked over to the nurse and submitted her to the same tests the doctor had made. He looked confidently at the sheriff. "There's not a damned thing the matter with her."

"Good," said the sheriff. "Michael Sterne and Margaret Burtt, I arrest you for the murder of Mrs. Winifred Tewksbury in Sausalito on June 8, 1945."

"It's a lie! You can't prove it," said Miss Burtt from the floor.

"And I must warn you that anything you say may be used against you."

Dr. Sterne, clinging for support to the back of a chair, was silent.

"Go ahead, Jameson, Buchholtz," said the sheriff dryly.

The deputies who had accompanied him slipped handcuffs over the wrists of Dr. Sterne and Miss Burtt. Redlick assisted Jameson in getting Miss Burtt to her feet, and leading her from the room. As Buchholtz and Zanetti were about to follow with the doctor, Mr. Weber, with Sugs in attendance, blocked the doorway. Mr. Weber was smudged, bleary-eyed and reproachful.

"What's this commotion? Can't a man sleep?" When he saw the doctor, he rocked with surprise and clutched Zanetti's arm affectionately. "Coincidence! That's what it is! I've been looking and looking for you. See this fellow here? He—He—" Mr. Weber's elation dimmed as he searched for an elusive memory. "I have something to tell you about him—" Frustration threatened tears.

"O.K., O.K., guy," said Zanetti soothingly. "You tell me all about it tomorrow. I'll help you back to bed now."

The congestion of figures removed itself from the doorway. The sheriff looked around the room at the others. "The rest of you may as well follow his example," he told them. "Tomorrow will be time enough to begin clearing up what those two were doing around here."

"That's a good suggestion," said the headmaster. "Van!" He held his hand out to the boy. "You did a fine job."

Van grasped it proudly. "Thank you, sir."

"And so to bed," said the headmaster.

"Yes, sir. Good night, sir."

The headmaster turned to the sheriff. "About Nils Berg. Your man Sugs will tell you that it was his cooperation that brought us over here in time to save Mr. Weber. Don't you think you can get the charges on that other business waived? He's returned the money. I'll put him to work."

"I'll see what I can do about it," said the sheriff.

"Let him bunk with Huggins. Walter'll guarantee to produce him when you're ready for him."

The sheriff pulled his ear. "It's not— Well, all right. I'll leave it like that for the night anyway."

"Sheriff, please—" It was Mrs. Cnut-Sorenson who spoke. "I don't understand—What happened to Mrs. Tewksbury?"

"Yes," said Mr. MacDowell. "You stole our climax. What's it all about?"

"Mrs. Tewksbury," the sheriff told them, "is said to have died for lack of attention during a heart attack. A servant discovered Mrs. Tewksbury's nurse, Miss Burtt, lying beside the body in insulin shock, and called her doctor, Dr. Sterne. Professional etiquette kept the episode from the attention of the police, and there were no near relatives to contest the will which left the bulk of her money to Dr. Sterne."

"Do you have a case there?" inquired Mr. MacDowell.

The sheriff smiled. "Well, I had enough to obtain warrants for their arrest. I understood that was what my deputies wanted me to turn up here with. When they go on trial, it'll be for the murder of Miss Breckenridge."

"What started you on that trail?" Mr. MacDowell was still curious.

"I was looking for the source of the money that enabled Dr. Sterne to buy a share of this school just six weeks after Mrs. Tewksbury died."

Dr. Sterne owned a share?" Mrs. Cnut-Sorenson questioned the headmaster.

"Yes," he said. "Torvaldson wanted it kept quiet on account of the other old gents. I knew that. And—so did Miss Breckenridge. That's probably what made her so confident that she had a strong club to hold over the nurse."

The sheriff looked at the headmaster. "I'm surprised you didn't see sooner what he was after. He was out to get control of the whole school property, It's a pretty profitable investment, isn't it?"

"Well yes, I guess it is," said the headmaster. "But I was more aware of another sort of— Oh well, skip that."

"But good lord," said Mr. MacDowell. "You wouldn't expect a fellow to go around murdering people in order to make a profitable investment!"

"It has been done," said the sheriff. "In the case of Mrs. Tewksbury, I imagine Dr. Sterne persuaded Miss Burtt to hurry along what he knew would happen anyway in the course of a few years by offering her part of his inheritance. Then he took advantage of a sudden opportunity to invest the whole thing in the school without consulting her. To keep her quiet, he brought her here and suggested that she could speed things up by undermining the headmaster. The way he'd taken hold of the school had made the picture less rosy. Her anger led her to go at her assignment too enthusiastically."

"I want to go home," said Mrs. Cnut-Sorenson. She was shivering from shock.

The sheriff assisted her to rise. "You came with Dr. Sterne? I'll have one of my men drive you into town."

"You look as if you needed to go back to bed too, Miss Blossom," said Mr. MacDowell. "How many times have you been knocked out in the last twenty-four hours? Walter was telling me, but I didn't count. Come on, I'll lead you."

"I've lost count too," said Miss Blossom, allowing herself to be helped down from the arm of the couch on which she had been perched.

With brotherly familiarity, Mr. MacDowell pushed her hair which she had been too dopey to rebraid out of her eyes. "You could pose as Lady Godiva. What is your first name, by the way?"

"Meredith. What's yours?"

Mr. MacDowell's voice floated back from the passageway. "Only the sheriff knows, and he's too big a man to tattle. You can call me Mac."

Monsieur Trougnac came out of his seclusion to stand before the headmaster. "I am much relieved," he said, and

held out his hand. The headmaster accepted it, and also
that of Mr. Dingle who had followed him. "And so am I,"
said Mr. Dingle. They both really felt that way; it had
been an upsetting week.

Mr. Pyke was released by their departure. He kicked
a footstool out of his way to rush forward and whack the
headmaster on the back. Walter closed in on the other side
with a *sotto voce* whoop left over from roundup days. The
three men, all over six feet, stood with their hands on each
other's shoulders and made Mrs. Maxwell feel maternal.

"You old polecat," said Walter. "Come up to the barn
and have a drink."

Mr. Pyke's countenance lit up still more broadly. "It's
Saturday night! What do you say, you lucky son of a bitch?"

The headmaster shook his head. "Make it next Saturday. I've got a couple of things—" His eye fell on Mr.
Arbuthnot who was hovering shyly behind Walter, waiting
his turn. "Take Arbuthnot with you. He'd love it."

"Why sure!" exclaimed Mr. Pyke. "What say, Ferdie?
Come on, Walter!"

With perfect timing, he and Walter tossed the depre-
cating and ecstatic Mr. Arbuthnot high in the air, made
him a queen's chair, and rushed him from the room. "I
say— Oh, look here! I say, fellows!"

There remained to congratulate the headmaster only
Mrs. Maxwell. She rose from the couch. Her cerise dressing gown covered her to the chin and fell in soft folds.
Her dark short hair curled back from her pale face, and
her dark eyes were wide with adoration. Her fingers were
locked across her breast. The discourse that flowed between them was not on the plane of speech.

"You'd better phone Lars Aakrog," she broke the silence
to remind him. "Did anyone tell you I have a telegram for
you?"

"Yes, I must. No, they didn't." The headmaster was a trifle incoherent while he strove to subdue an earthy impulse. "What did he say?" he managed to ask at last.

"It's in my room. I'll get it."

"I'll come with you." She felt his hand under her arm, and through it drank gladly of the reality of his presence. "No," he said, "not that way. Out here. It's not raining now."

They went out the north gate rather than through the courtyards. The sheriff and his men were backing and turning their cars on the edge of the cliff. As they walked away from the confusion along the seaward wall of the school, the headmaster said, "I've never liked the location of that parking space. The roof of the lean-to cuts off light from the infirmary in the daytime, and the headlights are bad at night." They took a few more steps. "That's it! There's a level place behind the woodshed." They considered this in silence. "There'd be a longer walk between it and the gate. The masters wouldn't like that." Then he decided. "But that's the place for it. I'll *make* 'em like it!"

He was as he had always been! She shivered with delight. He halted abruptly.

"Are you cold? This is a good night. The smell of rain clears the head after that roomful of smokers."

"No, no, you idiot!" She swung around in front of him and felt the muscles of his upper arms tighten under his light windbreaker as she laid the palms of her hands around them. He was back again! He was here—as adorably bullheaded and blind as ever.

"Frances," he whispered. His hands found her waist and encircled it. "You *don't* have much on," he tried to say matter-of-factly. The pressure of his fingers slid the robe over the satin gown beneath it, and with that sensation his grasp tightened. "Frances!"

She laughed at his discomposure. "Are *you* cold?"

"Frances! I don't think I ought— Next summer—" He lifted her off the ground and kissed the lips that were laughing at him.

The anger with which he set her down made her feel very sure of herself. "What better time than now?" she asked. "The headmaster needs a wife!"

"My God, I know! That's the trouble. I've been meaning to ask you for a year, and then to get around to it at a time like this!"

He looked down at her accusingly. The welcome in her attitude won out. He lifted her again and pressed his face against her breast. She rested her cheek on his hair contentedly. "You didn't need me before," she excused him softly.

The tide was at its ebb and the lazy waves were sighing back into the deep Pacific. The breeze was toying with the hem of her robe and moisture was settling in fine globules on her hair. There was no demarcation between her feeling of peace and the elements of the night. A mist wraith swayed at the end of the terrace and moved her to add, "You had Miss Breckenridge to look after you. I wonder whether I'll be able to live up to her."

He set her down again, the better to tell her the ways in which she was an improvement upon Miss Breckenridge. But before he spoke, he was arrested by a memory. A voice, in tones he had never before heard in it, had spoken his name with an intimacy born of long usage, "Alrik, what's the matter?" In response to its timeless veracity, he had come near flinging himself on his knees before the old woman and sobbing out his anger and bewilderment.

"Poor Miss Breckenridge," Frances was saying now.

"No," said Alrik out of an enlarged understanding. "No. She lived a long time. I think she had her innings."

Print-on-demand titles available at
CoachwhipBooks.com

Ebook titles available at
Coachwhip.com

BRUTAL Question

by
OLIVER WELD BAYER
author of
"AN EYE FOR AN EYE"

Crime
is of the
Essence
Joe Csida

DEATH
BEATS
THE
BAND

IDA SHURMAN

MAUDE PARKER

MURDER IN
JACKSON HOLE

THE
BEACON HILL
MURDERS

THE
BACK BAY
MURDERS

THE ROGER SCARLETT MYSTERIES
VOL. 1

CAT'S PAW

MURDER
AMONG THE
ANGELLS

THE ROGER SCARLETT MYSTERIES
VOL. 2

MURDER
IN BERMUDA

WILLOUGHBY SHARP

MURDER OF
THE HONEST BROKER

WILLOUGHBY SHARP

THE SERGEANT HARTY MYSTERIES
JOEL Y. DANE

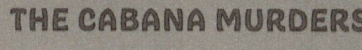

MURDER CUM LAUDE
— ① —
THE CABANA MURDERS

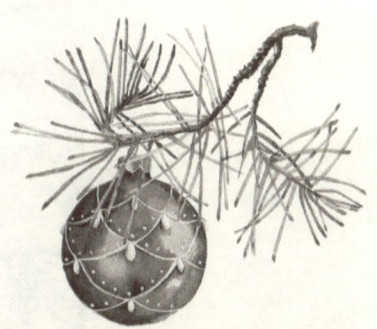

THE SERGEANT HARTY MYSTERIES
JOEL Y. DANE

GRASP AT STRAWS
— ② —
THE CHRISTMAS TREE MURDERS

LOUIS F. BOOTH

THE BANK VAULT MYSTERY
BROKERS' END

A
Matter of
Iodine

David Keith

THE
DARTMOUTH
MURDERS

THE
WAILING ROCK
MURDERS

CLIFFORD
ORR

MOST MEN DON'T KILL

MURDER IN BLACK AND WHITE

DAVID ALEXANDER

ODDS-ON MURDER

DANCE

JACK DOLPH

Jack Dolph

MURDER
MAKES
THE MARE GO

THE FIRES AT
FITCH'S FOLLY

KENNETH WHIPPLE

FULL CRASH DIVE

ALLAN R. BOSWORTH

THE QUINNY HITE
MYSTERIES

CHINESE RED · HERE LIES THE BODY

RICHARD BURKE

THE QUINNY HITE
MYSTERIES

THE FOURTH STAR · SINISTER STREET

RICHARD BURKE